"Thanks for dinner, Charlie." Paige turned to leave, but he touched her shoulder, shifting to step in front of her.

"Why do I have the feeling I said or did something wrong?" he asked.

"You didn't. I'm tired, but..."

"But?" he prodded.

"Charlie, I want you to know I had..." She knew she shouldn't lead him on when she wouldn't see him again. How could she explain what she was doing in Roseley or why she could never entertain a long-distance relationship with anyone here? Without mentioning Lucy or her past or why things were safest left a secret...she couldn't.

"A fun time? I really hope that's what you're trying to say." He blinked with the vulnerability of a child and eased into a sincere smile.

Paige's shoulders softened. She warmed under his gaze, powerless to draw her eyes from his.

"Couldn't you stay for a few minutes more? I'd really love to show you that view."

Dear Reader,

When I began writing this first book in my Lake Roseley series, I imagined the little town of Roseley as a place where the streets were paved with hope. So many of us can feel isolated even when we're surrounded by people, and Paige, our heroine, is no different. After suffering through a rough childhood, Paige has gone to great lengths to keep her distance from others, all while wishing for things to be different. After her heart leads her to Roseley and into the arms of a man who wears his loving heart on his sleeve, a new hope begins to take hold. She imagines a life where love and real connection are finally possible.

My hope is that some part of Paige and Charlie's love story will resonate with you, and if it does, I'd love to hear from you. You can follow the Elizabeth Mowers Author page on Facebook, or visit my website at elizabethmowers.com.

Wishing love to you and yours,

Elizabeth

HEARTWARMING

Where the Heart May Lead

—

Elizabeth Mowers

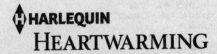
HARLEQUIN
HEARTWARMING

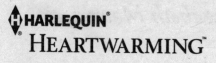

HARLEQUIN®
HEARTWARMING™

ISBN-13: 978-1-335-88975-1

Recycling programs
for this product may
not exist in your area.

Where the Heart May Lead

Copyright © 2020 by Elizabeth Mowers

This edition published by arrangement with Harlequin Books S.A.

For questions and comments about the quality of this book,
please contact us at CustomerService@Harlequin.com.

Harlequin Enterprises ULC
22 Adelaide St. West, 40th Floor
Toronto, Ontario M5H 4E3, Canada
www.Harlequin.com

Printed in U.S.A.

Elizabeth Mowers wrote her first romance novel on her cell phone when her first child wouldn't nap without being held. After three years, she had a happy preschooler and a hot mess of a book that will never be read by another person. The experience started her down the wonderful path of writing romances, and now that she can use her computer, she's having fun cooking up new stories. She's drawn to romances with strong family connections and plots where the hero and heroine help save each other. Elizabeth lives in the country with her husband and two children.

Books by Elizabeth Mowers

Harlequin Heartwarming

A Promise Remembered

Visit Harlequin.com for more
Harlequin Heartwarming titles.

To Danielle.

I dreamed of the best gift I could ever receive and there you were.

CHAPTER ONE

IF HEAVEN WAS a place paved with gold, then the morning sun cresting Little Lake Roseley made the quaint town snuggled beside it look like a place paved with hope.

White wicker baskets of flowers hung on either side of street signs, bright banners advertised an upcoming water ski show, and there were more pedestrians and bicyclists occupying the roads than automobiles. It was just the hometown Paige might have imagined for Lucy when she'd placed the tiny newborn in Dr. Hathaway's arms ten years ago. She had kissed a prayer to that baby-soft cheek and sent along all the hope in her heart. She envisioned a new set of parents, loving folks who would provide a home not just of love but of safety.

For the last decade she had been grateful to *not* know where Dr. Hathaway had placed Lucy, because the temptation to come out of hiding and catch a glimpse of the little girl would be too great. Circumstances, however, had changed in the last twelve hours.

Paige inhaled the lakeside breeze and bit her bottom lip in anticipation. She had only ever prayed and hoped and dreamed about Lucy, but today was different. Today she arrived in Roseley with the best intentions *for* Lucy. She had had no idea fate would send her on this quest when she'd awoken the day before, but she'd swallowed her fear all the same and had punched the gas pedal, heading west.

Life, until yesterday, had been pleasantly uneventful. Each day brought work to do and routines to follow. Each evening made way for dinner with her aunt and uncle, then quiet time to read and think. For life to continue this way for the next fifty years would have been not only a blessing but also the most she could wish for. She'd experienced enough turmoil during her formative years to now appreciate when the days and weeks and years drew out softly and slowly like the yawn of a calico cat. That was until yesterday…

Paige pushed through the front door of Mama's Cakes and scanned the shop as she did every year on this date.

"I'll be there in a second, sweetheart," a familiar voice sang from the back. "I finished your order this morning."

Paige fished a wad of cash out of her front pocket as she admired the intricate cakes in the glass case. The woven swirls of fudge and frosting made her eyes dance and her tummy grumble. She had worked through lunch to meet a deadline early. She wouldn't miss tonight for the world.

Madge, or Mama to the folks in town, hurried to the cash register. For a stout, round woman in her sixties, she could hustle. She placed a pink cardboard box on the counter, but before she could lift the lid, Paige waved her to stop.

"Leave it. I want to be surprised."

"Don't you want to see that it's right?"

"Madge, it's always perfect. You outdo yourself every year."

Madge dotted the perspiration on her brow with the back of her hand as her ebony-brown eyes crinkled in a smile.

"You're a gem, Paige. It'll be an even eighty dollars, please."

"Hmm. That's low," Paige said with a raised eyebrow as she handed Madge exact change. Madge shrugged and popped open the cash register.

"Cash discount. Sweetheart, you are one of a few customers who always pays cash. You don't like new technology, huh?"

Paige shrugged her shoulders and took the pink box, knotting it with the white twine Madge had started. It wasn't new technology she shied away from, it was that cash was untraceable.

"Thanks again, Madge."

"Take care, honey. Kiss your aunt and uncle for me. It was a long winter for them, I hear."

Paige hummed a sigh. "The warmer weather brought a bit of a resurgence for Uncle Craig."

"May it continue that way," Madge said, bringing a pair of prayer hands to her lips. Paige crinkled a smile of her own and slipped back out of the bakery shop. Throwing a leg over her bicycle, she pulled out onto the road, carefully dangling the cake box from her right hand.

Admiring her town at the slower pace of a bicycle ride was something she had looked forward to all winter. She just wished she could strap Uncle Craig on her back so he could enjoy the early June day too. He needed the sun, the fresh air and, most of all, the escape. They all did.

Paige smiled to children and mothers on the

sidewalk as a little girl pointed at her shiny new bicycle.

"Someday, kid," Paige chuckled to herself. She slowed to a crawl at the intersection to make a left turn onto her road. Without a free hand to signal, or a bicycle helmet, she needed to exercise caution.

It was something she was used to: exercising caution. Most of her life had been an exercise in staying low, staying discreet, staying off the radar. She, her aunt and her uncle had opted for life outside the city, shying away from cameras, social media and anything else that would prompt questions. Heck, she led Mama to believe today was *her* birthday just so she could purchase a fancy cake without sparking curiosity.

Parking in the garage alongside the brick duplex she shared with Aunt Joan and Uncle Craig, Paige sprang up the half flight of stairs to their back door.

"Knock, knock," she called, letting herself in. "Anybody home?" She heard a shuffling in the living room and muffled voices that hushed to silence before Aunt Joan appeared in the kitchen doorway. Paige paused, taken aback at her aunt's expression.

"Did I interrupt something?" When her

aunt's lips turned into a forced smile, she quickly concluded she had.

"Of course not," Joan said, hurriedly crossing the kitchen. She dead-bolted the back door behind Paige before wrapping her in a warm hug. Paige began to pull away after the respectable allotted time needed to give a good hug but found her aunt reluctant to let go.

"Is everything all right?" she whispered as Uncle Craig shuffled toward the doorway into the kitchen. His complexion was yellow, as if someone had soaked his entire body in turmeric. He braced himself against the kitchen doorway, wincing as he always did from the pains in his back. Joan's eyes moistened with tears as she pulled away and emphatically nodded.

"Everything is perfect now that you're here. What did you pick out this year?"

Paige held up the pink cake box proudly. "I have no idea, but I'm sure it's delicious." She turned to Uncle Craig. "Think you can eat a bite or two?"

Uncle Craig beckoned Paige closer with a calloused hand. "Heck, yes. Put it in the front room, honey. I need the sunshine."

Paige smacked a kiss on his cheek and placed the cake box on the dining room table as Aunt Joan followed with plates and forks. Paige raised an inquisitive eyebrow as she tied back the curtain sheers, letting the late afternoon sun stream through the windows.

"Don't you want to eat dinner first?"

"Life's too short," Uncle Craig answered from the kitchen as Joan winced a smile.

"What's going on?" Paige whispered again. "Did his doctor's appointment not go well?"

Joan waved away Paige's question as she would a mosquito and cut the white twine on the cake box, but she waited for Craig before lifting the lid.

"Okay," he said, managing to ease back onto the thickly cushioned dining room chair Joan had purchased especially for him. "Let's see this beauty."

Joan lifted the cake out of the box and placed it on the table.

"I love it, Paige," she said with a melancholy smile. "I was hoping you'd pick chocolate." She patted Uncle Craig's hand. "Your favorite, baby."

The round cake was smoothed with a chocolate ganache as perfectly polished as glass. White and blush-pink buttercream flowers cascaded around the perimeter while a lavender and pink fondant butterfly perched in the middle, just off center.

"Hmm," Paige said, studying the cake. "I brought a candle, but let's not use it. Mama outdid herself again, and I don't want to smush a candle in it. It's almost too perfect to eat." She slipped onto a chair next to Uncle Craig.

"Speak for yourself," he said. "I'll flip you for that butterfly."

After Aunt Joan had sliced out three generous pieces of cake and each person had savored the sweetness on their tongue, Paige turned her attention to them both.

"Are you going to tell me now or later?" she finally asked. "What did the doctor say?"

Aunt Joan studied her plate as Uncle Craig cleared his throat.

"My test results are pretty good. No improvement, but I'm definitely holding steady."

"Honest?"

"Honest."

Paige heaved a sigh of relief. "That's good news," she said, her face easing into a hesitant smile. "So, what has you both on edge?"

"Let's just enjoy our cake for a minute, huh?" Joan said. "You two had better catch up, because I'm already eyeing a second slice."

"Joanie," Uncle Craig said, his voice the hush of a gentle reprimand. "Come on."

Joan released a labored sigh and set her plate on the table. Clasping her hands tightly in her lap, she lifted her eyes to Paige with a resolute face.

"Today marks ten years since…"

"Yes, Aunt Joan, I know. I was there."

"Of course you do. Of course you do." Joan's fingertips had gone white from clasping them. "Your uncle and I have been talking, discussing really, the notion of…family."

Paige drew her plate closer to her as her eyes shifted between the only two people in her life who qualified as that. After her mother had died years ago, she'd moved in with them. It had been a blessing to all three: they had helped her get on her feet after a tumultuous childhood, and she'd already been a permanent fixture in their lives when Uncle Craig had first been diagnosed with cancer.

"As you know, Paige, our little family is not very big—"

"And getting smaller every day," Craig said with an eye roll. He patted the latest in his line of bandages on the inside of his wrist.

"Craig." Now it was Joan's turn to reprimand.

"We all know it, Joanie. Keep going."

Joan turned to Paige again. "We want to ask if…more like ask where you stand on…"

"Yes?"

Craig reached across the table to take Joan's hand before smiling at Paige. "Have you ever given thought to Lucy?"

Paige's breath hitched at the sound of the name. It had been all but forbidden between the three of them, no one even thinking her name for fear it would accidentally slip from their lips at the wrong moment and in front of the wrong person.

"Lucy?" she whispered. "I think about her all the time."

Joan smiled. "It's a silly question. We think about her all the time too, sweetie. What he really means is, have you ever thought of going to see her?"

Paige shook her head. She was confused. Her head had quickly clouded at the question.

"What do you mean *see* her? Like *in person*?"

Aunt Joan and Uncle Craig nodded.

Paige hadn't seen Lucy since the day she'd snuggled that baby-soft skin against her lips and savored the delicate fragrance of a newborn. She had daydreamed about that little baby every day and night for ten long years.

They knew they were asking her a question to which they already knew the answer.

"Your aunt and I have been talking about it for a while now—"

"Out loud?" Paige said, surprised by her irreverent tone.

"Only when we're here at home, of course."

"And you're serious…about me seeing her?"

"Do we look like we're joking, honey?"

"No," Paige replied, shoving a large bite of cake into her mouth for the mere excuse to work her jaw.

"We know giving her up was difficult for you. It was hard on all of us. But things are changing now and—"

"Nothing has changed," Paige said through a stuffed mouth. She jabbed her cake with her fork several times. "Nothing." She still paid cash. She still avoided people. She still went by the name Paige Cartman.

"What we really mean is, we think you should check on Lucy to make sure things haven't changed *for her.*"

Paige stopped and watched her aunt and uncle from beneath hooded eyelids. The suggestion of finding Lucy was so ludicrous, she wondered if they were in their right minds. It *had* been a long winter for the three of them. Uncle Craig's illness showed more on his face with each passing day, and though Aunt Joan exuded the demeanor of a warrior, she was nearly to her breaking point. She would chalk their suggestion up to wishful thinking, maybe even searching for something happy and fanciful to distract them from the pain... the inevitability of Craig's last days.

But their implication that the visit wasn't for her best interest but for *Lucy's* made her pause.

"Something *has* happened," she said. "When I walked in, you were discussing it. Your eyes were swollen, frantic," she said to her aunt. "Do you think I don't know the two of you by now? After all we've been through together? What is it?"

Her aunt and uncle sat in silence as if delaying the confession until the last possible moment.

"Today in the city," Joan said, "I thought I saw... I mean, I couldn't be sure...but his hair was always so *untamed*..."

Paige's stomach lurched. She slumped forward and Aunt Joan hurriedly scooted her chair closer as moral support.

"That hair? You think you saw him?"

Aunt Joan nodded. "I'm not positive, but I think so."

"Did *you* see him?" Paige asked her uncle.

"I never met him, honey. Remember? I wouldn't know him if he showed up at the front door, aside from Joanie's description. All I've ever seen is that grainy photograph you found of him on the internet a few years back. But if it was him, if he's made his way north—"

Paige touched a hand to her mouth. "It might be only a matter of time before he shows up at the back door." She imagined opening it one day and facing that wild, shaggy brown mane and coal-black eyes, the irises abnormally large and devious. "I should go."

"Nonsense. You just got here. Finish your cake."

"No, I mean I should go *away*."

"Neither of us is suggesting that, Paige. He'll never get a peep out of either of us, no matter what he threatens. We certainly didn't want to scare you, but if it really was him, we thought it wouldn't hurt if you got out of town for a few days and…"

"Checked in on Lucy." Paige finished her aunt's thoughts as if they were her own.

Aunt Joan shrugged her shoulders. "Or

maybe don't. You'll have to listen to your instincts on this one. I was never a mother, outside of loving you, so I don't have any maternal experience to bestow here. We've been discussing the pros and cons all afternoon. Whether you stay or go, we know you take a risk either way."

"We'd go with you if we could, Paige. You know I'd be right by your side if only…" Uncle Craig shook his head as he choked back tears. He turned his face toward the front window as sunlight pooled in his eyes. He wasn't looking outside or at the sun. He was looking ahead to a rapidly approaching end.

Paige studied his profile. Once so angular and strong, his sunken cheeks resembled those of a skeleton. It wasn't until she began living under his roof and sleeping on a mattress on his bedroom floor that she had begun to sleep the way normal people probably did—calmly, peacefully. He had offered her his strength at a time when she had been floundering to enter adulthood. And aside from overhearing him whispering to Aunt Joan late one night, expressing deep guilt and regret for not rescuing Paige sooner, he'd never brought up her past. He'd nod and listen intently if she had needed to talk, but he never asked first, never pried. His home, the one he had willingly and wholeheartedly provided, had been a clean and crisp break from her old life. So losing him, a fate foreshadowed every time she saw his face slip further into weariness, would be a new season of life she wasn't yet ready to acknowledge.

"I'm not going to leave you," she said quietly. He turned toward her again, his expression softening.

"I know you wouldn't want to, but a few days away won't hurt anything. My tests were good. I'm strong enough for now. I'm not going anywhere…at least, not yet."

"That's right," Joan said. "Trust us, Paige. We've discussed this for a while now, but today has sped up our timeline a wee bit."

Paige nodded. If she slipped away for a few days, she could always rush home if Uncle Craig's health took a sudden turn.

"How would I find her, anyway? All I know about her adoptive parents is that they were small business owners. I distinctly remember that, but that isn't much to go on. I can't exactly stalk every grade school for a little girl who looks something like me."

Joan batted her eyelids. "What if I told you I know *which* business?"

"How?"

"I contacted Bob…"

"Dr. Hathaway?"

Joan shrugged. "He's getting old, and he let it slip."

"Really? How?"

"I kept peppering him with questions until he got flustered and gave up a little golden nugget of information."

"Go on. Tell her," Uncle Craig said. "I know you're proud of yourself."

Joan swatted his arm. "I am proud. It's plenty to go on."

"He always had a thing for you. Cat-eyed Joanie called him up out of the blue—of course he was flustered."

Joan swatted his arm again, but this time they both chuckled.

Paige recalled Aunt Joan's friend, the doctor who had helped them anonymously put Lucy up for adoption, no questions asked. They had had to list her as abandoned, but that definition was anything from what Paige had done for her. It was a lonely, cold word to describe how much she loved that little baby and wanted to ensure her safety.

"He isn't supposed to give you any information, Aunt Joan. It was a closed adoption."

"He doesn't realize he did. Little Lakeside Sports…there's only one and it's in a Michigan town called Roseley."

"Roseley." Paige let the word hang in the air for a moment, imagining the place where Lucy had been living all these years. It was beautiful. "A sports shop?"

"I can place you in the right town and the right shop. You'll have to do some digging when you get there."

"Oh, my goodness. Am I really doing this?" Paige whispered. "I shouldn't take time off from work—"

"Nonsense. You're self-employed, you just finished your latest project and you can work from anywhere as long as you have your laptop."

"I know, but leaving you two—"

"We'll be okay," Uncle Craig said. "I have your aunt to scold me whenever I get out of line."

"You're never out of line," Joan said with an affectionate smile.

"Then you know you're doing a good job." Craig smirked and cut himself another piece of cake. "Pack a bag and leave tonight. Take it from me—life's too short."

"Yes," Joan said, touching Paige's hand.

"And when you find her, we wouldn't mind if you snapped her photograph. I'd love to see what she looks like now. And if she's… she's…"

"Safe?" Paige said.

Joan nodded. "And happy."

CHAPTER TWO

PAIGE HAD PACKED quickly and driven through the night. The dark highways heading north brought her plenty of time to think and, unfortunately, fret. She still wasn't sure that driving to Roseley was the best plan, but every time the worry in her stomach began to churn too much, Paige tried to imagine what the little girl looked like now. Would she be the spitting image of her and the women in her family? Would she see her own reflection when she peered into the ten-year-old face?

Having arrived in town eventually, she'd had several hours of decent sleep at the motel and felt refreshed enough to start exploring.

By the time the sun had breached the rooftops of the tiny shops stacked along Main Street like painted wooden blocks, Paige had wheeled her bicycle up the sidewalk to the front of the sports shop and locked it to the rack. She was in town to find Lucy, not joyride on her Schwinn, but she'd decided to bring it along in case she needed a solid reason for hanging around the sports shop. Who knew how long it would take to get information out of the staff.

The storefront faced the road but backed up against Little Lake Roseley. Paige had learned after perusing the website that Little Lakeside Sports was the place to rent or buy water skis, bikes, fishing poles and tackle and a wide array of merchandise for the outdoorswoman.

Paige also couldn't help but notice a floating plane docked on the calm morning water just kitty-corner to the shop. She could only assume, as she headed into the store, that it belonged to the store owners. She imagined Lucy riding in a floating plane with her adoptive parents. If that was the most dangerous thing she encountered in her childhood, Paige considered it a blessing.

Inside, Paige's eyes darted around for signs of life. The place smelled like new sneakers, she thought as she ran her hand over a carousel of men's T-shirts and pretended to check the price tags.

"May I help you?"

Paige jumped at the question, unaware anyone had been hovering nearby. Crouched down in a nearby aisle, a woman a few years older than Paige stood up and smiled. She was striking, as tan and brunette as she was tall and lean, with long, silky hair that fell loosely down her back, and big chestnut-brown eyes. *What a beauty*, Paige thought, as she admired the woman's perfect cheekbones and flawless complexion.

"I just rolled into town and wanted to check out your shop."

Beauty smiled. "Wonderful. We're happy to have you. Is there anything I can help you find?"

Paige floundered for one of her premeditated answers—the ones she had rehearsed on the six-hour car ride here.

"I just bought a new bike—"

"The Schwinn Signature Cruiser? I saw you stash it out front. How do you like it so far?"

"I haven't had much chance to ride it, but I'm glad to see there are a lot of cyclists around here."

"You and me both," Beauty said, leaning over the carousel to catch a better glimpse of Paige's bicycle. "It was a town initiative a few years back. The city approved funding to put in more bike lanes, off-road paths and bike racks. They started a bike share system too. Any neon orange bicycle is available to ride within the town limits. Just leave it at a designated bike rack when you're finished."

"I've heard of that happening in big cities. Nice to see it filtered down to places like Roseley."

"Right?" Beauty laughed. "I only had to push the proposal for years."

"It was your baby?" Paige said before catching herself. With Lucy so fresh on her mind, even the word *baby* sounded like a blaring alarm to her ears. "I mean, *your project*, to get it off the ground?"

"Staying active is important to me. I went to school to be a nutritionist and somehow ended up buying a sports shop."

Paige nodded, trying to slap on a smile that she knew was no better than an eager wince.

"Is this *your* shop?"

Beauty nodded proudly and placed her fists on her hips in a leader's stance.

"For the past eleven years."

Paige scrambled for another one of her conversation starters. She had to turn the talk to children—to Lucy.

"That's a lot of hard work. Your family must be really proud of you."

"Thanks for saying so," she said, tilting her head in appreciation. "It was difficult when my daughter was younger, but it gets easier, you know?"

"I can imagine." Paige swallowed hard, finding her throat had suddenly gone bone-dry. "How—how old is your daughter now?"

A warm voice called out from halfway across the store.

"Mara, line one!"

"I'm sorry, but I need to grab that. Look around and let me know if you need anything. Nice to meet you," she called over her shoulder as a silky curtain of hair sashayed behind her. Paige watched, her mind racing with a dozen follow-up questions.

"I need to know if you have my Lucy," she whispered to herself.

Without any better idea of what to do, Paige casually made her way through the store, occasionally lifting her gaze to study Mara. The woman got around. One moment she was working the cash register, then she was jogging to the back room, then she was stocking merchandise up front, then she was answering the phones. There was another woman working too, a middle-aged female with bifocals, but Mara was always quick to jump in as soon as something was needed.

After finally selecting a key lanyard, one

in the same cobalt blue as her bicycle, Paige slowly made her way to the front cash register, hesitating for a few moments until the other employee had drifted to the back room. She needed another opportunity to speak to Mara, and luckily Mara was eager to dart to the cash register to help her.

"Is this all for you today?" Mara asked, ringing up the lanyard and placing it in a small paper bag.

"No plastic bags, huh?" Paige said, for lack of a better question.

"Not for the last three years. If only some of the other stores would catch on."

Paige nodded, peeling several dollars off a wad in her pocket. "It looks like you could use some help around here. Any chance you're hiring seasonal workers?"

Mara rolled her eyes. "Is it that obvious?" She handed Paige her change. "My manager was supposed to stay on for the summer but found out last minute she was selected for an internship program out of state. Can you believe it? I barely got a two-week notice out of her."

"Could you use some help? I need a little work while I'm in town."

"Nah, I have a replacement starting tomorrow."

Paige snapped her fingers. "So close."

"But if you have retail experience," Mara said, fumbling for an application and pen, "you could fill out an application in case my new guy falls through."

"I've never worked in retail. Of all things, I'm a copywriter."

Mara's head snapped up. "A *real* copywriter?"

A smirk slowly spread across Paige's lips. "Is it that impressive? Most people give me a pitiful look. They assume I survive on beans and stale bread."

Mara chuckled and waved her hand apologetically. "It's just so funny that you said that. My husband and I were talking the other day about how he needs to drum up more traffic for his business. One of his ideas was to hire a copywriter." She gathered her long hair over her shoulder. "And here you are."

"Here I am," Paige said softly as her mind drifted off at Mara's words. "What kind of business does your husband do? Is he an entrepreneur like you?"

"For anyone who doesn't want to drive into the city every day, starting up your own place has its perks. You know what… I think I need to call him and strike while the iron is hot. That is, have you two talk immediately while the idea is still fresh in his brain. It'll take him six months to get around to hiring someone. Do you have a portfolio or anything you could show him if I set up a meeting?"

"If you could point me toward a store to make prints and copies, I can pull it together quickly. I have it all online, along with a list of my regular clients, but I know there's nothing like holding a physical copy in your hand."

"That would be amazing. Leave me your cell phone number, and I'll arrange a time."

Paige nodded before fishing a business card out of her purse. "I'm going to take a ride through town and maybe along the lake—"

"Perfect. I'll call him and set it up. Although I don't even know your name…" she said, glancing down at the business card. "Paige Cartman. Lovely. I'm Mara Selby."

Paige gathered her bag and slipped out of the shop as the other employee called to Mara. She had arrived at the shop looking for information on Lucy and was leaving with a great lead. If she could make a positive impression with Mara's husband, perhaps that would get her more access to their everyday lives and then access to Lucy—*if* he and Mara were Lucy's parents.

As she unlocked her bicycle and pedaled down the street, she rolled her eyes at herself. She had been so happy to have the opportunity fall in her lap, she had forgotten to get Mara's husband's name. No problem, she thought, she'd know it shortly. Although as this was her first, and perhaps only, lead to seeing Lucy, she knew she couldn't meet him soon enough.

Paige coasted around town for nearly an hour, though she wasn't exactly sure what it was she was looking for. She'd discovered a few cozy neighborhoods, including one with a grade school and playground nestled between quiet streets. She had stopped on the sidewalk outside the school as a classroom of children ran outside for recess, but they all looked younger than ten years old.

Finally, with her stomach growling, Paige pulled into a sandwich shop a couple of blocks from Little Lakeside Sports. She figured if Mara called while she was eating, she wouldn't be too far away to make that meeting with her husband.

She checked her cell phone and found a message from Aunt Joan. She texted back that she had found the sports shop and had a hot lead to finding Lucy's adoptive parents. That was the best way to describe it in a short text, anyway. She knew Aunt Joan could only check her phone in between her rounds as a nurse at the hospital and just wanted a sound bite. She was never much for chatting on the telephone—though Paige had never been away from her for longer than a day before.

She had no sooner slipped off her bicycle and tucked away her cell than she noticed a man sitting outside the sandwich shop. Sprawled on a wooden bench in the shade of the shop awning, he munched a sandwich and watched her with interest.

Paige was used to men noticing her. She wasn't oblivious to the fact that she had a cute figure, shapely legs and a pretty face. Plus, in her experience, men liked her silky blond hair. It had darkened to a dirty blond over the years, but a little bit of a lemon juice rinse in the summertime helped bring out the golden highlights she'd had as a child.

She wasn't surprised when the man pushed his sunglasses up on top of his head and offered a polite, noncommittal smile when she passed him. Once she caught a glance at his beautiful brown eyes, she managed a sincere smile of her own.

"Nice bike," he said, lowering his sandwich to his lap. Paige paused before pivoting to better see him. The light breeze had caught wisps of his moppy brown hair, lifting it off his ruggedly handsome face. He sported scruffy brown facial hair and an impressive tan. He was casually dressed in long khaki shorts and a black polo shirt with a Tour Guide logo over the breast pocket.

"Thanks. It's new."

"How does it ride?"

"Decent enough. Do you ride?"

He shrugged, taking another bite of sandwich. "Occasionally, when I find the time."

"Too bad. I always make the time."

His umber-brown eyes crinkled in an amused smile. "Is that so?"

"I love it. If I don't make the time, what's the point?"

"Of *life*?"

Paige joined him in a chuckle. *"Yes."*

He stretched his long legs out in front of him and contemplated her answer for a moment. As he slowly nodded, his eyes falling over her face, Paige found herself admiring his strong, masculine features with each passing second. He looked athletic. Basketball? Soccer? His frame was tall and broad, the gifted genetics of an athlete.

"Good for you," he finally said. "I like you already."

"Excuse me?" Paige said, unable to suppress a smirk.

"You heard me, Freckles." He took another bite and looked off in the distance, scanning the shops on the other side of the road. Paige only had a few freckles highlighting the bridge of her nose and tops of her cheeks. It would take an observant eye to notice so quickly. When he stole a glance at her, no doubt to surmise how his comment had gone over, his face broke into a lopsided grin that made her tummy catapult into backflips. "What are you going to get in there?" He held up his sandwich to further clarify before taking another bite.

"I don't know. I've never been here before. Is this place any good?"

"The best. Are you open to suggestions?"

Paige took a contemplative breath. "I suppose, if you're adamant about offering. What are you having?"

"Oh, no," he said. "To do this right, we need

to start with all the options. You need a trusted guide."

"I don't think that's necessary," she said, making for the door. As charming as he was, she couldn't afford to have someone asking too many questions about her. But before she could escape, the handsome stranger was on his feet, swallowing the last of his sandwich.

"Nonsense," he said, reaching across her to open the door like a proper gentleman. "It's what I do, and I'm very good at it."

Paige entered the shop. She sensed his eyes were on her, ogling her rear end the way men in her past always had, but when she glanced back, she found him scanning the menu above the counter. He seemed to be taking his job seriously. Paige squinted as she gave him a once-over.

"What do you mean it's what you do?"

He pointed to the logo on his shirt. "I'm a pro."

"You're a tour guide?"

"I used to be, not so long ago. Still have the shirt. Now, what do you have a taste for? Are you a crispy veggie delight kind of person or a heavy on the salty meats kind of person?"

"I'm a somewhere in the middle kind of person."

"My favorite kind." He smiled, eyes staring straight ahead. Paige snuck a peek at his profile as she pretended to study the menu too. She had veered drastically off target from finding Lucy. A potential job and a handsome flirt were not on her radar when she had arrived in town last night, and yet both were falling right into her lap. Why couldn't she meet men like this when she was at home and emotionally available? The thought no sooner crossed her mind when she answered her own question: because she never was emotionally available.

"Back so soon?" An older man with sparse gray hair entered from the back and slipped on a pair of plastic gloves. "What can I make for you?"

"I'm helping the lady," he said, motioning to Paige. "She heard wonderful things about your shop, Angelo, and she can't wait to sink her teeth into a signature sandwich."

"Is that right?" Angelo said with a wide smile, his leathery skin warping into a road map of wrinkles across his face. "I'm so happy to hear it. We get most of our business from word of mouth, you know. What did you hear about us? I love to hear compliments *word for word*."

Paige toyed with a lock of her hair and looked helplessly to her tour guide.

"Word for word, now," he prompted through a muffled laugh.

"Well, let me try to remember," Paige said as her cheeks warmed. "I overheard some people discussing lunch and someone said they had a taste for Angelo's signature sandwich. All three agreed yours are the best in town."

Her tour guide nodded his approval, his eyes dancing with mischievousness.

"The *best* in town, Angelo. Did you hear that?"

"Did they, now?" Angelo hooted, clasping his hands together. "You made my day, pretty lady. Lunch is on the house! Give me a second while I write that one down…best in town… I love it."

Paige gave her tour guide a wide grin as Angelo hurried to the back room, muttering happily to himself.

"Did you plan that?"

"I thought he'd kick in a free drink or something, but a free lunch is fantastic. He's in a great mood today."

Paige chuckled. "Yeah, and now I am too."

"Then that makes three of us." He settled on

a smile that warmed for a few beats too long. Paige blushed. The wise thing to do was cut and run before she swooned into this guy's arms. "Back to business," he said, sensing her unease. He shifted from one foot to the other and studied the menu again. "How do you feel about brioche buns?" Paige turned up her nose. He nodded as if recalculating. "Are you a classic Midwestern girl who puts ranch dressing on everything or can you venture off course and try new flavors?"

"Venture, please."

"Do you like blue cheese?"

"I do."

"Arugula?"

"I can't say I've ever had it."

He smiled. "Well, we're venturing, so I suggest you try it. How about the number five? It's salty, savory, and the apple slice in there offers just a hint of sweetness."

Paige nodded as Angelo returned.

"I'll take the number five, Angelo."

"Coming right up, pretty lady."

The stranger's eyebrows raised in surprise as he nodded toward the menu. "Aren't you going to read to see what else is in it?"

"I'm trusting my tour guide. We'll see how good you really are."

"I appreciate the vote of confidence. If you don't like it I'll have to spring for a giant chocolate brownie to make it up to you."

"I wouldn't get cross over a bad sandwich." Paige smiled, leaning casually against the sandwich case.

"No?" he said, mirroring her. Her eyes shifted in Angelo's direction before meeting his again. She lowered her voice.

"You got me a free lunch, after all."

"That is true," he said. "But just to make sure I stay on your good side, I think I'll buy the chocolate brownie now as an insurance policy."

"How proactive of you." She tried to suppress a smile, but the stranger's eyes were so intoxicating, she felt like a schoolgirl flirting with her first crush.

Paige took her sandwich and two plastic forks from the condiment console as her tour guide paid for the brownie. When he turned, she handed him a fork before settling behind a small table in the window.

"If we're sharing a brownie, I take it I can join you," he said, hovering beside the empty chair across from her.

"I think you invited yourself the moment

you followed me in here. I'm Paige, by the way."

"Charlie," he said, sliding into his seat. "How have I never seen you before?"

"Do you know everyone in this town?"

"*Most* of the people in this area. I grew up around here."

"Born and raised, huh?"

"Something like that."

"Well, I only arrived last night."

"Then welcome to Roseley." Paige held up her sandwich in a symbolic toast and took a large bite. She let a happy sigh escape with each chew. Charlie leaned back in his chair, smiling in amusement. "I think she likes it."

"I do. You did well."

Paige gazed at the stranger over the top of her sandwich. He really did remind her of the charming crush who would have made her heart race back in high school. Well, that was, if she'd had an upbringing that included things like attending a high school.

"What brings you to Roseley?"

Paige took another large bite to give herself a moment to think. She needed something as close to the truth as possible. Remembering too many lies had its downfalls. Trudy had taught her that. Finally, she managed, "I'm a writer. I needed some new surroundings."

"Are you looking for inspiration in Roseley?"

"Kind of."

"Are you staying on the lake?"

"No. Motel."

Charlie made a tsk-tsk sound. "Not even a cute bed-and-breakfast?"

Paige shook her head. "My funds are sparse now. Besides, I'll spend most of my time out and about."

"Well," Charlie said, scratching the scruff on his chin. "There are plenty of fun things to do this week. Let me be the first to invite you to the third annual Holy Smokes Food Festival, hosted by our very own Rotary and Lions Clubs. Are you a fan of smoked meats?"

Paige nodded. "I like barbecue."

"Excellent. It's been the talk of the town for the past two weeks. Starting the night before, you can smell smoke and barbecue from anywhere on Main Street. You'll eat yourself out of house and home for an entire day leading up to it just because your taste buds are in overdrive."

"Is that right?"

"That's what they say. And of course, you've

probably already seen signs for the Water Dancers' Ski Show."

"I did, but what are water dancers?"

"Ah, just the best water ski club this side of Little Roseley Lake."

Paige snorted a laugh. "The town isn't that big. Is that saying something?"

Charlie matched her grin. "They're actually pretty good. They perform every Wednesday night in the summer."

"I'll try not to miss it."

"No one else does either. You can walk up and down the middle of Main Street during showtime, because it's so deserted."

"It doesn't seem like it would take much to shut this town down."

"Are you getting inspired yet? Could a cozy little town like this be a great place for a murder mystery?"

"That's not my speed."

"Ah, too bad," Charlie said, snapping his fingers. A few moments passed as Paige sized up her lunch date. She was enjoying every second of his playful charm. Why, oh, why couldn't they be meeting under different circumstances?

"What?" she said as his gaze seemed to drift off while staring at her.

"Do you ever start the day with one set of goals and then life changes your course?"

Paige lowered her sandwich to her plate. She knew exactly what he meant and his mere mention of it reminded her of Lucy.

Before she could answer, Charlie's cell phone rang. As he raised it to his ear, Paige's mind drifted to what her next steps were in finding Lucy. There was a high likelihood that Mara was Lucy's adoptive mother. The middle-aged woman at the sports shop was over fifty and though she could be young enough to adopt a baby now Lucy's age, the chances that Mara was the mother were much better. The timeline worked too. She said she had owned the shop for eleven years. That made her a business owner at the time she would have been adopting Lucy.

Regardless, even if Mara wasn't Lucy's mother, a job at the sports shop could get her familiarized with the people in town and give her reason to talk to folks without sending up too many red flags. All of this was a moot point, she reminded herself, because she couldn't stay in Roseley forever. She had to find Lucy, confirm she was safe and happy and then get back home to Aunt Joan and Uncle Craig as soon as possible. Uncle Craig had assured her he'd be all right without her, but she knew better than to stay away too long.

"I'm at The Sandwich Board," Charlie said into his phone. "I can bring you back something."

Paige hesitantly took another bite, pretending not to listen. She hoped Charlie wasn't flirting with her over lunch while speaking to his girlfriend or wife on the line. She snuck a glance at his ring finger and found it bare.

"I'm enjoying someone's company, actually," he said, glancing briefly at her. "Thanks, Tully. I'll see you in a bit."

Paige found herself breathing a sigh of relief. Tully, as best as she could tell, was a man's name, but just as quickly as relief flooded over her, she was mentally kicking herself. She shouldn't care about Charlie's availability, because she wouldn't be around long enough to pursue anything further than this lunch…dessert included, of course.

"Do you need to leave?" she said when he was done. Charlie shrugged but made no move to get up. "If you don't mind me asking, how can you run a tour guide company in this tiny place? I mean, there's the lake and the state park, but it's not that big, is it?"

"I don't run a tour guide company. Not any-more." His expression soured as he stabbed a corner of the brownie and shoved it into his mouth. It led her to believe she'd wandered onto a delicate subject. He stared silently out the front window before taking another stab at the brownie. "Life has a way of making its own plans."

Paige knew all too well how true that was. She took a stab of the brownie herself to show her solidarity, but before she could ease the chocolaty bite onto her fork, Charlie swiped it off her fork and popped it into his mouth.

"Hey!" she said, laughing. His crooked grin made her try again. "No fair. I haven't had a taste yet."

"So sorry," he said, holding up his hands in defeat. "Go ahead. It's *really* delicious."

Paige jostled a large bite onto her fork again just as Charlie swiped it and popped it into his mouth a second time.

"Seriously?" she said with a laugh.

"I can't help it if you're slow. This is sur-vival of the fittest, Freckles."

Paige held a protective arm between Char-lie and her brownie before managing to take a bite. He chuckled as she closed her eyes in satisfaction.

"Now that *is* good."

"Angelo's is the best in town. Your words, not mine." He smiled for a moment before shifting in his chair. "Listen, Paige, I do have to get back to something. I know you're new in town, and perhaps don't have dinner plans yet…at least I'm hoping you don't."

She blinked up at him. "Are you asking me out?"

"Only if you say yes." There was that lopsided grin again. "If you turn me down then I'm going to pretend it's all an embarrassing misunderstanding…on your end, of course."

She knew he was trying for a laugh, but her sudden unease made her avert her eyes back to the brownie. Dating was a step in the wrong direction. She was in Roseley for one reason and one reason only. Besides, what kind of happily-ever-after could she really expect when she couldn't tell him about her past or who she was or why she was in Roseley in the first place? They had had a nice little lunch, a few beautiful moments to distract her from her troubles but that was all.

"That sounds really nice, Charlie, but I don't think…"

"Don't say yes right now. In fact, you might

say yes for the wrong reason, considering I *did* get you a free sandwich."

"Are you still bringing that up? I'll never hear the end of it."

He grinned harder as he stood and made his way to the front door.

"If you're interested, meet me tonight at the Bayshore Bar around seven o'clock. If you don't show, then I'll have a pretty lakeside sunset to watch as I cry into my drink."

Paige took a breath to respond, but Charlie had already slipped out the front door. After watching him disappear down the block, she picked up her brownie and eyed it carefully.

"How was it, pretty lady?" Angelo called from behind the counter. Paige sunk her teeth into the chocolaty goodness.

"Completely unexpected," she sighed. "And wonderful."

CHAPTER THREE

CHARLIE STILLWATER RAPPED lightly on the screen door before swinging it open.

"Hello! Where the heck are you?" he called.

"Back here."

He followed the direction of the voice to find his best friend, Tully, sprawled under the kitchen sink.

"How on earth do you not have a basin wrench?" he asked, placing his own on the floor beside Tully.

Tully slid out from underneath the sink and wiped his hands on an old rag. "I can't find it, and I've been tinkering with this plumbing all morning." He stood with a sigh and cracked his neck. He was a bear of a man, bigger than any fellow Charlie had ever encountered. However, anyone who got to know Tully knew he was a big teddy bear. A teddy bear with a sharp wit and discerning mind.

Charlie claimed a bar stool on the other side of the counter as Tully glanced around.

"Sandwiches?"

"What?"

Tully raised his eyebrows. "You said you'd bring me the wrench and some lunch. I'm starving."

Charlie ran a hand down the length of his face. "Oh, man, I'm sorry. I forgot."

"I talked to you not twenty minutes ago—"

"I know. I can't explain it."

Tully tipped his head and studied his friend. "Oh, no."

"What?"

"I've seen that look before. Who is she?"

Charlie rolled his eyes. "Trouble."

"I like her already."

"She has my head spinning, man."

"When did you meet her?"

"About ten minutes before you called."

Tully let out a snort as he yanked open the refrigerator door. "You always do this. Why am I not surprised?"

"Do what?"

Tully placed a can of tuna fish and condiments on the kitchen counter across from Charlie. He chuckled again as he fixed himself a tuna fish sandwich and a pickle.

"*This*. Jumping in with both feet without

checking to make sure there's water in the pool."

"But you haven't met this woman, Tully. She's—"

"Beautiful?"

"Gorgeous. Butter-blond hair, bright green eyes—"

"A deviance from your usual type."

Charlie frowned, not wanting to think about the past. He had agreed to help his family, but that didn't mean he had to put his romantic life on hold. He wanted to move on. He desperately needed to move on and that meant not thinking about…

He shook his head. He needed to move forward without looking back.

"She's a writer and the conversation was so easy…"

"You can make conversation with a tree stump easy—"

"She's funny too. *Witty.*"

"That's a definite departure from—"

"Don't say her name, man."

Tully shrugged. "I'm sorry. I just mean… so far so good."

"The one catch is—"

"Here it comes."

"She's only in Roseley for a little while.

She doesn't live here and didn't say when she was leaving."

"A minor setback."

Charlie snatched a pickle out of the jar as his friend chomped down on his sad little sandwich. He made his way to check Tully's refrigerator: beer, an open can of tuna fish and a bulk package of spicy snap sausage. "Don't you grocery shop?"

Tully shrugged and glanced back at him. "It needs a woman's touch."

"Does it ever. How's it going in that department? Any new cadets catch your eye?"

"Oh, no. Don't change the subject. When are you seeing your next heartbreak again?"

"Hopefully tonight, if she decides to show. I'll have to stalk every motel in the county to find her if she doesn't."

"She'll show."

Charlie leaned back against the refrigerator, picturing Paige's perfect face.

"Oh, yeah?"

Tully chomped down on another bite of sandwich and grinned. "Have you ever known a woman to turn you down?"

He hadn't. But that hadn't really been his problem with love. He fell fast and hard and didn't see the warning signs until they clocked him in the face. Maybe this time things could be different if he only practiced some restraint. He wouldn't fall in love again until he knew, without a doubt, that his feelings were completely requited.

"Do you need help with this?" Charlie asked, motioning to the kitchen sink.

"Do you have time?"

"I'll make the time. I need the distraction."

"I know what you mean. Home repairs are the only thing that get my mind off working a case."

Charlie squatted down in front of the pipes. When it came to Paige, he wasn't sure a home project was strong enough to do the trick.

PAIGE THREW HERSELF over her motel room bed and pressed her cell phone to her ear as her aunt's voice came over the line.

"Was it a productive first day, honey?"

Paige ran her finger along the powder blue swirl design on her bedspread.

"Sort of."

"What does that mean? Didn't you find the sports shop?"

"I did, but I'm not sure if Mara, the owner, is Lucy's adoptive mother or not. I'm still working on that part."

"Couldn't you ask her if she has a ten-year-old daughter?"

"I could if I wanted the conversation to end right there. I don't only want to find Lucy. I want to make sure she's okay—safe, happy. I need to know we made the right choice."

"I never doubted whether or not we made the right choice, Paige. Neither you nor I were in a position back then to raise a child, considering—"

"I know. I know it was the right choice in my head…"

"But?"

"My heart is still longing to know her."

Aunt Joan sighed into the phone. Paige could picture the heavy frown lines deepening between her eyebrows, the way they did when the doctor delivered more bad news about Uncle Craig. Those lines had been permanently seared years ago.

"I know, kid. Mine is too."

"I'm supposed to meet with Mara's husband at the shop tomorrow. He's interested in hiring a copywriter."

"What? How did you swing that?"

"I still don't know, but if I can make a great impression tomorrow, perhaps the job can put me in the right place to meet Lucy. I can't just keep wandering into the sports shop every day, hoping she's skipping school and hanging out there."

"Any idea which school she attends?"

"I'm not about to go stalking every elementary school within a ten-mile radius."

"True. Well, I'm happy for you, Paige. For only arriving last night, I'd say you're on your way. Are you going to call it an early evening and rest up for your meeting tomorrow?"

Paige flopped to her back and covered her eyes with her arm. She was still entertaining the idea of meeting Charlie for dinner. Every time she convinced herself that getting involved was a foolish idea, she'd picture his dreamy brown eyes smiling back at her and the butterfly wings fluttering in her stomach made her reconsider.

"Something like that," she said. "I still have to grab some dinner."

"Let me know how the meeting goes tomorrow. Love you, honey."

Paige hung up and stared at the clock on her phone. If she jumped in the shower right now, she could easily make it to Bayshore Bar before seven o'clock. Paige let out a labored groan and sat up on the bed. She technically didn't have to decide right this instant. It was probably a good idea to take a hot shower before bed, and taking one didn't mean she *had* to go out to dinner with Charlie. At least, that's what she concluded as she trotted off to the bathroom.

PAIGE RAN A FINGER around the top of her glass and gazed out over the restaurant. Without even trying, she had found herself dressed and sipping a spritzer at the Bayshore Bar much earlier than seven o'clock.

"So much for just taking a shower," she muttered to herself. She wanted to remain calm, cool and collected. After all, she *had* to eat. It didn't really make much difference if it was greasy takeout eaten on her bed in front of the motel television or a Cobb salad at the bar. If she happened to talk to Charlie while eating that Cobb salad, what was the harm in that?

She had casually taken another glance around the restaurant when she spotted a stout little man scurrying toward her. The stout little woman at his side had curly gray hair and a ruby-red smile flashing straight at her.

"Pretty lady!" he called over the light instrumental music and chatter. "Hey there, pretty lady!"

"Hi, Angelo," Paige said, accepting Angelo's waiting hand as he turned to introduce her.

"This pretty lady—" He paused and looked expectantly at her to supply a name.

"Paige."

"*Paige* here told me that our shop is the best in town. *The best*, CeCe."

"Honey, the best, you say?" CeCe powered into Paige's personal space and grasped her hands in hers.

"It's true," Paige said, hoping Angelo and CeCe didn't ask her what other restaurants in town she had recently patronized.

"CeCe and I started The Sandwich Board almost twenty-seven years ago, didn't we?"

CeCe nodded. "It was just a sub shop when we bought it. We moved here from New Jersey when our daughter got accepted to the university."

"You moved halfway across the country to open a sandwich shop?"

"And to be near Tracy, our daughter." Angelo smiled. "Although I don't know how happy she was about it. She thought she was getting some freedom and we traipsed right into town behind her."

Paige shook her head. "How could she not appreciate you moving closer?" The story made her long for parents who would have done the same for her. Luckily, she'd had Joan and Craig, but not until she was nearly Tracy's age.

"Honey, where are you sitting?" CeCe asked, patting Paige lovingly on the cheek as if sensing a maternal energy was needed. "We already got a table. Come join us. Please don't eat alone. It isn't right to do such a thing. Is it, Angelo?"

He furiously shook his head. "Food needs to be experienced with company. Come on over."

"Would you like another wine, miss?" the bartender asked as Paige tipped back the last of her drink, contemplating CeCe's invitation.

"A water with lemon, please." She needed to eat something before the white wine went straight to her head. But as she turned and spotted Charlie cutting through the crowd, his handsomeness garnering the attention of plenty of nearby women, she knew it was too late. Either the drink was making her woozy or the easy way his body strode swiftly toward her was.

"My friend just arrived," she said, motioning toward Charlie. CeCe had to mask a squeal of excitement as she tugged at Angelo's arm.

"Angelo, she's on a *date*," CeCe emphatically whispered as Angelo flailed to figure out what was happening. "We didn't mean to interrupt," CeCe offered, shooting Paige a sly smile.

"You didn't," Paige said as Charlie shook Angelo's hand in greeting.

"Hello, Charlie," CeCe said, nodding approvingly up at him. Her eyes sparkled like a seasoned matchmaker. "Good to see you're doing well. We heard you got back into town."

Charlie side-glanced at Paige as she hid a smile behind her water glass.

"News travels fast."

"We'll just be over here. Come on, Angelo. The kids need to order."

Angelo waved goodbye as CeCe whispered in his ear and tugged him toward their table. Charlie muffled a laugh.

"I was hoping to act suave and open with a line," he said, cozying up in front of her. "But I couldn't keep a straight face right now if I tried."

"No?" Paige said, smoothing her cool linen skirt over her crossed knee. "Why is that?" She could barely keep her hands from fidgeting as he stared at her, as if he'd wandered in out of the desert and couldn't keep from drinking her all in. It had been a long time since she'd reciprocated feelings for a man, and as he slid onto the bar stool beside her, she wanted to savor every moment with him.

"I'm so happy to see you. I wasn't sure you'd come."

"A girl has to eat."

"Thank goodness for that. Are you hungry?"

"Starving," she said with an eye roll as she motioned to the bartender. "The wait for the deck is at least an hour, so let's eat here. I already eyed the menu, and after very seriously considering a Cobb salad, I realized there's a bacon cheeseburger calling my name."

"A woman after my own heart." He took a sip from her water glass. Paige hid a smirk. The familiarity of it had her leaning closer as he ordered them two bacon cheeseburgers.

"How long have you been here?"

"Long enough to get some dirty looks for holding your bar stool. I had some thinking to do. How's Tully?"

Charlie blinked. "He's... Tully. You'll have to meet him. He was a high school linebacker, but there's not a mean bone in his body. He has the biggest heart."

"Does he work with you?"

"He's a longtime friend. His father and my stepdad went way back, so he and I grew up together. He's more like my brother."

"I'm close to my aunt and uncle like that. We live in the same duplex."

"On either side?"

"It's a good fit for us. I live on my side of the house, but I'm close enough to help if they need it."

"Are they elderly?"

"Sick. My uncle has advanced-stage pancreatic cancer." The words tumbled out fast and matter-of-factly as if she was ripping off a verbal Band-Aid. It was her best coping method to keep from getting choked up about it, as if doing it quickly would keep her from feeling the pain.

Charlie's face fell, grave. "I'm so sorry." With his arm resting on the bar, he grazed the length of her pinky finger with his own. Paige's arm prickled. She wanted to move closer, to slip her hand under the heat of his and wish her sorrows all away.

"Me too."

"How advanced is it?"

Paige bit back a shaky voice as the thought of losing Uncle Craig suddenly came over her again. Just when she thought she was prepared for the end, the thought of saying goodbye made her want to fall apart.

She shrugged, her eyes beginning to glisten at the thought of it. Charlie, as if sensing her pain, covered her hand with his own. She felt nothing but sincerity under the weight of his palm and welcomed it with a wispy smile. Uncle Craig had always been her rock, comforting and strong. And as her tearful eyes met Charlie's, she saw something in him that reminded her of that strength.

"We were happy he made it through the winter. Every day is a gift."

Charlie squeezed her hand slightly, sending a jolt to the nerves up her arm.

"I can tell you love him very much." The timbre of his voice was low and gentle, each word cared for like a treasure. She wanted to draw every comfort from him that he could offer with his voice, his words, his touch. She blinked hard, unable to break his spell over her. If there were others in the restaurant, she was blissfully unaware of them.

"I do. Thank you, Charlie."

"Is there anything I can do?" His brow

tensed in seriousness. Though she found herself believing the sincerity of his offer completely, the darkness that shadowed her heart
every time she thought of Uncle Craig reminded her there was nothing anyone could
do. Not really.

Her eyes dropped to his hand placed snugly
over hers, and the sight brought her a happiness she hadn't known in a long time. Perhaps it was no more than a silver lining, but
it was something, and she had needed it more
than he could imagine. Paige turned the face
of her palm and clasped his fingers in hers.
They stayed like that for a long time, neither
of them shifting, neither speaking.

When the bartender approached with a
water pitcher and topped off her water glass
without a word, Charlie lifted her hand to his
lips and brushed a delicate kiss over it. Her
mouth went dry, any hope for words lost in her
throat as she watched him. He was so tender,
so kind. And the gesture caressed a wound
in her soul that had been formed such a long
time ago.

Her eyes fluttered shut, willing him to
kiss the heartache away completely. When
she opened them again, they had filled with
tears. As if retrieving it from thin air, he of-

fered a tissue and she dotted her eyes. She hadn't wanted to start their dinner by crying at the bar, but one glance at Charlie made her certain he didn't mind.

"And your aunt?" he asked as she took a sip of water, grateful now it was nothing stronger.

Paige focused hard to regroup, her mind shifting to Aunt Joan. "I think she had the flu twenty years ago. She's tough as nails."

Charlie chuckled. "Are they from around here?"

"Ohio."

"Then how did you find your way to Roseley?"

Paige took another sip, searching for a chunk of ice to crunch. That was a sticky question to which she didn't absolutely have an answer. It wasn't just that she didn't want to get into the story about looking for Lucy. For so long, she hadn't spoken the little girl's name out of a desperate need to protect her. As much as she saw Charlie as a trustworthy confidant, she knew old habits died hard.

"I wandered in, I guess. It seems like a nice place to spend a few days." Truth be told, she thought it seemed like a nice place to spend a lifetime.

"Now you're talking. It has a small-town

feel, but the lake gives you a bit of an escape when people are a bit too invasive."

"Like CeCe?" She felt grateful for a topic that would let her chuckle away her emotions rather than tear up again.

"Exactly. I've known Mr. and Mrs. Takes for many years."

"Twenty-seven, would you say?"

Charlie paused. "Ah…probably. How on earth did you know that?"

"They don't hold much back. You saved me from being their dinner companion."

"They would have made you feel like family in under five minutes. That's what you can expect in Roseley."

"Do you have family in the area?"

Charlie grinned as the bartender brought them a basket of pub chips. "Why is family always so complicated?"

"I think they were designed that way."

"You talk as if you know."

She knew all too well. The last ten years had been a pleasant calm after the storm. She'd seen a movie once of a woman who had ridden out a hurricane in a tiny ocean-front bungalow. She'd finally emerged, two nail-gripping hours later, dirty and bruised but grateful to be alive. That, Paige thought, was exactly how she'd felt ten years ago. Hurricane Mommy had wreaked havoc on her life for seventeen long years and then...

"I heard a band goes on at seven thirty," Paige said, eager to lighten her mood.

Charlie tipped his head toward a small stage at the edge of the bar. A few musicians milled about, setting up equipment, as a microphone powered on. "Oh, yeah? How do you handle yourself on the dance floor?"

"It's been a long time. I'll probably surprise the both of us." Dancing? Paige thought. Had she ever?

He grinned. "I would have taken you for a dance kid. You know...the ones who take lessons six days a week."

Her mother certainly hadn't been a dance mom, that was for sure. She hadn't had the desire to shuttle a kid around to frivolous ventures like dance classes or dentist appointments or...school.

"Maybe *you* were the dancer," she said. "You look like you have a strong build for dance."

"Checking out my build, were you? I'm very flattered."

"No," Paige said, fumbling as her cheeks

flushed. "I was only saying…well, you do have a strong build."

He laughed hard, making her cover her eyes with her hands in embarrassment for a moment. When she reemerged, his lopsided grin widened.

"I played sports growing up, but in recent years I've found other interests."

"Such as giving tours?"

"Ah, you remember," he said sadly. "If only I still was. The tour guide business was a good fit for me."

"Why do you say that?"

"I liked owning my own business and talking to new people every day. I'd have a difficult time working behind a desk all day, every day."

"What are you doing now?"

Charlie groaned. "Good question, Freckles. I haven't quite figured that out yet."

Paige rested her hand on his forearm. At her touch, his eyes moved to find hers.

"You will," she said, the reassurance in her voice surprising even herself. "I can tell by talking to you, you're a man who will always figure it out."

"You can tell all that just from talking to me for a few minutes?"

"Definitely."

"Do you consider yourself very perceptive about people?" She nodded. Little did he know her survival growing up had depended on it. He leaned forward as if sharing a secret. "Now I'm curious."

"About?"

"Where you came from, Paige…?"

"Cartman."

"Paige… Cartman…" He mulled her name over in his mouth as he rested his hand on hers again. Her skin prickled with goose bumps, and this time he smirked at noticing. He brushed his hand down the length of her forearm as if to smooth them away. Paige repressed a sigh as she imagined Charlie brushing his hand over the rest of her body. There was nothing like a man's touch, she thought, tipping her head to better study the crinkle of lines around his eyes. She stared at this new person who suddenly felt so right. It was hard to remember a time when she hadn't known him.

Paige held up her glass, prompting Charlie to clink his against it.

"Here's to figuring it all out," she whispered. "And making new friends."

"To making new friends with Paige Cartman," he said before taking a sip. "Wherever it is she came from."

PAIGE SLIPPED INTO the bathroom to catch her breath and swipe on more lip gloss. Washing her hands in cold water, only to help cool herself down, she smiled at her reflection in the mirror. Her hair had become greasy at the crown from sweat earned from dancing, and she didn't care. Why didn't the world provide more opportunities for dancing and laughing? she thought as she let the cold water beat against the insides of her wrists. She had missed out on so much in the past and tonight, dancing with Charlie, felt like an awakening.

As she dried her hands, her cell phone chimed, alerting her that a message awaited her. She discovered four text messages from Aunt Joan—all relating to Uncle Craig and all missed amid the loud music.

"Honey, there you are," Aunt Joan said in lieu of a standard hello.

"What's happened?" Paige said, sinking into an upholstered chair stationed by the bathroom door. She pressed her phone to her ear to hear Aunt Joan's shaky voice through the chatter of women in the bathroom. "I thought he was holding steady."

"He was, but you know how these things go."

Paige knew all too well. A few hours could make all the difference in the world to a person suffering from a debilitating illness. Uncle Craig could awaken in the morning with enough energy to announce he was taking them out to breakfast, but by lunchtime he'd zonk out into bed and sleep until the next day. Days like that were difficult to watch, but the emergency room visits were harder.

"Where are you?"

"Where else?" Joan said with a sigh. "I rushed him in a couple of hours ago."

"I'm having a difficult time hearing—"

"Where are *you*? I thought you were hitting the hay early tonight."

"Something came up."

"That's how my evening played out too. I hope yours is more fun."

Paige could hear the pain in Aunt Joan's voice. She had always been a strong, upbeat woman, but things had begun to shift six months ago. It had been a long, hard winter on all of them and Aunt Joan had emerged that spring much wearier, despite how hard she tried to hide it.

"I'm grabbing dinner. How's Uncle Craig?"

"He was in a lot of pain and kept rating it at a level ten. He's admitted for the night. The painkillers they gave him knocked him out, thank heavens. They told me to go home and get some sleep, but you know how I can't. Not when he's here and…and…"

"You should. You won't sleep on that crappy, plastic love seat. Uncle Craig needs you to take care of yourself. For him."

Paige strained to hear if her aunt had responded, uncertain if she missed a barely audible "Uh-huh," but she couldn't be sure. Finally, as she was about to repeat herself, her aunt sighed loudly into the phone.

"You're right, honey. I'll do that in a bit. I'm just going to check in on him again."

"But you're going home?" Paige pressed.

"Mmm-hmm."

"Joan."

"I'll try, honey, but it's raining here, so maybe camping out in his room wouldn't be such a bad idea…in case it storms. I wouldn't want to get home and not be able to get back to him…because of the storm."

Paige pinched the bridge of her nose. She had relied so heavily on her aunt and uncle after Aunt Joan had rescued her and Lucy. She and Craig had embraced her fully and unconditionally, loving her like the mother and father she'd never had but had always deserved. And in the years since, the pendulum had swung in the opposite direction as they had begun to lean heavily on her. Since the day they'd taken her in, she had never been away from them overnight and now, only one day into her mission to find Lucy, she sensed Joan was floundering. "Everything is going to be just fine. Go home, get some sleep, and I'll call you tomorrow. I love you."

"Love you too, kid."

Paige made her way to the bathroom door but couldn't bring herself to open it. What was she doing here laughing and dancing while her family was barely holding it together back home? She could feel her absence weighing heavily on them—could hear it in Aunt Joan's voice. What she hadn't said conveyed volumes compared to what she had.

Paige shook her head and shoved her cell back into her purse. She couldn't live for herself. She had responsibilities and couldn't afford to waste time with a handsome young man. Not when she had to stay focused on her main objective: finding Lucy and making sure she was okay. Once she did that, she'd never see Charlie again. *Who am I kidding?* She'd be on the road home, and the bliss of tonight would be a long-lost dream she'd recall once in a while years from now. He'd be the one she would miss deeply. The one she'd let slip away, but at the end of the day, she had to do just that.

"S'cuze me, sweetheart," a robust woman said, swinging open the bathroom door. "Delivering five babies *au natural* gives a woman a one-track mind after two Long Island iced teas! Oh, my stars in heaven, ladies! Make way!"

Paige smiled with amusement as the woman hurried past her to the first available stall, her friends hollering and cackling behind her. Emerging from the ladies' bathroom, Paige spotted Charlie standing at the bar.

"I didn't know if you wanted something other than water. I thought we could take some drinks out on the deck. It's a little quieter and the view is—"

"I need to call it a night, Charlie."

"You do? Is something wrong?"

Paige shook her head, but she knew her face was anything but convincing. Charlie moved closer, gently touching her arm.

"I'm fine," she said, waving away the bartender, who waited for a drink order. "I need to get back to…" She couldn't muster the right word. She needed to get back home, to Uncle Craig, but not until she checked on Lucy. "*My motel.* What do I owe you?"

"I already settled up with the bartender. I asked *you* out, remember? Buying your cheeseburger was the least I could do in exchange for a fantastic dance partner."

She knew he was trying for a smile, but the ethereal pleasure of the evening had dissolved as soon as she'd heard Aunt Joan's voice. It had been a rude reality check, but a necessary one.

"Thanks for dinner, Charlie." She turned to leave, but he touched her shoulder, shifting to step in front of her.

"Why do I have the feeling I said or did something wrong?"

"You didn't. I'm tired, but…"

"But?" he prodded.

"Charlie, I want you to know I had…" She shouldn't lead him on when she wouldn't see him again. How could she explain what she was doing in Roseley or why she could never entertain a long-distance relationship with anyone here? Without mentioning Lucy or her past or why things were safest left a secret… she couldn't.

"A fun time? I really hope that's what you're trying to say." He moved closer, his eyes blinking with the vulnerability of a child as his lips eased into a sincere smile. Paige's shoulders softened. She warmed under his stare, powerless to draw her eyes from his. "Couldn't you stay for a few minutes more? I'd really love to show you that view." He tousled a lock of her hair and when he did, his fingers delicately grazed the slope of her neck. The heat of his hand drew a current down her spine, electrifying each nerve along the way. Her lips parted, wanting to welcome his lips to hers for just one small taste of him before she left. His mouth would be warm and inviting and would mold perfectly against hers in the way she'd been imagining all evening. She could fall into his arms tonight with complete abandon if only…

"You're a good man, Charlie," she said softly enough that he leaned closer to keep from missing it. She wouldn't repeat it; the words were meant for her more than him. "Thank you for a fun evening, but I do need to go."

He reached for her hand. "I don't have your phone number for the next time."

"There won't be a next time."

Charlie shook his head as he grappled with her answer.

"I don't understand."

"I can't really explain, Charlie, and I do need to go."

"Freckles, you're breaking my heart here," he said, forcing a laugh, though his face had fallen. "Talk to me for a second. I thought you and I had something special. I felt it from the moment we met, and I have to believe you feel it too."

She wanted to cry and tell him she did. From his first playful smirk, she had felt drawn to him like the tide pulled by moonlight. His gravitational pull was so captivating, she knew she had to walk away now to keep herself from drowning in him completely. When she'd come to dinner tonight, she knew she could only keep his company for the evening. It was never meant to last longer, and she had to make sure of that—now.

"It doesn't matter."

"I find that hard to believe. Tell me where you're staying, at least, so I can call you in a couple days and talk you into meeting for coffee or—"

"I don't know how to make myself clearer, Charlie. It doesn't matter how I feel about you. I can't get into a relationship."

"Can't or won't?" His voice tinged with an edge, and she knew she'd hurt him. They'd both be hurting tonight, but there was no way around it.

"Good night, Charlie." And without daring to look back at his pleading brown eyes for fear they'd convince her to stay, she darted out of the restaurant.

CHAPTER FOUR

PAIGE PUMPED THE BRAKES of her Schwinn Signature Cruiser at the bottom of the path that led along the outskirts of the Michigan town. To her left, Roseley was just coming alive as cars and bicyclists cruised to work. To her right, Little Lake Roseley was calm and still.

A pair of mallards, disturbed by her presence, cut a path through the grass, heavy laden with early summer dew. A half dozen newly hatched ducklings, nearly tripping over their own feet, hurried quietly behind.

Roseley was serene. She could tell it had been carefully nurtured and preserved for the treasure it was. Landlocked on three sides, between Little Lake Roseley and the heavily wooded Roseley State Park, the town reminded her of wildflowers that had managed to squeeze through concrete slabs and thrive despite not having much room to grow. That was what she needed to be, she thought, as she popped a leg to the ground as a kickstand. She was proud of the life she'd managed to maintain for the last ten years, but now, she needed to keep trying until she could find Lucy.

The cool morning air enlivened her senses, every breath bringing hope and strength she desperately needed in order to power through her meeting with Mara's husband.

She rolled her shoulders and envisioned her flawless presentation. She had polished her pitch over the years, appealing to her clients' emotional triggers more than any logical ones. She was such an excellent copywriter, with the results to prove it. It was rare she didn't land a job she sought.

She could thank her aunt and uncle for setting her on the writing track. After the three darkest years of her life, when she hadn't done much more than scribble out journal entries to keep her from unraveling, they had hired her a full-time tutor so she could not only finish school but excel. It was only one of the gifts they had given her, and she'd never taken it for granted, approaching her studies and later her work with a ferocity to succeed.

But this job was different. So much hinged on it, and it made Paige nervous she'd lose her edge. Along with preparing for the job meeting, she'd spent the rest of the night inventing leading questions to figure out if Mara and her husband were Lucy's adoptive parents. If they were, she'd have to think of another way to learn more about Lucy.

It was hard to push thoughts of Charlie out of her mind. She'd finally collapsed on the bed in her clothes and drifted off into a fitful dream about her mom, Trudy. Paige scowled recalling it all.

So lost in her thoughts, Paige nearly toppled over from the surprise of hearing a voice behind her. She jerked around to discover a gang of retiree-age women speed walking up the path. Dressed in sweat suits and colorful windbreakers that had fallen out of fashion years ago, their older frames made good time.

"Left!" one woman cried, arms locked at ninety degrees and swinging madly on either side of her. Paige scrambled to walk her bike to the side of the path when the voice shrieked again. "Oh, Paige! I didn't recognize you!"

CeCe.

Paige quickly donned a smile before turning.

"Good morning, CeCe."

"Ladies, halt!" CeCe cried, bringing her roving gang of speed walkers to a standstill.

"I want you all to meet the newest addition to Roseley."

"I'm not a resident," Paige tried to explain as the posse milled closer to check her out.

"No? You haven't just moved here?" CeCe asked, though her questions sounded more like accusations.

"I'm just passing through. Your town is charming, though."

One of the women, with curly violet-grey hair, stuck out a hand. "I'm Dolores Mitchell. I own the tea shop on Main."

"Nice to meet you—"

"Are you the new woman Charlie is courting?" Dolores continued, her eyes widening with interest as she shook Paige's hand.

"What?" Paige's cheeks flushed. Did people really use the word *courting* anymore? "We're friends, Dolores. I only met him yesterday."

"She's the gal I was telling you about, ladies," CeCe continued, as if not hearing Paige.

"She's as much a looker as you described, CeCe." The women continued to chat about Paige as though she wasn't still standing there in front of them.

"And he couldn't take his eyes off of her…" CeCe continued before reaching out to pat Paige on the arm. Paige smiled awkwardly.

Word certainly did travel fast in Roseley. For a person who prized her anonymity and privacy, she was quickly gaining a reputation among the townspeople.

"You'd better move fast, honey," Dolores said. "Charlie was quite the catch back in the day."

CeCe nodded knowingly. "Then he met that gal and…well, I'm glad he's come to his senses about her."

Paige's cell phone rang, jerking all six women to focus intently on her jacket pocket as if they were puppy dogs following a strip of bacon.

"It might be my aunt. Please excuse me," Paige said, grateful for the interruption.

"Come by my tea shop," Dolores said as she and the women picked up their pace again. "The first cup will be on the house!"

"And The Sandwich Board!" CeCe called over her shoulder. "I work tomorrow ten to close!" Paige waved goodbye as she pressed the phone to her ear, expecting Aunt Joan.

"Good morning!" the voice on the other line chirped. "Any chance you're already up and about?"

"I'm up," Paige said, frowning at the unrecognizable number on her cell phone screen. "Mara?"

"I'm calling from the shop. Listen, I know you were supposed to stop by later this afternoon, but is there any chance you could come now?" Her voice carried out over the quiet trail like a melodious wake-up call. "I know it's super-duper early, but my husband, make that soon-to-be *ex-husband*—" She laughed, but Paige could hear a man grumbling in the background. She waited patiently as Mara emphatically whispered to someone. "*Somebody* has to get to the city early this morning and that's after *somebody* woke up in a foul mood." More whispering transpired and Mara corrected, "Make that came home late last night in a foul mood. You drive me crazy, Mr. Selby. *Anyway*," she continued in an agitated voice. "Can you come now?"

"Uh, of course." She could tell she was about to get pulled into whatever marital strife was going on between Mr. and Mrs. Selby, and the possibility Lucy was living in that strife plucked a nauseous nerve. "I'm out riding at the moment, Mara, but if you can give me time to shower and grab my portfolio—"

"No, no, no, Paige. Just swing by. We don't care if you're sweaty with helmet hair. You'll fit right in around here." She laughed again. "It won't be a formal meeting, just a quick meet and greet. Can you do a…what do those writer folks call it? An elevator pitch? Minute or less?"

Paige clenched her jaw.

"Mara, I don't really feel comfortable flying by the seat of my pants. If you can give me just a half hour to get back to my motel and grab my portfolio, I have a brief but very informative presentation prepared."

"Look, sweetie, I'm not sure I can keep him longer than fifteen minutes. Something came up, and he's driving to Detroit this morning." The man's voice on the other end grumbled something more at Mara, making her snap at him in reply. The stress in Mara's voice had Paige cringing. "I'll leave it up to you. If you can make it—great. Otherwise, I don't know when he'll next be available."

Paige hung up and glanced back down the path where the crushed gravel led toward her motel. Even if she sprouted wings and flew to collect her portfolio, it would take at least a half hour to just get to the motel.

She needed to wrap up her visit and get back to her aunt and uncle. Landing this job might not be her one and only chance at meeting Lucy, but it was the most immediate opportunity, and it at least gave her a connection with Lucy's parents if Uncle Craig's health forced her to return home quickly. Ready or not, she had to take it.

Shoving her phone in her jacket pocket, she pedaled hard and fast, picturing the tiny, fresh-faced baby she'd placed in Dr. Bob's arms all those years ago.

Paige locked her bicycle in the rack and hurried to the sports shop. The door was locked as the shop didn't open for business for over an hour. She rapped loudly on the glass and paced along the sidewalk in front of it. How on earth would she reduce her presentation down to a minute? It was already short and snappy and most importantly—it worked. Not normally one to get nervous, Paige found herself shaking out her hands and forcing several deep breaths. After almost a minute, she cupped her hands around her face and pressed her forehead to the glass front door, searching for some sign of life amid the darkened merchandise.

Finally, she spotted a tall figure toward the back of the store and rapped loudly again. The figure turned, but after taking a few steps in her direction, stopped short and stared. She felt certain it was a man due to his sheer height and broad build, but his face was darkened. Whoever he was, he didn't look too anxious to let her in. If it was Mr. Selby, it seemed she was already in big trouble.

"I'm not a customer, Mr. Selby," she muttered to herself, rapping on the door again. "I was invited." The figure slowly made a move, prompting her to whisper encouragements as he did. "Come on…come on…open the door. You're slower than dripping molasses, bub. Yep, you can do it. I've only aged a thousand years."

Finally, a figure sprinted past him to the front door. Within seconds, Mara's bright face appeared from the shadows.

"Paige, you made it!" she said, unlocking the door and swinging it open. "I hope you weren't waiting long. I told Charlie to keep an eye out for you while I started some things in the back. Come on in, and I'll introduce you."

Mara strode briskly in front of Paige, who had suddenly downshifted into a dripping molasses pace of her own.

Mara had already made her way halfway across the sales floor to the back office, passing the tall, shadowy figure along the way. Paige half hoped that she had misunderstood

Mara, inserting Charlie's name in her head over whatever real name Mara had spoken. The obsessive loop of the handsome tour guide that had played in her head all night and morning had obviously messed with her, she thought. But as she drew closer into the darkened room, she realized she hadn't made any sort of mistake. The whites of Charlie's bold brown eyes caught in the light pooling from the back office. And they were locked on her.

She hesitated in front of him. She owed him something. Some word of acknowledgment that she was happy to see him, but her surprise overwhelmed her. She could barely manage a half-hearted grin under such confusing circumstances.

"What...what are you doing here?" she said. Charlie slung his hands into the front pockets of perfectly pressed gray trousers and tipped his head casually to the side.

"What am *I* doing here?"

His face was most likely a mirror image of her own, she thought. Eyes wide, mouth hanging slightly agape, breath caught. She made a mental note to force her mouth shut. Aunt Joan would warn her she would catch flies if it fell open any further, but under the circumstances, she couldn't help it. The last person she expected to see today was Charlie, and by his surprise, she knew he felt the same way.

"Come on, you two!" Mara called from the back office. "This meeting isn't going to run itself!"

Paige's eyes shifted from the back office doorway to Charlie. "Are you coming in here too?"

"That was the plan, yes."

"To listen to my presentation?"

"Yep."

Paige's chest constricted as a wince creased her face. "Please don't tell me that you're the one who woke up in a foul mood this morning."

"What?" Charlie frowned, making a study of her expression. When she didn't elaborate, he motioned for her to follow Mara. "After you, Ms. Cartman."

Paige could feel a red rash beginning to prickle her skin, working its way from her chest, up her neck and over her throat. It had happened a few times during her youth, during times of extreme stress, but over the years living with her aunt and uncle, it had become a very rare occurrence. The heat would usually stop short of her face, only ripening her cheeks to the blush of a Pink Lady apple, but her neck would turn a hot fiery red. As much as she willed it away, it always lingered at the worst moments, and she knew this situation couldn't be any more deserving.

Mara motioned for Paige to sit on the opposite side of her desk. "Paige, you can take the big chair over here. Make yourself comfortable."

"It's Ms. Cartman," Charlie said as he moved slowly past her to lean back against the desk. Paige's eyes flashed. Mara would realize she and Charlie had met before, and when she realized *that*, she'd want to know where they met and then she'd want to know—

"What was that?" Mara said as she shifted a pile of papers out of the way.

Paige cleared her throat. "Feel free to call me Paige. There's no reason for formalities."

Mara smiled up from her stack of papers. "I feel the same. And don't worry about having any helmet hair. You look great."

"I don't wear a helmet," she mumbled.

"What? Why not?" Charlie's voice cut through the small space like a submarine commander. Mara cocked her head to scold him as Paige replied.

"I don't like the feel of it."

"Would you rather have the feel of your head cracking open like an egg all over the sidewalk?"

Paige's eyes rounded as Charlie's had darkened. For a man so jovial and warm the night before, she was not at all prepared for his hostility.

"Babe, that's disgusting," Mara said, crumpling up a wad of paper and throwing it at him. He didn't flinch. Paige shook her head. She had come to Roseley to check in on Lucy and as of seven o'clock last night, might have made the little girl's life even worse by dating her father. "What has gotten into you, Charlie? You're supposed to make Paige feel at ease. You're usually so great at that."

"I'm not on my game today, Mar." He smiled weakly at Paige, but his eyes remained unchanged, as if he was hollow inside.

"Don't mind him, Paige. He's been acting strange all morning. Was there a full moon I didn't know about?"

Paige smiled politely even if she was smiling at a cheating, no good, big scamming jerk face. She'd make the pitch as quickly as she could out of respect for Mara, but as soon as she was alone with *Mr. Selby*, she'd tongue-lash the cad across Roseley and back again.

This, *this*, was who Dr. Hathaway had entrusted Lucy to?

"Charlie is excellent at hospitality," Mara continued. "I've been asking him for a few years now to work here with me and make this shop a family business."

Paige's eyes shifted between the two of them. "I'm still unclear what sort of business I'm supposed to write copy for…that is, if you like my pitch."

Charlie sat on the edge of the desk. "As best as I can explain it, it's a sports marketing start-up. Promoting events—"

"Direct to consumer?"

Mara nodded. "They'd like to branch out, though. If they could get hired on with a few local sports teams to handle all their event marketing, maybe they could eventually take on professional sports teams. Might as well shoot for the moon."

Paige nodded in turn. "The best advertising sells the product without drawing attention to itself. You probably got into sports marketing because it's something you've always loved whether by playing or watching. Sporting events are about passion, excitement, drive. Fans feed on the camaraderie of cheering with others and rooting for the hometown team. It's a full-on experience. Your marketing strategy capitalizes on this so you should bring that kind of excitement when you're trying to bring on a new team as your client. Where are you in the start-up? Are you actively trying to book sports clients now? Athletes? Arenas?"

Charlie frowned at her, but Mara was quick to respond.

"He and his partners want to start targeting and representing sports teams, exclusively. He's heading out today for a pitch meeting with a minor league baseball team."

Paige nodded, processing what that meant. "To convince a team to sign with you is to convince them that you have their best interests at heart—always. You must convince them that no one else can share their story to the mass market the way you can. It's about building a relationship within the first few minutes. When they look at you—"

Paige's voice trailed off as Charlie's eyes locked on hers. What was he taking from her words? More importantly, what on earth was she trying to say? From the first moment he'd talked to her in front of the bike shop, she'd felt a connection to him unlike anything she'd ever experienced before. If only…

"When they meet you," she continued and

cleared her throat, "they have to feel like they've found the solution to all their problems. You must make them feel like the long-lost member of an amazing family. I can help you do that."

Paige placed her hands on her hips in a superhero pose. She usually had more time to paint a story, but as Charlie and Mara caught each other's eye, she knew she'd left the right impression. She didn't want to work for Charlie now that she knew he would sneak behind Mara's back with another woman, but she desperately wanted to see Lucy. She *had* to see Lucy, no matter what the cost.

Mara's face finally broke into a wide smile.

"I think that's exactly what we were looking for, Paige," she said. "Now take a few deep breaths and say that when Peter gets here."

"Peter?"

"My husband."

Paige's hands slipped off her hips. "Your husband?"

"I don't know where that man is. He said he was on a tight deadline and yet, once again, here *I* am waiting on *him*." Mara slipped around Paige and through a door. "Peter, for real? Paige is waiting."

Paige side-glanced at Charlie, who flinched his eyebrows upward.

"So, if you're not…"

"Mara's husband? I realized you thought that about ten seconds into your pitch. Thanks for assuming the worst of me."

"I did think… I mean…it was a misunderstanding…"

"But still not the reason you ducked out on me last night."

Mara darted back into the office with her husband hot on her heels.

"Thanks so much for waiting, Paige," Peter said, crossing the floor to shake her hand. With brown hair peppering to gray and muted blue eyes, his demeanor conveyed the gentleness and patience of a yoga guru. "My business partner was supposed to present at a convention in Detroit tomorrow, and I learned last night that he came down with meningitis. Unfortunately, I'm off last minute to fill in."

"Traveling puts Peter in a bad mood," Mara said. "And not waking me up to tell me your change of plans puts *me* in a bad mood."

"What would you have done last night that you couldn't do this morning?"

"I would have woken Lucy up earlier so she

could spend a few extra minutes with you. You're going to be gone for several days."

Paige brought a hand to her mouth to mask an audible gasp. Mara and Peter were too caught up in their own soap opera to notice, but Charlie's slightly furrowed brow told her *he'd* noticed. Quickly, she balled her hand to a fist and forced a cough. Their daughter was Lucy, but was it *her* Lucy? Had they really kept her birth name?

"Would you like a drink of water?" Charlie asked.

"Water?" Mara said, surfacing from her squabble with Peter. "I can grab you one, Paige."

"No, thank you. Let me get on with it. I'm so excited to talk about what I can do for your business, Peter."

"You know what," Peter said, holding up a hand. "Before you launch into anything, this was all Mara's idea. Truth be told, Paige, I'm not in the right frame of mind to listen to a pitch. Even if you completely sell me on the idea, which I'm sure you could, I can't decide right now. I'm sorry for wasting your time, but maybe I can better consider this next week."

"Peter," Mara said, pressing her fingers to

either side of her temples. "You always do this."

"Always do what?"

"This."

"I apologized to Paige, but I can't do this right now. I have to leave, and you're obsessed with hiring a copywriter."

"*You* are. It was your idea. I'm just trying to help."

Paige cringed as Mara and Peter lobbed accusations back and forth at each other like champion tennis players. *This* was who had been raising Lucy for the last ten years?

It was all falling apart: the dream life for Lucy she'd carefully constructed in her mind to ease the pain of letting that little baby go. The heat that had crept up her throat now turned to a surge, fueling her desire to outshout Mara and Peter. If she wanted to preserve any chance of seeing Lucy, she had to get out of here before she did just that.

"Thank you for your time, but I should go." Hurrying around the desk, she didn't wait for Mara or Peter to reply. Wanting to leave the door open for further contact, at a time when her heart wasn't pumping her into an early grave, she called over her shoulder, "I'll be in touch!"

CHAPTER FIVE

CHARLIE STILLWATER STILL couldn't put his finger on what had gone wrong last night. He'd spent the entire evening reliving every minute of his date with Paige Cartman, calculating the width of her smile and how her eyes crinkled in delight when he made a joke. If she hadn't been enjoying herself, he was sure he would have picked up on it sooner than the moment she had practically sprinted out of the restaurant.

If there was one thing he knew, it was how to read people. He prided himself on the fact that it was one of his greatest strengths. Well, it had been one of his greatest strengths until Crystal had pulled one over on him, and Freckles had thrown him for a loop. Sadly, he probably needed to reexamine his greatest strengths.

He had eliminated the likely possibilities of what could have happened with Freckles. If she had gotten sick or overheated, she would have wanted to leave quickly, but she wouldn't have made a point to completely sever all future contact. Perhaps she had a boyfriend or husband back home and had wandered too far down the rabbit hole with him, a stab of guilt finally hitting during a quiet moment in the bathroom. There was also the possibility that she didn't really like him, but if that was the case, she was a brilliant actress. She had no motive for leading him on—unless she was making a fool of him for sport. But the way she spoke of her uncle and aunt didn't lead him to believe she had no empathy for others. The depth of her heart was one of her most endearing qualities, which he had concluded after only a few minutes into dinner.

Charlie had awakened that morning still thinking about Paige when Mara had called, asking if he could come in early for his first day at the sports shop. He had planned to get an early bike ride in and blow off his skunky mood, but instead agreed to arrive early. Mara could be a little tightly strung, but he could sense she needed him.

He had had that sense for a while. It was one of the reasons that had persuaded him to move back to Roseley. If Mara and Peter were struggling through a rocky phase in their marriage, Mara would need family support, and if he were honest, he needed a little of his own. Living with Mara and her family until he could sort out a place of his own certainly took some adjustment, but he suspected she was glad to have him around, if only for moral support.

He had just arrived and wandered out onto the sales floor to give Mara and Peter some privacy to bicker, when he thought he'd heard someone rapping on the front door. Mara had briefly mentioned on the phone that a copywriter was stopping in, but he had assumed it was during business hours.

Through the dimly lit front of the store, he squinted at the figure standing on the other side of the glass in the sunlight. Of all the people he had wished to see at that moment, he had had to blink several times to convince himself she was real.

Freckles.

It made sense. She was a writer, although he had at first pictured her as more of a novelist, hibernating in a woodsy cabin and looking for inspiration from the whispering of gently swaying tree branches. And to be honest, he wasn't exactly sure what a copywriter did. Was she supposed to be some sort of ad man?

She moved quickly, he thought, as Mara

welcomed her through the front door. For only just arriving to Roseley, she'd managed to get a job interview with Peter. She'd also managed to get dinner from a hopeless romantic who had been instantly smitten by those kissable freckles and jungle-green eyes.

Paige had stopped in front of him, her eyes widening the way a cat's did spotting birds on a window ledge. They were hypnotizing, yet not as sincere as he'd remembered from the night before. Getting rejected had put a damper on his memory of the evening. Of her.

Following her into the office, he'd wanted to ask again about what had happened at the restaurant. He wanted to know if she had led him on purposely. His heart was still very raw since arriving in Roseley, although she wouldn't have known that. Disclosing his relationship history was more appropriate for a fourth or fifth date, which now wasn't in the cards for them.

She had spunk. He had to give her that, he'd thought, as he listened to her pitch. He had taken enough from her presentation to know she was good at her job. Peter would be a fool to turn down her expertise, although, the way Mara told it, Peter hadn't been making the wisest decisions lately.

But when Paige had sprinted out of the room, he knew he'd regret not following her this time.

"Paige," he called, pushing through the front door to find her furiously unlocking her bicycle. "Hold up a second."

"What for?" she asked, eyes averted, from a crouched position.

"What's your hurry? Are you really going to run out on me again?"

She looked up and shielded her eyes against the morning sunshine.

"I wasn't running out on you, Charlie. I had to get out of there. That bickering…"

"It drives me crazy too. Heck, it drives them crazy. But it's quieter out here, so give me a minute, huh?"

He wanted to offer a hand and help her to her feet, but at the same time he already felt too exposed. If she refused to take it, it would turn the rusty nail in his heart another quarter inch. And if she did accept it, he wasn't sure he could stand to let it go.

Paige stood and crossed her arms.

"So, if you're not Mara's husband, I take it you're her new hire? She said she had a new person starting today."

"Sort of. I moved back to Roseley to help Mara and Lucy—"

"Lucy?"

"My niece."

"Your *niece*? Are you Mara's brother?"

"That's usually how it works," he said with a chuckle. "I'm her big brother."

"I never would have guessed. You don't look that much alike, aside from the height."

He shrugged. He'd heard that plenty of times before.

"My father died shortly after I was born, and my mother remarried quickly. Mara's father, my stepfather, Glenn, is Polynesian. She was blessed with his ridiculously handsome good looks."

A smile slipped over Paige's lips. "You're not too bad looking yourself." He shrugged, avoiding her compliment. "How old is Lucy?"

"She just turned ten."

"Was she blessed with Mara's supermodel good looks?"

He laughed. "In high school Mara was voted most likely to be a secret supermodel. I think they added the category that year just for her. She always jokes that she never took full advantage of her high cheekbones." Paige nodded, solemn, as if waiting for an answer. "But no. Lucy is adopted."

"Does she know she's adopted?"

Charlie made a face. "Of course. Have you known adopted kids who don't know they're adopted, or something?"

She dragged the toe of her sneaker against the sidewalk before kicking at a loose shard of concrete. "Yeah, something like that. What are you helping Mara with…if you don't mind me asking?"

"I do, actually."

"Oh," she said, her neck reddening as it had earlier during her pitch. He had to fight the urge to touch her blushing cheek.

"Look, I followed you out here to get a little closure after our date last night. I had a nice time with you and wanted you to know that." What was he saying? What was she supposed to say to that? If anything, he was grasping for words to keep the conversation going.

"I know I left quickly, Charlie, and I probably got you confused. I'm so sorry if I hurt you."

"I wasn't hurt," he said, but he knew it was a lie.

"That's a relief," she whispered, lowering her eyes. Had she worried about hurting him last night when she'd run out on him suddenly? Did she regret leaving now that the intimacy of last night had dissolved?

"If I moved too quickly last night," he began, not sure how to finish his sentence. He certainly hadn't felt like he'd moved too quickly. He'd only let himself drift along on their date, like a raft carried downstream by the current. If that current had moved too rapidly for her, who was he to say?

"You don't need to—"

"No. If things moved too quickly for you, I'm sorry about that." The truth was, after all that had transpired between him and Crystal, things last night should have felt like they were too fast paced. But somehow, they hadn't. "I should have given you a bit more space for a first date."

"Thanks," she muttered. He wondered if her response was an admission of sorts. He'd been warned before of falling in love too quickly and not seeing the warning signs until they were flashing right in front of him.

"Anyway, there isn't much more to say about it, especially since Peter's away for a few days and has put off any hiring. I guess our paths won't cross again, huh?"

"Not unless you head back to The Sand-

wich Board and help me order my next sandwich." By the way she angled her head to look
up at him, he could swear she was flirting
with him.

His lips parted in surprise. He shifted his
weight to his heels, deciding whether he
should leave, when his mouth rambled on with
another question. "How long are you planning
to stay in Roseley?"

Paige squinted up at the morning sunshine
as if contemplating the question for the very
first time.

"Are you that anxious to get rid of me?"
When he didn't answer, she continued. "I
haven't decided, Charlie. My life is complicated right now, but if I stay, I know one thing
that's for certain."

"Yes?"

"I *will* be going back to The Sandwich
Board, and if you happen to show up too, I'd
be very…"

"Very?" he prompted.

She bit her bottom lip and smiled up at him,
the sunlight reflecting tiny bits of gold in her
bright green eyes.

"Excited."

"Excited?" It was hardly the word he'd expected. *Glad, fine, okay*—any of those words

were polite enough, but *excited*? Just the word rolling off her glossy lips made something inside him leap.

"I did a lot of thinking last night after I left you, Charlie. Perhaps finding you here at your sister's shop was fate's way of handing me a second chance. Do you believe in that?"

"In fate?"

"In second chances."

Charlie dipped both hands into his front pockets. For a woman who had been so hellbent on getting out of here this morning, she had certainly pulled a one-hundred-eighty-degree turn, now lingering on the sidewalk with the ease of a retiree. Perhaps because he apologized for moving too quickly before…

"I don't know, Paige. I need to get some work done before the shop opens."

"What time do you get off work?"

His fingers toyed with a loose string in his trouser pocket, plucking it taut as he processed her question.

"Three. I'm picking Lucy up from school today."

Paige smiled. "Good for you. I didn't mean to pry or insert myself where I don't… Never mind. You'll be too busy with your niece this afternoon. I'll let you go."

She rolled her bicycle to the curb and swung a leg over the seat. A jolt of anxiety flooded his blood. If he let her ride off without another word, he knew he'd regret it for the rest of his life.

"Why don't you meet me here at three? I'm taking Lucy down to the lake, and you're welcome to join us."

Her face broke into a teary smile as she quickly slid her sunglasses into place. It made him hopeful she had regretted the way the night had ended as much as he had.

"Are you sure? I don't want to impose."

"Be here no later than three," he said, heading back into the shop. "And wait until you meet Lucy. She's the greatest."

PAIGE RAN HER hands nervously over the tops of her thighs. Of all the places she had dreamed of being when she woke up this morning, on her way to meet Lucy wasn't one of them. She couldn't believe her luck. No matter how much she wiped her hands off, they continued to perspire. It was almost a release valve; every cell in her body was humming. She hadn't been this nervous since the night she'd wrapped Lucy in an old sweatshirt and huddled in the darkness, waiting for the flash of

Aunt Joan's car headlights. Although these nerves were due to excitement and not to fear.

Heart pounding, she noticed Charlie. He was riding casually in the driver's seat, watching her.

"Is everything okay?" he asked, pulling his eyes back to the road.

"Just peachy. How was your first day on the job? Did you sell any mountain bikes?"

He rested his hand on the top of the steering wheel. "I love my sister, but she doesn't know what's good for her."

"How do you mean?"

"Have you ever met a person who didn't get it?"

Paige twisted her mouth, thinking. Truth be told, she didn't really know that many people. She had lived the past decade keeping her distance, carefully shielding herself from the harmless conversations that could quickly diverge to pointed questions she didn't want to answer. The fatigue of thinking several steps ahead to avoid those questions had led her to avoid most people altogether. Aside from staying close to Aunt Joan and Uncle Craig, she mostly kept to herself. One of the first times in a long time, when she had let her guard down was when she'd met Charlie. She had deviated from her standard cold shoulder, and all because the gentleness of his handsome smile had lulled her into conversation.

"Family has its challenges," she said as her mind wandered to sad memories of Trudy. "And as a matter of fact, I do know what you mean. Some people really don't get it, Charlie, and they never will." She knew thinking of Trudy made her tone bite.

"Whoa. Who burned you?"

"Nobody worth mentioning," she said with a forced smile. "That's a pretty extremist attitude to hold, huh?"

"Not if your life experience gives you the right to hold it. People can be pretty awful sometimes." Paige nodded in agreement, tightly clasping her hands in her lap. *"But,"* he said. "People can come through in pretty amazing ways too, you know."

She turned quick enough to catch his eyes as they squinted into a grin, and even though it wasn't exactly a logical conclusion, she had a feeling he was referring to the two of them. She tore her eyes away and cleared her throat.

"Tell me what Mara doesn't get."

Charlie released a groan. "For starters, she doesn't see how she's the root of most of her problems."

"Most people are."

He shrugged. "I'll give you that, but the way she talks to Peter immediately puts him on the defense. Then he snaps back at her. Then she begins to emotionally unravel…"

"And Lucy lives in that?"

"Unfortunately, but it's only a recent thing. I visited them eighteen months ago, and I don't remember any arguing. They've always been happy, so something must have happened."

"Mara might now be ready to tell you."

"I hope she trusts me eventually. All I want to do is help."

Paige inwardly sighed at the sincerity in his voice as he looked out over the road. His words rang with nothing but compassion, and it stirred a deep desire in her heart that had been hidden away for so long. She had always believed that trust was something a person had to slowly earn, as they came through time over time. Once a person had plunked enough trustworthy tokens into her bank, she'd consider trusting them. And every time they failed her, she'd dump out the bank and write their balance sheet back to zero. After all, her entire childhood had been a sad exercise in dumping out her trust bank. It was an experience she had never wanted Lucy to face.

"I'm sure you'll get to the bottom of it...
for Lucy's sake."

"Wait until you meet her. She's going to win
you over in about two seconds."

Paige's palms began to sweat again at the
prospect of it.

"How soon until we're there?" she asked,
staring out the window. Charlie swung his
pickup truck into a half-circle drive in front
of a wide redbrick building and rolled down
Paige's passenger window.

"Here she comes." He motioned to a little
girl bounding out of the school. "My little
jackrabbit. She has more energy than anyone
I've ever known. I hope you're ready for her."

Paige brought her fingertips to her lips. She
had been ready for this moment since she was
seventeen years old.

CHAPTER SIX

CHARLIE CHUCKLED AS Lucy galloped up the sidewalk before clinging to Paige's car window. She batted thick brown eyelashes back and forth between him and Paige, the shadow cast by the truck giving her normally bright green peepers a gray and brooding look.

"Uncle Charlie, are you on a date?" she said, raising a dramatic eyebrow at Paige. He waited for Paige to laugh or shake her head or at least look at him, but she seemed almost transfixed by the little girl. He couldn't blame her; Lucy sometimes had that effect on people. Mara liked to refer to her as having an old soul, but he hated that description. It was true that she did pick up on things other ten-year-old children didn't, but her balance of spunk and decorum was entirely hers.

"This is my new friend, Paige."

"Paige?" Lucy said, leaning farther into the truck to get a look. "Like a page in a book?"

Again, Charlie waited for Paige to respond,

but after several moments of silence, Charlie explained.

"It sounds the same, but it's spelled differently."

"Oh," Lucy said, tipping her head back in eureka. "That's a good name. I've never heard it before. Is it your nickname? Do you like to read a lot?" Before Paige could respond, Lucy's eyes widened mischievously. "My nickname is Cat. Can you guess why?"

When Paige slowly shook her head, Lucy ducked down out of sight before leaping back up into view and clawing her hands in the air. She made a playful meowing sound before erupting into laughter. Charlie chuckled and motioned for her to hop in the back seat as Paige spun around to get a lock on Lucy again. She leaned on the center console, the scent of her citrusy shampoo filling his senses like a spring morning.

"It's nice to meet you, Lucy," she said as if finally finding her voice. "Your uncle Charlie has told me so much about you." She smiled up at him, as if realizing she had moved much closer into his personal space.

"I've never heard anything about you before," Lucy said, buckling herself into the center seat. "Charlie usually tells me everything."

"We only met yesterday."

"Where?"

"At The Sandwich Board."

"The Sandwich Board?" Lucy made a face and slugged Charlie on the shoulder. "You found your new girlfriend at Angelo's? That's not very romantic."

"I found a new *friend*, yes."

"Well, you need to find a new *girl*friend. Mom says the only way to heal a broken heart is by falling in love again. It's the gold sold... soldering the broken pieces of your heart back together again."

Charlie gripped the top of the steering wheel tighter and shifted in his seat. From the corner of his eye, he could tell Paige was working hard to not look at him.

"What grade are you in, Lucy?" she asked, noticeably changing the subject. She really was nice.

"Fourth. It's the best grade, because we celebrate Storybook Characters Day next week for the end of the school year."

"What's Storybook Characters Day?"

"We wrote and illustrated our own chapter books. Our teacher helped us print and bind them, and next week, we each get to read them to a first-grade class. We're supposed to dress up like one of the characters in our story but—" Lucy sighed. "Mom hasn't gotten around to helping me with my costume."

"She has a lot on her mind, kiddo," Charlie said. "Don't worry. I'll help you figure it out."

"But I need her to sew me this." Lucy dug through her book bag to retrieve a sketch of a girl wearing a simple purple dress. "This is what it's supposed to look like."

He glanced at his niece in the rearview mirror. "That looks easy enough, Lucy, and I can wield a glue gun. I'm sure we can pull something together."

"Maybe I can help," Paige said. "I sew a little."

Lucy leaned forward. "Did your mom teach you?"

Paige shook her head.

"Self-taught. No matter what problems come my way, I tend to buckle down and figure them out on my own eventually."

"Why would you want to do that?" Lucy said.

"I grew up having to do things on my own."

"Didn't your mom help you?"

"Uh… I didn't have a mom like your mom."

"Do you know my mom?" He noticed Paige hesitate. After a few quiet moments, Lucy became impatient. "She's a good mom, but I've already reminded her about this costume three times."

"We'll help you make a costume, Lucy," Charlie said. "As long as it's not a cat costume."

Lucy giggled.

"Do you really love cats?" Paige said, hugging the back of her seat to better angle her body toward Lucy.

"Who doesn't?"

"I can think of a few people."

"People who don't love cats? Why? They're only the best animals on the planet."

Paige caught eyes with Charlie and muffled a smile.

"What makes you say so?"

"For starters," Lucy said, heaving an exaggerated breath, "they're smart. They can hunt for survival. They clean themselves. They can climb the sides of buildings like superheroes. They have nine lives. And…they're the cutest wittle things I've ever seen."

"You're forgetting the best reason," Charlie said, spying her in the rearview mirror. His niece's face broke into a self-conscious grin as she pointed at him to explain.

"Which is?" Paige asked, leaning closer.

Charlie laughed as Lucy covered her face in embarrassment.

"Lucy has the biggest, greenest cat eyes of anybody I've ever seen. Cats are pretty much her spirit animal."

"That's the *real* reason my friends sometimes call me Cat. Plus, I love to wear headbands with cat ears." She dug through her book bag before placing a headband with purple metallic cat ears on top of her dark brown mane.

"Okay, you've convinced me. Cats are the greatest animal on earth."

"But you didn't like them before, Paige?"

"A person I used to live with had way too many cats, so I didn't like them very much."

"Why didn't you move out if they bothered you?"

"I couldn't at the time. I just had to learn to live with them."

"Couldn't your roommate keep them in her room?"

"There were too many to do that. Plus, our…uh…*home*…was really tiny."

"How many cats did she have?"

Paige paused to think. "I don't really know. At least eight at one point."

"Eight?"

Charlie's head snapped at the number. "Whoa. That's a lot. Who was this roommate?"

Paige tucked her hair behind both ears. "It was a long time ago. It wasn't even worth mentioning. I'm not sure why I did." She turned back to Lucy. "What do you prefer to be called? Lucy or Cat?"

Lucy bounced forward in her seat as they pulled up to the beach. "Both. Unfortunately, there are two other girls named Lucy in my school, but I'm the only Cat."

"How did your parents come up with the name Lucy?" Paige asked.

"They said it means *light*, and I'm the light of their life. How did your parents choose Paige?"

Paige flinched.

"They, uh, didn't," she mumbled. Charlie cut the truck's engine. He flipped his keys in his hand.

"Why?" Charlie asked. "Was it a family name they felt obligated to use or something?"

Paige threw open her truck door and hopped onto the hot asphalt. By the time he had climbed out to join her, the question had been lost to the summer breeze, which carried the call of seagulls and the mist of lake water.

Before he could blink, Paige had kicked off her shoes, tossing them up on the hood of the truck. She sprinted toward the sand, taunting Lucy to follow.

He laughed and shook his head at the two scampering up and down the beach like puppies meeting each other for the first time. And as he watched Paige with her sun-kissed locks chase Lucy out toward the water, he couldn't help but think the entire scene, with their instant camaraderie, was all somehow so familiar.

PAIGE KICKED A FAN of water at Charlie, splashing him just above the knees.

"What was that for?" he said, reciprocating with an even larger water spray. She dripped from head to toe, blotches of watermarks spreading on her purple tank top, but she didn't care. She couldn't remember a day that came close to the joy she felt now. It was as if she'd woken up in a television commercial, strolling along the beach with a picture-perfect stand-in family of her own.

"Come on, Paige," Lucy shouted, leading her down the beach. "I have an idea!" Paige followed the little girl behind a sand dune and squatted down beside her. "I'll lure him this way," Lucy said, her voice tinged with excitement. "Then you run around and jump on his back. We'll bury him in the sand. He won't know what hit him." Paige nodded in approval as she worked to lock the girl's face to memory. They had the same silky textured hair, but Lucy's was a dark brown that contrasted against her cream-colored skin. Running had flushed her fair cheeks to deep pink. She was a rare beauty, Paige thought. Lucy's features reminded her so much of both her own and of the women in her family. She noted how Lucy had the dark hair of her own grandmother, and the button nose of her mother.

"Don't you want to be the one to tackle him?" Paige said in a whisper. Considering her only contact with Charlie consisted of light dancing the night before, she hesitated at the thought of jumping on him in a full-body tackle.

Lucy peeked out from behind the sand barrier. "He's coming in hot. There's no time. Go!" Lucy jumped out and waggled her fingers at Charlie in a na-na-na-na-boo-boo fashion as Paige took her cue and scurried around the sand barrier. But when she was no more than a few yards around it, someone caught up with her from behind, tickling her.

"Get away from me!" she hollered as Charlie sent her into convulsions of squirms and squeals. Paige could barely grasp for breath between her howls of laughter as Lucy jumped on top of them both. Charlie tickled his niece then, until she tried to tickle him back.

Charlie burst into laughter and held Lucy off with one arm. "You can try your hardest, kid, but I'm not ticklish, remember?"

"You're not ticklish?" Paige said, brushing off sand.

"Not a bit."

"That's no fun."

He grinned as Lucy helped pull him to his feet.

"Why? What did you have in mind?"

Paige scrambled for a witty response, but before she could muster a reply, she was struck by the kindness reflected in Charlie's smile.

"I'm surprised," she said. "I've never met anyone who wasn't ticklish."

"You're more than welcome to try." He raised his arms out to his sides and beckoned her with a naughty grin. When she scowled back up at him, he tenderly brushed sand off her shoulders and ran a thumb over the tops of her cheeks.

"That ought to do it. I hope you didn't have fancy dinner plans for tonight. I'd hate for you to show up to a date looking like this, Freckles."

"No date tonight unless you're asking."

His eyes fell serious as the short gap between them seemed to close without either of them moving. Paige wavered a step closer just to feel his breath warm her skin, but Lucy tugged at her.

"What now, Paige?"

"How about some ice cream?" she said, clasping the little girl's hand snugly in her own.

"For dinner?"

"Why not? You only live once." She blew a wisp of hair off her face and offered a sly smile.

"I can already tell you're trouble," he said, answering his ringing cell phone. "Luce, it's your mom." His face fell in a serious grimace as he turned away to talk.

"Not again," Lucy muttered, sinking onto the sand.

"What's wrong?"

"It's always something these days. They probably fought again."

"Do your mom and dad fight a lot?"

Lucy shrugged her shoulders. She scooped a handful of sand and let it run slowly between her fingers. Paige held a hand to shield her eyes from the sun as Charlie returned.

"Hey, kiddo. Mom wants you home for dinner, so let's head back."

Lucy nodded and silently made her way to the car. Paige lagged, tugging on Charlie's arm.

"What was that all about?"

"I need to get her home. Can I drop you somewhere?"

"You can drop her first if you need to. I don't mind."

He nodded and hurried ahead to let Lucy into the truck. Paige picked up her pace but wondered why. What was going on with Mara and Peter that had put Charlie and Lucy so immediately on edge? Whatever it was, she thought, she couldn't go home until she was certain Lucy was safe and happy here.

CHAPTER SEVEN

PAIGE IMAGINED CALLING Aunt Joan to tell her the news: she had found Lucy, and she was lovelier than either of them could have imagined. She didn't want to act too eager, but it was all she could do to keep from desperately concocting a plan for another outing. After the playtime on the beach ended so abruptly, she needed another outing to snap a picture of Lucy. She knew it would be one of the first things Aunt Joan would ask about. Perhaps they could go pick out fabric for Lucy's storybook costume or grab dinner or hit the beach again or go for a bicycle ride or...

As Charlie swung his truck into the driveway, Mara popped up from the porch steps and sprinted to them. For as beautiful as Paige had originally thought her, she now looked tired and anxious. Her silky brown hair was twisted in a ratty topknot, and dark circles had appeared under her eyes as if developing just from that morning.

"Uh-oh," Charlie muttered under his breath as Mara hurried for the back door of the cab, bypassing Charlie completely. He rolled down his window. "What's the matter, sis?"

Mara wrapped Lucy in a bear hug before the little girl could wrangle her book bag and body out of the truck. Paige watched in envy as Mara squeezed her eyes shut and buried her nose in Lucy's hair. Perhaps if she hung around town long enough to get close to Lucy, she could soon hug her that way too.

"You were gone too long. I missed you, baby," she said, pressing Lucy's cheeks between her palms. Lucy groaned and slung her book bag up over her shoulder.

"Mom, I was only gone an extra hour."

"I know, I know. I'm only teasing. Go wash up for dinner."

As Lucy jogged toward the house, Mara leaned into Charlie's door.

"Paige, I'm sorry about how things went this morning. I don't know what's wrong with my husband. He needs a copywriter even if he doesn't know it."

"No worries." Paige smiled. The truth was, things were working out just fine for her on their own. Mara glanced between her and Charlie.

"You two seem to be getting along."

Paige smiled politely. "Charlie and I met yesterday."

"Charlie told me the story after you left the pitch meeting."

"What's going on, Mara?" he said. "Why did we have to get Lucy home?"

Mara rubbed her fingers against her temple. "I wanted her back as soon as I heard. It figures Peter would be gone when things hit the fan. He's always away or busy these days when I really need him—"

"Mara," Charlie said, his tone growing impatient. "What on earth is going on?"

"I got a phone call today from Dr. Hathaway."

"Who?"

Paige clenched her jaw, attempting to keep her face as neutral as possible even as the name completely shocked her. Dr. Hathaway had been there during the darkest time of her life, although back then she'd called him Dr. Bob.

"The doctor who helped us adopt Lucy. He called all in a tizzy, and now *I'm* in a tizzy."

"It doesn't take much, sis. You freak out quickly these days."

"Ha ha. Very funny. Well, this is serious,

and I have no idea what I'm going to do."
Mara smoothed her hair off her face as her
eyes darted to Paige. "I'm sorry to go on about
this in front of you, Paige. Just the joys of
motherhood."

"You don't have to talk about anything personal in front of me," Paige said even though
her ears were pricked with a desperation to
hear every word.

"Paige is fine, Mara, but if you don't spit
it out—"

"Dr. Hathaway talked to someone who
helped put Lucy up for adoption. He told us
back when he brought her to us that he knew
Lucy's adoptive mother, but he didn't disclose
her personal information, just like he didn't
tell the mother where Lucy was going.

"The birth mother, or someone who knows
her, contacted him this week trying to get
information. The two of them went twenty
rounds, as he described it, until he finally
managed to end the conversation. He didn't
think much of it until this afternoon when it
dawned on him that he had slipped and mentioned Little Lakeside Sports by name. At the
time he didn't think he gave anything away,
but then today—"

"Slipups happen. Isn't he an old man by now?"

"He was an old man ten years ago when he brought us Lucy, so yeah."

"Does he think the mother wants to hurt Lucy?"

"I don't think so. If he trusted her then, I don't see why he wouldn't trust her now. What I'm really concerned with is…"

Paige held her breath. What dots had Mara connected in the short time since speaking with Dr. Hathaway? Her heart hammered the inside of her chest, waiting for Mara to suddenly snap her attention and point an accusatory finger at her.

"We didn't go through the proper channels to adopt Lucy. Lucy practically fell in our lap overnight, thanks to Dr. Hathaway. He fudged paperwork to make it all happen. To protect her."

Charlie's brow furrowed. "Why on earth would he cut corners on something as important as an adoption? Why would you? Was it anything illegal?"

"It was all in Lucy's best interest, Charlie. I assure you. He told us Lucy was in a lot of danger and needed to be adopted as quickly, and discreetly, as possible. But now, based on the conversation he just had..." Mara's eyes flooded with tears as she croaked out her words. "It's been ten years and then to have someone call out of the blue? What if the birth mother wants her back?"

Charlie gently cracked open his truck door and slipped out in a seamless maneuver to embrace his sister. His tan biceps flexed as Mara's face disappeared into his chest.

As she watched the siblings sway gently back and forth, Paige couldn't help but wonder how fragile their adoption contract really was. Mara was worried enough, that was for sure. If Dr. Bob hadn't gone through the proper channels, Lucy's future could have veered in a completely different direction, if the right people, *or person*, knew about it. Aunt Joan and Uncle Craig had been right: checking in on Lucy had been the wise decision if only to learn this tiny, but important, detail.

"It's going to be fine, Mara," Charlie said. "We won't let anything happen to Lucy. She's your daughter, and no one can take her from you. I won't let them."

Paige drew her focus out her own window. Her shortsightedness had been foolish. Instead of hoping for the next outing with Lucy, she needed to think what was in her best interest for the long run. Even though she wanted to tell Mara and Charlie the truth, after ten years of not allowing herself to utter Lucy's name out loud, she couldn't bring herself to spill the little girl's ugly past now. There was a reason she and her aunt and uncle had vowed complete secrecy. There was a reason she had changed her name and stayed off the grid as much as possible. As much as it pained her to realize it, just being in the same town as Lucy might be a tragic mistake. If she had been followed here…

She glanced longingly at Charlie, wishing she could tell him the truth and then slip up into his arms with complete vulnerability like Mara did. No one had ever made her feel the same sense of peace and safety as Charlie had in just two short days. But the sad truth was that carrying on with him any longer might only lead to trouble, not just for him but for Lucy as well.

PAIGE REACHED FOR her door handle before Charlie had even downshifted to Park.

"In a hurry?" he asked, removing his sunglasses. She bit the inside of her cheek. She could spend every waking moment enjoying his presence, but she'd used the drive back to her motel to convince herself of the truth: hanging out with Charlie would only hurt them both. He'd been quiet on the drive, no doubt thinking about Lucy and Mara, so it had given her enough silence to get her thoughts in order. There wouldn't be a future for them, no matter how much they liked each other. There *couldn't* be a future. Life had dealt her a complicated hand, and Charlie would end up as her collateral damage if they continued.

"It's been a really long day, Charlie."

He cut the engine and rested his head on the seat back. "It sure has. I know now why I moved back here."

"You didn't already know the reason?"

"I knew *a* reason, but I didn't know *the* reason. Do you believe things happen for a reason?"

She shrugged. Her entire childhood had been one long continuous game of playing hot lava. Her days with Trudy consisted of one giant leap after another from stone to stone, trying to not get scorched. Unfortunately, wherever Trudy was involved, Paige had always been burned. Had there really been a reason to any of that?

"I'm not sure, but you apparently think so."

"I knew I moved back here to help Mara—"

"And to escape some kind of heartbreak?"

His lips parted in surprise. "Well, aside from that, I think it's a good thing I'm back. If any trouble with Lucy's adoption develops, Mara will need the support."

Paige moved to touch her door handle again. "It looks like you have your hands full, then. I should get going."

"Are you brushing me off?"

"I'm only in town for a bit, and you're getting over a breakup of some sort. Then there's this thing with Lucy's adoption…" She sighed. "Starting something up with me right now is bad timing. You know it is."

"I know meeting you is probably the best thing that's happened to me in a while, but if you don't feel any chemistry between us, I can take a hint. I know when I've scared a woman off."

Paige rolled her eyes. "You haven't scared me off."

"Good." He smiled. "Because I've never actually scared a woman off before. I'm really likable."

"Not modest, though."

He smiled wider. "I could feign modesty if it would keep you in the truck longer."

"Look, Charlie," she said, shifting in her seat. "It's not that I don't like you…"

"Not handsome enough for you?"

She blinked hard at the perfect lines of his rugged face and playfulness in his eyes.

"I don't think either of us are in a place to get involved."

"I don't either."

"You don't?"

"Nope. I do not want to get involved with you, Paige Cartman. It's a bad idea right now. In fact, I should kick you out of my truck and drive away forever. But…" He lowered his eyes. "I also really like having you around."

"You do?" Paige whispered.

"So much."

"I don't know. Maybe if we're just friends—"

"We don't have to name it. There are people I like to spend time with and people I don't. Maybe you could be a person who I like to spend time with. How can there be any harm in that?"

Paige looked away if only to break the lovable trance he held her in. He certainly made it difficult for her to cut and run. The truth was, just sitting beside him filled her senses with a peace she hadn't known in years. And that smile…

"I think… I think I'm tired."

He fired up the truck engine. "Rest up. You never know when I'll bump into you at Angelo's."

Paige slipped out of the truck and into her motel, hesitating at the front door to glance back at Charlie. As much as she knew she shouldn't see him again, the possibility that she might had her grinning all the way to her room.

PAIGE FLOPPED ON her bed and dialed her aunt, but it went to voice mail. She quickly shot off a text; she had so much to tell her.

Call me. I need to talk.

She startled when her room telephone rang immediately.

Bringing the phone slowly to her ear, she paused a few seconds before speaking.

"Hello?"

There was a pause on the other end before a familiar voice came over the line.

"I forgot to mention something."

Charlie.

Paige made herself more comfortable on the bed, cradling the phone in the crook of her neck.

"Aren't guys supposed to wait a few days before calling after a date? I think you're breaking some sort of guy code."

"Nope. It's not guy code."

"Why not?"

"Because you and I weren't on a date. We are two people who like to spend time together, so you joined me while I hung out with my niece. Easy peasy."

Paige laughed. "Did you just say 'easy peasy'?"

"Yeah. Do you have a problem with easy peasy?"

"It's ridiculous."

"What did easy peasy ever do to you?"

"Every time you say it, it sounds weirder!" Paige laughed as she tucked a pillow under her head. "What did you forget to mention?"

Charlie's voice crackled like a fire, warming her ear. "I called because I wanted to hear your laugh again." Paige closed her eyes. He was an open book, just saying what he felt and asking for what he wanted. She didn't know people like that really existed in the world. They had never existed in hers.

"Give me something to laugh at."

"Is easy peasy all used up?"

She grinned. "Yup. You have to try harder."

"How about if I try harder tomorrow night? Remember the Holy Smokes Food Festival? The signs are plastered over every square inch of this town."

"You're a barbecue meat kind of guy?"

He sighed. "I'm a takeout kind of guy. I only eat well if Mara invites me over for dinner."

Paige's smile faded as she thought of Mara, tooling around in her kitchen, her mind reeling with worry of the unknown.

"Is she okay? I mean, *really* okay?"

"Hard to tell. She has a legitimate reason to be worried, but her emotions have also been exaggerated for months now."

"Is she a good mom?" Charlie paused on the other end of the line, sending a nervous wave over Paige's skin. "I mean, she seems like a good mom, but…"

"She's the best mom I've ever met." Paige nodded silently, momentarily forgetting she was on a phone. "You're catching her at a low point. We all get them."

No truer words had ever been spoken, Paige thought. If Mara had met her ten years ago, she might have judged her harshly too. Anyone would. Heck, she still did.

"What are you going to do about Lucy's storybook costume?" she said, eager to change the subject.

"Why? Have you been brainstorming ideas since I dropped you at your motel?"

"Yeah. I have my sketchbook open in front of me."

"Ooh. Ms. Cartman can dish the sarcasm."

She smiled. "I can give you a hand with the costume, if you want?"

"Lucy would like that. She likes you."

Paige tucked her hair behind her ear.

"I like her. She's a great kid."

"You haven't seen anything yet."

She wanted to see everything. She wanted to be a part of Lucy's life, and nuzzle a nose into her hair the way Mara had. Paige wasn't sure the bond of family would mean so much to her after all this time, but now that she'd met Lucy—touched her, listened to her giggle— she wanted it all.

"I'm here to help," she said in a peppier voice than she had meant. She knew she was trying to convince herself as much as Charlie. That *was* why she'd sought out Lucy, wasn't it? To help?

"We can discuss it over barbecue tomorrow afternoon. My shift ends at five."

"Are you bringing Lucy?"

There was a brief pause. "I suppose I could…since it's not a date."

"Bring whoever," Paige said, hurrying to hide her eagerness to see the little girl. "Maybe it would be good for Mara to get out too. I can meet you all there."

"What's your cell number?" he said just as Paige's cell phone rang. "As much fun as it was calling the motel and having them connect me—"

"I've got to go, Charlie. I'll see you tomorrow after five." Replacing the phone on its base, Paige answered her cell.

"Hi, honey." Her aunt's homey voice sang over the line. "I may have jumped to conclusions a wee bit when I read your text message. It is good news, isn't it?"

"Where are you?"

"Hospital. But Craig's doing much better."

"You stayed all night, didn't you?"

"Guilty as charged," she said as Craig called

out something in the background. Joan laughed. "Your uncle thinks I like it here because of the fancy furnishings."

Uncle Craig was chuckling. Paige sighed with amusement. Charlie was right—listening to someone's laughter was reason enough for a call.

"Now, what's your news, honey?"

Paige had so much to tell her aunt and uncle. So much to ask them. She needed their guidance about what she should do and what she *shouldn't*. But as Uncle Craig said something else to make Aunt Joan giggle and cover the phone before responding, Paige knew it could keep for another night.

"I wanted to hear your voices, that's all."

"Aw, honey, I'm glad, and don't worry. You'll find her. If she has your same sparkling green eyes, she'll be difficult to miss."

CHARLIE ARRIVED AT The Copper Kettle, the best breakfast nook within a thirty-mile radius of Roseley, and immediately spotted Tully at the far end of the counter. As it was usually packed with locals coming off the night shift, he was glad Tully had snagged them counter stools.

"Coffee?" Gemma asked, turning Charlie's mug over. He nodded.

"How are you doing today, Gemma?" He and Gemma had gone to high school together. After marrying Rick Murdock, a fellow Roseley High alum, and quickly becoming mom to three little boys, she had settled into managing The Copper Kettle. Whenever he had come home to visit, he'd usually stop in for a chat with Gemma and a tall stack of buttermilk pancakes.

"Ricky Jr. was up sick all night. My mom's watching him today, but was he ever sour with me for leaving this morning." Her wide brown eyes drooped with guilt.

"Motherhood's the hardest job there is, Gem."

"You're telling me, Charlie. I gotta work my job like I ain't a mother, and I gotta mother like I don't have to work a job."

"He's still pretty young," Tully said. "He'll have a better understanding when he's older."

"He'll be eight in July. He's my fierce and quiet one, you know. He communicates just as much in what he *doesn't* say. Anyhoo, what'll I get you, fellas?"

"The special," Tully said, passing her his menu. "As is."

"I'll just stick with coffee, Gemma." She winked and slid an order slip to the back kitchen.

As soon as she had gone, Tully smoothly switched into detective mode, turning his full attention on Charlie. "What is it?" he asked in a low monotone.

Charlie raised a brow. "What's what?"

Tully leaned an elbow on the counter and sized up his friend. "I know when something's up. You're as jittery as Mara on two pots of coffee, and I've never known you to come here and eat anything less than a tall stack of pancakes. It's your new lady friend, isn't it?"

"My new lady friend?" Charlie chuckled. "Is that what we're calling her?"

"I was hoping you two were still just friends since you only met her yesterday."

"Technically it's been two days—"

"Two *whole* days—"

"And, yes, we're *just* friends." He could feel Tully boring holes into his temple, waiting for the other shoe to drop. His friend sometimes knew him better than he knew himself. Charlie raised his coffee to his lips, holding it there for a moment before muttering, "For now."

"There it is."

"What?"

"Tell me you're not jumping in too quickly."

"Define *quickly*."

Tully curled a discerning lip. "When are you seeing her again?"

"You mean when are *we* seeing her?"

"Excuse me?"

"I'm meeting her at Holy Smokes tonight…"

"And?"

"And I'm bringing Lucy…"

"Because?"

"To keep it light. You know, like you said. We're just friends and going to Holy Smokes together will feel like a date if we're alone. I don't want to scare her off."

"Why would she scare so easily?"

Charlie hesitated. He hadn't told Tully about how she'd run out on him the other night at Bayshore Bar. Tully would take it as a red flag that something was wrong. He'd warn him not to ignore the incident. He'd tell him to stay more guarded and take things more slowly. And if he had to admit it, Tully would probably be right. He still didn't understand why Paige had run out on him and then why she seemed to warm up again on the sidewalk in front of the shop the next morning. It didn't make sense, and at the same time, he didn't want to overthink it. The bottom line was, he just wanted to see her again.

Charlie looked up, realizing he'd hesitated too long. Each second was making Tully more suspicious of his plan.

"I want to start things off on the right foot, on a good foundation. So I invited her to join Lucy and me and…you."

"Me?"

"I need your help, Tully. After we all eat—"

Tully nodded knowingly. "I can take Lucy and give you two some alone time."

"Don't act as if you weren't going to go anyway. Barbecue meats and all?"

Tully shrugged and readjusted his suit blazer. "I think I can make it work. I don't get off until five—"

"That's fine."

"Unless a case comes up—"

"We'll make it work."

Tully smiled. "Anything to help you out, buddy. You really like this woman, huh?"

"She has my head spinning."

"And what's her name again?"

"Paige."

"Last name?"

Charlie shot him a scowl. "Oh, no you don't."

"What?"

"No, Tully, I like this woman. If she has anything dark in her past, I'll leave it up to her to tell me in good time."

"So, you think there might be something dark in her past," Tully said slowly with a suspicious nod.

"That's not what I said."

"I surmised."

"No running her name in the database. No background checks or calling in a detective favor."

"There's no harm in having a full picture—"

"I have the full picture," Charlie said, knowing it was a lie. He flashed back to the look in Paige's eye just before she sprinted out of Bayshore Bar.

"I'm only giving you a hard time, buddy."

"I doubt that."

"Well," Tully sighed, slapping a hand on Charlie's shoulder, "I'd run her name if you let me, but only if you gave me the green light. The truth is, I can't wait to meet her."

"You'll love her."

"Just promise me something."

"What's that?"

"Don't fall in love with her too quickly."

Charlie grinned and waggled his eyebrows

over the rim of his coffee cup. "I can't make any promises, Detective."

"Yep," Tully said, running a hand down his face, but grinning all the same. "That's what I was afraid of."

CHAPTER EIGHT

PAIGE LOCKED HER bicycle to the rack in front
of a sushi restaurant she'd found online and
reached heavenward in a long stretch. She'd
put a lot of miles on her Schwinn and would
have the aching muscles the next day to show
for it.

Kicking around Roseley for the morning,
counting the minutes until she could see Charlie and Lucy, had left her looking for ways to
pass the time. She'd checked online for where
the school district lines were drawn so she
could remember which school might be Lucy's.

She'd then considered biking past Little
Lakeside Sports in the hopes Charlie would
be outside on a break but decided against it.
As much as she wanted to believe they could
just be friends, the truth was that she was aching to see him again.

Was this what it felt like to fall for somebody? It was a first for her, because she'd
never let herself get close enough to men to

try. Aside from her aunt and uncle, she'd never let herself get close to pretty much anyone. Forget dating. Over the years what she could have used the most was a good girlfriend or two to gossip and share secrets with and lean on during the hard times. So as much as her excitement grew whenever she was around Charlie, the prospect of making a friend, a real friend, had her heart bursting with hope.

From the sidewalk, Paige scanned the street blocked off for the Holy Smokes Festival. Food trucks, tents and tables lined either side, stretching several blocks in either direction. The permeation of hot grease and smoked barbecue delighted her senses and saturated her skin along with the humid evening air. As police officers trotted by on horses and pedestrians swarmed at the entrances, Paige realized it might take a while to find Charlie. She'd no sooner kicked off the curb to begin looking for him when she heard a bubbly voice.

"We thought we might see you here!" Angelo and CeCe hurried up to her. Each was holding a tray of barbecue ribs and a beer.

"I heard this was the place to be," Paige said. Angelo nodded.

"The first year they did this, they had a surprisingly large turnout. It practically guaranteed it would be an annual event. Plus, the fact they can get away without charging an entrance fee—"

"No need to," CeCe said. "The shops around here think of it as Christmas. Helps get them in the black before the summer tourists turn up."

"Is The Sandwich Board open tonight?"

"Oh my, yes, but we're not working!" CeCe laughed. "Angelo and I couldn't miss this. It'll be an annual tradition for us, don't you think, Angelo?"

"Whatever you want, C."

CeCe turned her attention to Paige again, motioning for her to follow her to an open picnic table. "Now, honey, tell us about yourself. Where you from? How long are you staying?"

Angelo and CeCe slid onto the picnic bench next to each other, leaving Paige to reluctantly slide across from them.

"I'm from Ohio."

"Where exactly?"

Paige swallowed and shrugged. "Near the lake."

"I have a niece near Shaker Heights. Where are you?"

Paige fumbled to her favorite distraction:

follow-up questions. "Shaker Heights? What does your niece do there?"

CeCe's eyes set into two little slits. Paige could tell she was the one used to asking the questions.

"Married with two kids. Where near the lake?"

Paige wondered if she should lie. There wasn't necessarily anything wrong with telling CeCe a little information about herself, and remembering a lie was always risky. Still, she wasn't in Roseley to make friends and build relationships. Chatting with locals was the last thing she needed.

Just as she was about to draw a breath, she heard the voice of an angel, soaring in to save her.

"There she is! Paige! Paige!"

Lucy's dark brown hair streaked through the crowd like a swooping raven. At the pace she moved, Paige expected her to leap directly into her arms. She stood and held out her arms haphazardly in front of her in anticipation. But at the last moment, Lucy stopped short and beamed up at her, her cheeks pink and round like two little macarons. After a moment's pause to catch her breath, Lucy slung an arm around Paige's waist and squeezed her in a hug. But Paige dared not bend to kiss her head, as much as she wished to.

"You've won her over," Charlie said, strolling up to them. In long khaki shorts and a navy polo shirt, he was casual and tidy and worth taking a long look at…when CeCe wasn't there to scrutinize her every blink.

At his side was a tall, broad man who was no doubt just as handsome. He looked like a football linebacker.

Charlie motioned to the man. "I want you to meet Tully."

"It's a pleasure to meet you, Paige," Tully said, shaking her hand. "Charlie speaks kindly of all, but what he said about you was especially charming."

Charlie gave Tully a playful slug in the arm as Lucy giggled.

"Is that so?" Paige chuckled. Tully wrapped an arm around Charlie's shoulders as CeCe and Angelo exchanged a satisfied look.

"Sorry, Charlie. Was I not supposed to say that in front of her?"

"I was playing this one a little closer to the vest, buddy."

Paige laughed. "It's nice to meet you, Tully. You're a longtime friend of the family, aren't you?"

Tully turned to Charlie. "You've been talking about me too, huh? I'm touched."

"Of course, buddy. Now get off me with the lady watching."

Tully smacked a kiss on Charlie's temple, sending Charlie into a hearty laugh.

"Ready to eat?" he asked. "Angelo, those ribs look delicious."

"Bayshore Bar used a dry rub from The Spice Trader and it's divine," CeCe said, sinking her teeth into one.

"That's where we're heading, then," Charlie said, as he and Paige waved goodbye and moseyed toward the food trucks.

Paige looked around. "Where's Mara?"

"Mom didn't want to come," Lucy called as Tully motioned for her to walk ahead with him. "But she said to eat an ice cream for her."

"Crowds aren't really her thing," Charlie said in a lowered voice. "And she wanted to talk to her lawyer about the birth mother situation."

"Oh," Paige mumbled. "About what exactly?"

"How locked down the custody paperwork is—or *isn't*."

"Does it look like there are any loopholes?"

"I don't know. They've been Lucy's parents

for ten years. I can't imagine any judge in the world would reverse that based on some faulty paperwork. The trauma of placing Lucy with a new parent out of the blue—"

"Anything is possible." When she felt Charlie's eyes land on her she hurried to clarify. "Nowadays you never know how a court would rule. It's good she's meeting with a lawyer and not just hoping for the best."

"Thanks for saying so, but that won't help Mara relax."

"How can she? If I were in her position, I wouldn't either." Paige's stomach churned at the thought of how desperate Mara must feel. She wanted to ease her anxiety, but to say anything would mean she'd have to say what happened ten years ago and she'd sworn to herself she'd never do that—ever.

Charlie turned his attention to a fiddler. "Don't you love things like this?" he said as the fiddler nodded to them both and played a jaunty tune.

"I really do," Paige said, watching Charlie more than the musician. Meeting him really had been a breath of fresh air.

"My mouth has been watering for some sweet barbecue all day. Remember, it's our duty to sample as much as we can. This is, after all, a contest to declare the best smoked meat this side of Lake Roseley."

A woman with sticks of skewered meats waved to them.

"Hello, there, honey! Would you care for an all-meat shish kebab?"

"She's a little shy," Charlie called, striding closer. "She's never judged a contest before and the responsibility is really weighing on her tonight."

The woman's face burst in excitement as Paige inwardly rolled her eyes.

"Honey, step right up! I have the house special ready for the judges."

Charlie quickly put a finger to his lips and shushed her. "Ma'am, I wasn't supposed to say that. Please don't tell anyone she's a judge. It's a secret judging, after all."

"Of course not. Of course not," the woman said, whose name tag read Connie. "This is the judge sampler. This pork has been smoked for nearly twelve hours. It's fall-off-the-stick, melt-in-your-mouth perfection."

Paige accepted a sample, gearing up for her best food critic impression.

"It has a nice flavor."

"Yes…*and*?" Connie prompted, leaning heavily over the truck counter. Charlie coughed to catch Paige's eye, and when she focused on him, he looked ready to explode with laughter.

"And..." Paige said. "I really love...um... how the meat falls apart. It's very tender."

"It surely is!" Connie burst. "Twelve hours of smokin', honey! I already told you that. And?"

"Don't be shy, *honey*," Charlie said. "They picked you for this job because you're a professional food critic from Chicago. This is the time to let your expertise shine."

Connie nodded approvingly as Paige shoved a bite of meat in her mouth. She had to come up with something good and fast.

"The fats blend together to sear not only a hardwood flavor but also a texture that plays with your tongue. If I could invent another taste other than salty or savory, I would categorize this as...smokified."

Charlie turned away to mask his laugh as Connie stood straight and pressed her fists to her hips.

"Honey, I don't know what on earth you just said. Are you a critic at one of those fancy-pantsy art food magazines? This is *real* food. As my daddy used to say, it's putting-hair-on-your-chest food. Smokified? Am I supposed to know what in the heck that means?"

Paige scowled. "*Smokified.* I know it isn't a word, but it *could* be. Smokified!"

Charlie quickly slapped some money on the counter and wrapped an arm around Paige, escorting her away as Connie huffed. He burst out laughing as soon as they were out of earshot.

"Quit doing that!" Paige said, tearing a bite of meat off her shish kebab. "You owe me another chocolate brownie for putting me on the spot again!"

"I didn't know I was getting dinner *and* a show," Charlie howled as Paige's scowl broke into a reluctant smile. "You're something else, Freckles."

Paige shrugged. "Thanks, friend."

"Are we friends now? I thought we were still just being friendly."

"People who like to spend time together. Right."

"Right."

Paige slid onto a picnic bench as Charlie bought them a few more meat samples.

"Here. I even found you coleslaw and fried pickles to count as vegetables."

Paige nodded appreciatively. "Did you grow

up here? Has it changed much?" With the streets blocked off, little children scampered around them, some sticky faced with cotton candy. She turned her attention upward. Two- and three-story redbrick buildings lined the streets, each storefront with a different colored awning. Charlie nodded as Paige pointed to a burgundy one.

"There's The Spice Trader that CeCe was talking about," Paige said. "Can they make rent selling *spices*?"

"Somehow these shops survive. Mara's does."

"But Mara is the only sports shop in a lakefront town. She seems like she would do great business."

"She does and mostly all on her own."

"That would be hard."

Charlie nodded and pointed to a shop with a pink-and-white-striped awning. "My first job was there at The Lollipop. Mallory, the owner, was hesitant to hire me and rightfully so. I ate most of the profits when she wasn't looking."

"What's that place?"

"That's an antiques store called Grandma's Basement. I'll have to take you in there. Miss Jenkin dresses like she stepped out of the 1940s and '50s. And that," Charlie continued, "is a hardware store that's been on this street for three generations. Tully worked there briefly in high school."

"Is Tully your best friend?"

"He sure is. He'd do anything for me."

"Must be nice," she said, shoving a bite of coleslaw in her mouth.

"Who's your best friend?" he asked, softly.

"I'm going through a bit of a dry spell when it comes to friends, I'm afraid." She studied her lap. Admitting she didn't have any friends hurt.

"It's probably been hard taking care of your uncle."

"Aunt Joan and Uncle Craig are it. They're all I have in this world." His eyes softened at her admission before gently kicking her under the table.

"Well you have a friend in me, Freckles. Deal?"

Paige kicked him back but couldn't bring herself to give an audible answer. How did one even make a friend? She really didn't have a clue, but maybe this was it.

"What does Tully do for a living? He looks like he could be a professional wrestler."

"Nah. He's more of a gentle giant with a sharp mind. Man, is he smart."

"Paige!" Lucy called, sprinting. "Look what I'm having for dinner." She proudly held out a three-scoop ice cream cone.

"That thing is bigger than your face," Charlie said, lifting an eyebrow in Tully's direction.

"She promised me she wouldn't get sick," Tully said. "Don't tell Mara."

"Are you scared of Mara?" Paige teased. Tully nodded as Lucy tried to lick her ice cream faster than it could melt over the top of her knuckles. If Lucy was hers, really hers, she'd let her bathe in the ice cream. There was so much she wanted Lucy to experience that she, herself, had missed out on as a child. And there was also so much she wanted to spare her from.

CHARLIE SAT WITH Paige on the edge of his truck tailgate, watching the crowd slowly begin to dwindle into the early evening sunset. Tully had taken Lucy to a kid attraction at the end of the street, complete with bouncy house, ball pit and inflatable games. He was the perfect wingman.

"It's a nice kickoff to summer," Charlie said, motioning to the festival. "The weather isn't too hot this early in the season."

"I'm surprised Lucy is still in school."

"They start earlier and go later than I ever remember as a kid. There's a lot more pressure on them too. I wish I could take some of it from her."

"It'll make her stronger."

"Do you think?"

Paige leaned back on her hands. "I had a rough childhood, and I'd like to believe it made me stronger. Although most days I can't tell."

Her voice had whimpered out at the end, making him wonder what "rough" meant. He leaned back on his hands to mirror her, admiring the soft profile of her face. She was a true beauty, not that he could see anything else with the soft sunset highlighting her delicate features.

"Have you spoken to your uncle?"

"He was in the hospital yesterday and the night before, but he's home now."

"And I take it you were raised by him?"

"No."

Her response was resolute as if punctuating a sentence she hadn't wanted to speak.

"I wondered what a *rough* childhood meant for you, but you don't have to talk about it."

She drew and released a deep breath. "My

grandmother raised me until I was fourteen. She didn't have much, but she was a good woman and we made do. My mother was a flake, flitting in and out of my life for the first fourteen years."

"What about your dad?"

"I didn't know him. Neither did my mother much, for that matter. Anyway, my grandmother died when I was fourteen and life after that was…rough."

"What about your aunt and uncle?"

"They wanted to adopt me, but my mother refused. It was a huge point of contention between the three of them. I remember a lot of fighting about it back then."

"Is that why you feel a connection with Lucy?" She turned at the question, and when she didn't answer, he shrugged. "I can tell you see some of yourself in her. The day you met her, I couldn't help but wonder if you were adopted too. I know there's a strong connection between kids who are."

Paige stared off into the distance for a long time as the silence hung between them. He was about to apologize, about to ask her to forget what he'd said, fearing he'd unintentionally exposed something she wasn't ready to reveal. But just as the words rose to his lips, she continued.

"Trudy thought she could make it as a country music star. She dragged me around from one lousy situation to another."

"Trudy?"

Paige hung her head, her voice very small. "My mother."

"Was she any good?"

"I couldn't say. Grandma said she had talent when she was young, but I didn't know her before she started using."

Charlie's face fell, grave. He'd grown up with a healthy set of parents. He'd never known his birth father, who'd died shortly after he had been born. He'd only known Glenn, his stepfather, and had only ever thought of him as Dad. Glenn had loved him and Mara and his mother every day. He couldn't begin to imagine what life had been like for Paige if her mother had been an addict.

"I'm sorry to hear that. How bad was it?"

Paige sat up and ran her hands over her face.

"I'm still feeling the repercussions of it every day, Charlie, and she's been dead for a long time." She looked back at him and winced a smile, drawing him to sit up to be close to her. "Let's not talk about it. It's not something I usually share when I first meet someone."

"Whatever you want."

"Whatever I want?" she said, drawing a different meaning out of his remark than was intended. "I want to know what happened with that old heartbreak." He groaned, making her side-bump him with her shoulder. "Come on. Your turn. I know there's a story there, and it's more than coming home to help Mara."

"It's the oldest story in the book. I came home to nurse a broken heart."

Her eyes narrowed. "I'll kill her."

He side-bumped her in return. "I'd rather forget her altogether."

"Did she leave you at the altar or something?"

"No. She had the courtesy to break my heart before I put down the deposit with the caterer."

"You were engaged?"

"Yep."

"Is that why you were willing to walk away from your tour guide business?"

Charlie nodded. "She was one of my business partners."

"Ouch."

"I thought the business would be my life for the next thirty years—the sea, children, Crystal. Life can certainly change in an instant."

"Sometimes there are warning signs. Did you have any inkling she didn't want to get married?"

Charlie leaned over the edge of the truck tailgate, dangling his feet.

"In hindsight, I can put my finger on a few things that didn't add up, but when it finally came to an end, it was a sucker punch to the gut. I didn't think I'd ever put myself out there and risk that kind of pain again, but the past few days have changed my mind. *You've* changed my mind."

When he checked to see how his words had been taken, their eyes collided. Her cheeks had flushed, looking tempting enough to touch.

"Aren't we just friends?" she whispered as he leaned closer. He matched the soft timbre of her voice.

"We can stay friends if you want. That's option one."

The colors in her eyes transformed like a kaleidoscope in the warm sunlight, the emerald green morphing to jade as tiny flecks of gold sparkled up at him. He yearned to pinpoint every color he saw. He had fallen for her from the first moment he'd seen her, coasting up the street on her bicycle to stop short in front of him. He'd admired her trim physique and the way her golden hair had shone as slick as yellow fish streaking through the water. In that moment he'd somehow foreseen that she would change his life.

"Beautiful," he murmured. Her eyes fell to his lips.

"I think I want option two," she breathed. At her words, his skin pricked, the energy between them pulling him closer. Her blush-pink lips parted and when they met his, her eyelashes fluttered closed, sending his mind swirling. He felt he had sunk under water and could hear nothing but the pounding of his heart until her fingers toyed with the collar of his shirt. With her delicate whimper of satisfaction reverberating against his lips, he drew out his kiss, wanting to savor every taste of her.

He'd forgotten he was supposed to be licking his wounds opened by Crystal. He'd forgotten what it had felt like to hold a woman close and feel completely lost in her. When he wrapped an arm around Paige's shoulders, she maneuvered closer, and for the first time since arriving in Roseley, he felt like he was rewriting what his future could look like.

PAIGE WAITED WITH Tully and Lucy as Charlie scrounged for something in the front seat of his truck.

"Are you sure we can't give you a lift back to your motel?" Tully asked. "You'd have to sit in the back seat with Lucy, but we can throw your bicycle in the bed."

"No, thanks. I love riding at night."

"But it's getting cold," Lucy said, hugging herself in a shiver. Tully wrapped his arms around her. "You're like wearing a winter coat, Tully."

"Happy to be of service, little Lucy."

Charlie emerged from his truck. "I'd prefer to give you a lift back to your motel," he said as Paige shook her head. "But if you won't let me, then you'll have to take these instead." He helped her slip into a gray zippered hoodie that smelled of him and all things good. "And because I care deeply about your safety and because you don't want me to worry..." He held out a brand-new bicycle helmet. It was cobalt blue with silver streaks.

Paige twisted her mouth. "Are you serious?"

"The color is a perfect match to your bike," he said as he placed it on her head. After snapping the straps under her chin, he gazed at her like a man very pleased with what he saw. It made her heart leap that she was the object of his loving gaze. "And it looks good on you."

She balked. "I look like a bowling ball head."

"Nah, Freckles, you can't look anything other than pretty. Let me take your picture and prove it to you." He went for his cell phone but Tully had already held up his.

"I'll take it," Tully said. "Lucy, get in there with the two of them."

When Paige saw Tully and Charlie exchange a glance, she smiled a little to herself. *Very cunning, Charlie Stillwater*, she thought.

"Uncle Charlie, did you call her pretty?" Lucy said, dissolving into giggles. Charlie tried to ease a hand over her mouth, but Lucy squirmed to freedom. "You like her more than a friend, Uncle Charlie. You can't fool me."

"Everybody say 'cheese,'" Tully said, trying to interrupt Lucy. The little girl's giggles finally subsided as she posed for the picture.

Charlie's arm slipped around Paige's shoulders, like it should always be there.

"I'm not posing with this thing," she said, slipping the helmet off her head. She wished for a copy of the picture for herself and wanted to look like herself in it. She'd cherish a picture of Charlie and Lucy forever, after she'd left Roseley and returned home. She tossed her head to fluff her hair and found Charlie watching every movement.

"You do look great, you know," he said.

"Thanks. I'd better get going," she said, a sadness falling over her suddenly. The thought of leaving was sobering in the least. She strapped the helmet to the back of her bicycle. "Thanks for the helmet, Charlie, but you really shouldn't have. I don't like to wear them."

"You should wear it," he called, helping Lucy into the back seat of the truck. "Better safe than sorry."

"Yeah, yeah."

She waved goodbye and coasted to the end of the road, hanging a left toward her motel as Charlie fired up his truck. Even with the cool night air filling her nostrils, she could still smell his scent wafting from the hoodie.

By the time she reached her motel, her

cell phone had vibrated several times in her pocket. She smiled to herself as she slipped off her bike. She imagined what Charlie would text her about their first kiss, and as she relived the sensation of cozying up to him, she wished it wouldn't be their last.

It took her a moment to remember he didn't have her cell number. Digging for the phone, she trekked in the front doors of the motel and stopped short in the lobby as she illuminated the phone screen.

"Miss? Is everything okay?" the young man behind the front desk asked. She was sure the horror on her face had startled him almost as much as her aunt's text messages had scared her. A cold chill crept down her spine as she lowered herself onto a lobby chair.

Call me immediately.

Thorne was at the house.

It's only a matter of time.

CHAPTER NINE

PAIGE PACED IN front of the fabric store, picking at the skin around her fingernails. She hadn't managed much sleep the night before after talking to her aunt. The early morning hours had dragged by from one anxiety-ridden thought to the next. She didn't want to leave and miss out on time with Lucy, but Thorne was moving faster than she had expected. Her phone call with Aunt Joan was proof of that.

Her aunt had been nearly hysterical on the phone as Uncle Craig's calm, reassuring voice in the background did little to quell the squall.

"Honey, he knows where we live. He knows where *you* live. A cop car was here. They'll be back. I'm sure of it."

"Please calm down," she'd told Aunt Joan. "I can't see you in person and the way you're rambling on makes it difficult to understand you."

"I'm trying but I—" Paige could hear Uncle Craig in the background.

"Joanie, sit down. *Sit down*, baby."

"Okay, okay. I'm sitting."

"Deep breaths, love," her uncle said.

Paige followed suit as she listened to Aunt Joan heaving exaggerated breaths into the phone receiver. After a few moments her aunt continued.

"I tried calling you—"

"I know," Paige said. "I didn't hear my phone. I was out."

"Out where?"

Paige closed her eyes tightly and whispered into the phone as if the words were a treasure meant to be kept only between the three of them.

"I found her."

Joan gasped on the other end of the line. She could imagine her aunt clasping Uncle Craig's hand and nearly toppling out of her chair.

"She found her," Joan said, her voice breathy. "Is she everything we imagined?"

"She's perfection."

There was a long silence on the other end of the phone. "Perfection," her aunt repeated as she broke down in tears. "I have to pass the…here, Craig… I can't…"

"Honey?" Uncle Craig said, taking the phone. "I'm so happy for you. Where did you see her?"

"I met her. We talked, we played. I'm seeing her again tomorrow, and I'm making her a costume for school."

Now that the secret was out, it was all Paige could do to keep from running one fact after another in a hurried conglomerate of excitement.

"You met her?"

"She met her?" Aunt Joan squawked in the background, raising her voice for Paige to hear over the line. "How! Does Lucy know who you are?"

"Oh, for goodness' sake," Uncle Craig said. "I'll just put it on speakerphone. But you'd better not talk over me, Joanie."

"She has no idea," Paige said. "But I met her uncle. He and I have been talking and spending time together. He's so kind and funny. The past couple of days have been so… I mean, I've been feeling…"

"You have feelings for *the uncle*?"

"I don't… I don't know."

"What's his name?"

Paige rolled her eyes in an embarrassed smile. "Charlie."

Uncle Craig muffled a chuckle. "Charlies are usually good people."

Aunt Joan's voice was louder now. She imagined her nearly hovering over the phone speaker. "Have you told Charlie who you are?"

"How can I?"

"That *is* sticky territory," Uncle Craig said. "What was it like meeting Lucy?"

"It was like looking in a mirror. Her hair is nearly black, and her complexion is fairer, but her green eyes are a spitting image of mine."

Aunt Joan let out a whoop and a holler. "She has our eyes! Are you sure this Charlie fellow isn't going to suspect anything?"

Paige began to shake her head, then stopped. She hadn't considered that anyone would notice how strikingly similar their eyes were. She'd gotten her eyes from Trudy, who had gotten hers from Grandma. Aunt Joan's eyes were a green-hazel, not quite as bold as theirs, but still similar. She'd always loved how her eyes had been like a telltale sign of where she belonged, even when things with Trudy had been tumultuous. Deep down, her green eyes had felt magical to her, like they could help her survive whatever situation Trudy dragged her into.

But she'd never stopped to think that what she'd always considered her biggest asset could jeopardize her time with Lucy. Even Charlie had noticed a connection she felt with Lucy. If he began to suspect…

Paige shook out her worry, at least for the time being, and directed them back to the matter at hand. "Tell me what happened with Thorne."

"I'd better tell you," Craig said. "Your aunt is furiously scrubbing the cabinet under the kitchen sink."

"It's filthy under here!" she called. "How have I not noticed this before? Where's all the bleach, darn it."

"Take me off speaker," Paige said.

"I already did, honey."

"She's unraveling. Should I come home?"

He sighed. "Not until we know what Thorne knows. It's no use coming home and walking smack dab into his trap. The best place for you is probably anywhere but here."

"Did you talk to Thorne?"

"I didn't see him. I was sleeping when he came to the door. Joanie silently watched both him and a police officer through the peephole but pretended no one was home. He and the police officer talked for a minute and left, but she's worried he's casing the place."

"I'm surprised he was only accompanied by one person. I've never seen him without a clan."

"Your aunt says he looks the same—ratty long hair and coal-black eyes."

Stone-cold eyes, Paige thought, as goose bumps rose along her skin. She knew a person couldn't possibly have jet-black eyes, but every time she had ever looked into his, all she could see were two large lumps of coal leering beneath hooded eyelids. Time wouldn't have changed them. When her aunt had punched the gas ten years ago, speeding off into the ink of night, Paige hoped it would be the last time she'd ever have to see those eyes again.

"She should stop calling us," Joan called. "The police could trace it."

"They're not going to tap our line, Joanie. They need a warrant for that."

"We can't be too careful! That's all I'm saying!" They'd ended their call after that.

Now, Paige wandered back and forth along the curb in front of the fabric store, Pleats and Patches. Her aunt's words had been ringing in her ears all morning. To keep Thorne from finding her, she really couldn't be too careful. Any calls made to her aunt and uncle might put her location in Roseley at risk. As unlikely as it was, it was still possible. With as careful as the three of them had been for the past decade, she wasn't about to start slipping up now. For the time being, she needed to cut all ties and buy a disposable phone.

Pulling her cell phone from her purse, she held it in her hand, deciding if she was ready to trash it. She gently placed it on the ground and stared at it for several moments before crushing it with her heel. It took many stomps before she could convince herself the phone was completely broken. Scooping up the pieces in her hand, she glanced around for the nearest trash receptacle and spotted Charlie striding up the sidewalk.

The sight of him made her skin prickle with anticipation. After their kiss the night before, the sight of his perfect lips made her nervously lick her own. In faded Levi's and a distressed red-and-black Roseley High School T-shirt, he moved toward her with a casual cool. The corners of his lips curled as he got closer and found her watching him.

"Hey, there."

"I take it you're a Roseley High School alum?"

"Go, Falcons." He glanced down at her hands. "What do you have there?"

"I dropped my phone in the road and some-one drove over it."

"Maybe we can fix it…" Charlie began until she opened her hand to reveal the pieces. "Nope. That thing is destroyed. You know, if you don't want to give me your cell number, just say so. I can take a hint. You don't have to crush your phone."

Paige smiled at his teasing as she tossed the pieces in the trash. "Where's Lucy?"

"She and Mara had to take Leapsters to the vet."

"Leapsters?"

"Her British shorthair cat. He hasn't been eating well so they're getting him checked. That leaves just the two of us on fabric duty. Mara told me to thank you profusely and give you this dress pattern. She also borrowed Miss Jenkin's sewing machine for you, which I have in the truck."

"It's my pleasure," Paige said. And the truth was, part of the pleasure was that she was doing something normal. Something her own mother had never done for her. Something family did for each other. It really was a true pleasure.

The chemical scent of new fibers met them at the entrance. Bolts of multicolor fabrics, stacked three shelves high, lined the rows on either side of the shop.

"I can't say I've ever been in here before," Charlie said.

"I love little places like this, though I haven't sewed anything in ages."

"Good afternoon, Charlie." A voice nearly sang to them from over the tops of fabric bolts. Paige recognized the violet-gray hair before the face.

"Hi, Ms. Mitchell," Charlie said. "Are you sewing something?" Dolores shuffled around the bolts while holding out a handful of fabric swatches.

"Charlie, you're old enough to call me Dolores, for heaven's sake. And yes, I'm sewing new curtains for the tea shop. I want something a little brighter. I can't afford a complete renovation, but maybe a few small changes will be enough of a face-lift."

Charlie began to motion an introduction, but Dolores waved him away and embraced Paige in a gentle hug.

"We already met on the trail. Paige, you

need to come by my tea shop while you're in town. You too, Charlie. Come after you're done shopping."

Paige glanced at Charlie. "Maybe. Thanks, Dolores."

"Toot-a-loo, dears," Dolores said, making her way for the door.

"For someone who doesn't have any friends, you certainly can make them easily," Charlie said. "Would you mind introducing *me* around town?"

"She was with CeCe the other day."

"Ah, CeCe. She makes it her business to know everyone and everything."

Paige nodded, taking mental note. As she checked the price tag on a pink paisley print, he leaned close to her ear, dropping his voice to a whisper.

"I feel a little out of place here. Every customer and employee is female and in the fifty- to sixty-five-year-old range."

Paige rose to her tippy toes and scanned the store. He was right.

"I'm sure you can find a way to use that to your advantage."

"I'm great on scoring free sandwiches, but I'm not sure I can manage a discount here."

She stretched out an arm's length of amethyst-colored fabric. She knew the color would complement Lucy's fair complexion.

"Perhaps you only need a little motivation. We could put a wager on it."

Charlie leaned against a concrete pillar. "You've got my attention, Freckles. What did you have in mind?"

"I came up with the idea. Do you need me to come up with the terms too?"

He chuckled. "I wouldn't dream of putting you out like that."

Paige grazed her fingers over the selection of purple spools of thread. She selected a few, along with some buttons.

"It can't be that difficult," she said, breezing past him toward the cutting table. Charlie slid up beside her and lowered his voice even though they were alone.

"If I can't get a discount on this order, I have to take you out for dinner tonight—my choice of place."

"Define *discount*."

He thought for a moment. "Twenty-five percent."

"Seventy-five."

"Fifty."

"And if you *do* get a discount?"

He placed a palm on the cutting table and leaned down to look her square in the eye.

"You have to start wearing your bike helmet."

Paige cocked her head and let out a snarl. "You've got to be kidding me. No way."

"You're that convinced I'll win, huh?"

"No, but I—"

"If you can't take the heat, Freckles—"

"Going out for dinner is grossly different than agreeing to—"

"Taking your safety seriously?"

An employee, a drab-looking woman named Flo, lumbered behind the cutting table and spread out the fabric.

"Three yards, please," Paige said. Flo barely flinched her facial muscles in reply before smoothing out the fabric and taking to it with scissors. Paige turned to find Charlie's eyes on her.

"Deal or no deal? And may I remind you that betting was your idea."

"Only because I believe you are overly confident and in need of a little humbling, I will agree."

Charlie's face spread in a satisfied grin.

"A little humbling? I'll remember that in a few minutes when I'm gloating."

"Good luck."

"Ma'am," he said. "Do you have any sales or promotions going on now for that fabric?"

Flo didn't acknowledge that she'd heard the question. Several long seconds passed before she uttered something under her breath.

"You'll have to check our mailer."

"I don't get the mailer. I'm a new customer."

Flo scanned the price of the fabric and printed Paige an order slip. She slid it across the table to her.

"Anything else?"

Paige shook her head, pleased. "All set. Thanks, Flo."

Charlie followed Flo as she began to lumber away.

"Flo, do you give any discounts to new customers?"

She shook her head. "Not anymore."

"What about if I download the store app to my phone? Any coupons for signing up?"

"It takes forty-eight hours to process."

"Forty-eight hours? That long?"

"That's what I said." Flo didn't wait for a follow-up before turning for the aisle she had previously been working in. Charlie glanced back at Paige, who pantomimed a mock cheer for his efforts. But because he looked so determined to win with the only payoff being she'd have to wear a safety helmet, she had to admit he was quite sweet. She still wouldn't wear the helmet if he lost, but the effort he was going to for her made her smile difficult to suppress.

"What if I open a store charge card? Or sign up for the mailing list?"

Flo paused and tapped her foot. She angled her head back at him as if waiting for permission to finally leave. Paige figured it was safe to say that Flo wasn't in the habit of winning employee-of-the-month awards for good customer service.

"I'm not aware of any discounts," she said. "It's a wonder this place hasn't gone belly-up with them raising rent downtown…" Flo drifted off muttering barely audible words as Charlie hung his head.

"I don't know anything about that," he said. "I only just moved here from North Carolina." He turned and shuffled back to Paige, a mopey look hanging off his face.

"I didn't think I was hungry until now," Paige said, tugging on the front of his shirt. "But as I have a free dinner coming—"

"You know," Flo called. They both startled and turned. "My manager mentioned in a staff meeting this morning that we're giving out coupons for the Welcome Committee."

"Welcome Committee?" Paige said.

"Sponsored by the Chamber of Commerce. They send you coupons to local businesses if you move to town."

Charlie's face brightened. "Please go on, Flo, because I have a feeling you're about to become my new best friend."

Flo's scowl faded slightly.

"Let me check behind the register. They may not have sent them out to the Welcome Committee yet."

"Flo, that would be amazing. You're really helping me out here."

"It has to be fifty percent," Paige reminded him in a hushed voice, "or it doesn't count."

"Shh," he said as Flo hunched down behind the cash register and came up with a canary yellow coupon slip.

"It's for fifty percent off your first purchase of ten dollars or more. You qualify. Would you like to use it today?"

Charlie slapped the counter before taking the coupon.

"Flo!" he said. "You came through for me. I think I am really going to like Roseley after all."

"If you just moved to Roseley," Paige said,

"where did you find the vintage Roseley T-shirt you're wearing?" She innocently looked up at him as Flo considered her words. Charlie's mouth drew into a straight line, but Flo didn't seem to care. She shrugged as Charlie slipped around the counter and wrapped an arm around Flo.

"Do you want to hug me, sir, or do you want me to ring up your order?"

"I want both, Flo. You may not understand it now, and I can't really explain it to you, but you may have just saved a life today. You, Flo, are a lifesaver."

Paige watched in shock as the grumpy cat of fabric store employees managed a half smile.

"You're right, sir. I don't understand."

"And you never will, Flo, but I appreciate you more than you know."

After Charlie paid for the order, Flo clicked her tongue. "I can't say anyone has ever called me a lifesaver before. Glad I could help." She hustled off to what appeared to be the break room without looking back. Charlie pushed out into the sunshine and waited patiently on the sidewalk as Paige slunk out behind him.

"Flo's words really *humbled* me," he said. "Should you consider that a win-win?"

"I thought you were going to get a discount by charming someone in there. Not flat-out asking for a coupon."

"Did you see Flo? I charmed the socks off her."

Paige groaned. "Are you really going to hold me to this?"

"Cheer up, Freckles. You look cute in that helmet."

"It's so uncomfortable."

"I'll tell you what. I'll still take you to dinner. It's a really classy joint, and my favorite ten-year-old is the hostess."

CHAPTER TEN

CHARLIE LED PAIGE through the front door of his sister's house in one fell swoop.

"You don't knock first?" Paige said, lingering in the doorway. Charlie raised an eyebrow.

"That's right. You don't have siblings. Trust me, this is normal."

It was another piece of the Paige Cartman puzzle he was slowly able to place. She'd had a rocky childhood with a mom who was an addict. No siblings. No father. Grandma died when she was fourteen. She had somehow managed to make it to adulthood relatively unscathed and a kind, sweet person. She was highly creative and helpful. After all, she'd offered to sew Lucy's costume after only just meeting her. She was sporty and pretty and whenever she blinked those sparkling emeralds up at him, he couldn't stop himself from smiling.

"We need propane," Mara said, bustling out of the kitchen. "Peter used it up last weekend and didn't replace it, of course. Charlie, would you? Hi, Paige. Welcome to the crazy. Charlie, seriously, would you?"

He turned to Paige as Mara chased Leapsters off the kitchen table.

"I can get propane and be back in ten minutes. Do you want to hang out here and maybe…" He lowered his voice and winced at the kitchen. The clamor of pans tumbling out of the cabinet made Paige cover her mouth in a laugh. "Help Mara?"

"Sure thing."

He gave her an appreciative nod and strode to his truck. She was nice. He loved nice.

"Leaving already?" Tully called from the curb as he crawled his truck up alongside it.

"You're driving me to get propane." Charlie hopped in the front seat. "She has me walking on air, man."

Tully punched the gas in response, fishtailing down the residential street.

"I can tell, brother. You're in all kinds of trouble."

"I never thought I'd feel this way so soon after Crystal, but the more time I spend with her, the more I think she might be the one."

"The one? Charlie, you only met her a couple days ago."

"Just because you don't want to get married and avoid the subject like the plague—"

"It's not about whether or not I *want* to. I'm just not cut out for it. I've seen the ugly underbelly of what happens when marriage goes wrong."

Charlie bit his tongue. Tully hadn't had the easiest childhood where his parents were concerned, but that didn't mean all marriages ended brutally.

"Maybe if you met the right woman..."

Tully shrugged. "How do you know once you've found her? Wasn't there a time when you thought Crystal was the right woman?"

"That's what has me so crazy," Charlie said, looking out the window. "It took me two years to propose to Crystal. Meanwhile, I'm already imagining marrying Paige."

"Subconsciously you knew marrying Crystal was a mistake. If it took you two years to talk yourself into it."

"Wow. Don't soften what you're thinking on my account."

"Am I wrong?" Tully pulled up to a red light and shot his friend a discerning glance.

"Two years is an appropriate amount of time to wait before getting engaged." Tully furrowed his brow. "Okay, I knew on some level that marrying Crystal was a huge mistake, even if I couldn't put my finger on why back then. I dodged a bullet."

"But not until the damage was done."

Charlie couldn't help but remember the damage. He'd returned to his office late one night and overheard his best friend and business partner, Benny, speaking sweetly to someone. When he'd pushed open the cracked office door and discovered Crystal there too, he had immediately broken out into a cold, sick sweat. The truth was, there was nothing happening in the room that would suggest Benny and Crystal were engaged in something romantic. They weren't kissing or touching or even standing too close to one another. It should have appeared innocent since he and Benny and Crystal were all business partners. Each had legitimate reasons for being at the office late at night. Another person, a stranger wandering in, would see nothing amiss.

But in that instant, Charlie had known better. It had been something in Benny's voice that had given him away. And the blaze in Crystal's eyes as she listened to him was something Charlie had never seen when she looked at him. When Benny and Crystal had turned to see Charlie standing in the doorway, the expressions on their faces had confirmed his suspicions. Crystal's look of guilt had been faster than a flash in the pan before she had hurried to hug him, but he had seen it and he had known, instinctively.

The night he had confronted her, she hadn't been able to muster a response quickly enough. She'd been fooling around with Benny since before they had bought the tour guide company. She had agreed to marry Charlie because Benny hadn't moved quickly enough to propose himself. And, Charlie surmised, neither she nor Benny would have stopped their affair after the wedding. They'd both been making a fool of him for a long time and the fact that they had both been his best friends…

"I couldn't tell she was hiding the truth until…"

"Until she shot two bullets straight to the chest," Tully finished for him.

Charlie heaved a sigh and hung an arm out the window. That was certainly how it had felt.

"Uh-huh. Until it was too late."

"Too late would have been after you had said 'I do.' But I get your meaning."

"Benny should have had my back. He should have told me if things with Crystal

felt off, but you know how that turned out."
As Tully swung into a parking spot in front
of the store, Charlie faced him, his expression serious. "I don't trust myself, Tully. Not
anymore."

"Then take it slow. There's no need to rush
into anything with Paige." Charlie knew
Tully was right, but he felt no control over
his senses anymore. If Paige was no good for
him, he knew he wouldn't see it until it was
too late again.

"I need someone to watch my blind side,
because I feel like my heart is on a runaway
train."

"It's one of your most endearing qualities
but…"

"A giant fault too?"

"It can be, if you're not thinking straight."

"You need to be my wingman, Tully. Tell
me if you sense anything is off about Paige."
Tully smacked Charlie lovingly on the shoulder and gave him a gentle shake.

"A true wingman never needs to be asked,
buddy. I'm already way ahead of you."

CHARLIE TWISTED ON the new propane tank.

"What are we grilling?" he asked.

Mara placed a plate of marinated steak and vegetable shish kebabs beside the grill.

"I hope you like shish kebabs, Paige. Lucy was helping me spear these before you arrived."

"We just ate them at Holy Smokes," Charlie said, causing Mara's face to contort. His eyes widened, realizing the mistake he'd made. "And Paige loves them. She said they're one of her favorites."

"Really?" Mara squawked as Paige nodded enthusiastically from the porch bench.

"I could eat them every day," she lied. She let her eyes wander to Lucy, who swayed back and forth with Leapsters, whispering sweet things into the cat's ear.

"What's wrong with Leapsters?"

"The vet had to pull a cracked tooth."

"Will he be able to eat now?"

Lucy nodded. "He'll be fine. That's why you always get your checkups."

"That's why I take you for your yearly checkup too, you know," Mara said, lifting a parental eyebrow at Lucy.

"But, Mom," Lucy said. "It's the flu shot I don't like, not the checkups." The little girl turned her attention to Paige. "Did your mom make you get a flu shot every year?"

Paige shook her head. She couldn't remember Trudy ever taking her to the doctor. Her first year of living solely with her mother, she remembered coming down with the flu and dialing Aunt Joan, who lived four states away. Joan was ecstatic to hear from her, and desperately wanted to know where she was so she could come get her. But Trudy had overheard the conversation and disconnected the line before flying into a rage. She'd brought Paige a Coca-Cola and some orange juice later that day to make peace, but that had been the full extent of her maternal instinct or bedside manner.

"The flu shot wasn't popular when I was a kid."

"Lucky you," Lucy said as Leapsters sprung from her arms and darted into the house.

"I can see why you call him Leapsters," Paige said with a smile as Charlie handed her a sweet tea.

"They should call him Doctor Destruction with the mischief he gets into," Charlie said. "You can't train him to leave anything alone."

"Do you have any pets, Paige?" Lucy asked.

"Nope. Just me."

"She probably doesn't have much time for a pet, she helps take care of her uncle." Charlie had no sooner said the words than he tilted his head at her as a pseudoapology. She appreciated it as Uncle Craig wasn't really a topic she enjoyed discussing with others.

"What's wrong with him?" Lucy asked.

"He has late-stage pancreatic cancer."

"I'm so sorry," Lucy said, touching her gently on the shoulder. Paige rested her hand on top of Lucy's and smiled warmly at her.

"Thanks."

"Paige," Tully said. "With your uncle sick, how long will you stay in Roseley?" She could sense Charlie shooting him a look as she grappled with a reply.

"I'm not sure. I was really only passing through for a couple days to write and clear my mind."

"I can imagine," Tully said. "Being a caregiver is the hardest job there is. It's wise to get away for a few days if you can manage it. But how did you end up out here? It's a far sprint from Ohio."

Paige nodded and brought her tea to her lips to buy herself a moment. She normally didn't allow herself to be drawn into social settings where people could ask her questions. Even the most harmless of settings could lead to twenty questions, such as this.

"I met with a client in Chicago last week, and he suggested I pass through Roseley."

"Really," said Tully. "How come?"

"Uh…he used to own a place on the lake."

"Which pier?" Tully asked. "I know almost everyone. I'm a second-generation Roseley bumpkin and proud of it."

Paige plastered on an interested smile and raced to change the subject. "Why on earth would you call yourself a bumpkin? You're anything but, Tully."

"Thank you, kindly. What was the fellow's name?"

"Who? My business client?"

"Whoever owned a place on the lake. You say he's in Chicago now? What does he do?"

Paige took another sip of tea. "He was trying to start up a small engineering firm, but after our meeting he sounded like he was close to throwing in the towel."

"And his name?" Tully's face was relaxed and pleasant as if he had just asked Paige if she'd like a bit more tea. "You must remember it."

"Palmer," she spit out. "But it was his wife's family that owned a place up here, and I don't think he ever mentioned their name."

"I don't know anyone who married a

Palmer," Mara said, sprinkling seasoning on the shish kebabs. "But this lake is huge. If you knew them, Tully, I'd really be impressed."

"Shoot. It was my one chance to impress you, Mara," he said. He gave a low chuckle as Paige allowed herself to ease back onto her seat just a hair. But relaxing was premature. "Are you originally from Ohio, Paige?"

"Originally?" she sputtered. Mara was so frazzled most of the time and engrossed in her own troubles, she wouldn't be one to ask too many prying questions, and Charlie seemed to sense she didn't want to talk much about herself. But Tully, with his easy demeanor and smiling eyes, was landing one question after another and making her inwardly squirm. "I mean…yes… Ohio."

"Whereabouts?"

"When it comes to Ohio, it all looks about the same," Paige forced, rolling her eyes.

"Nah, you've got that confused with the entire Midwest," Tully said, accepting a tea from Mara. "East or west?"

"Up toward Cleveland," Paige admitted. She needed to tell as few lies as possible to keep her story straight.

"What are your plans after you hang around here, Paige?" Mara said.

She laughed uncomfortably. "Who knows. I'm not in a rush to figure it out. Why?"

Mara stole a glance at Charlie. "Just curious."

"You two make a pair," Tully said, thumbing toward Charlie. "He doesn't have any idea what he's going to do next either. Only time will tell what he figures out."

"What is there to figure out?" Mara said sternly. "Don't bail on me, Charlie. You just started working at the shop."

"He can't do that forever," Tully interjected.

"Why not? He always wanted a family business, and this is a family business."

"But it's not *his* family business. He doesn't want to sell fishing poles the rest of his life."

Mara let out an exaggerated groan. "Then what's he going to do with his plane, Tully? It's an eyesore. He can't tour up here like he could in the Carolinas."

"He's more at home on that plane than in any other business."

"Wait a minute," Paige said turning to Charlie. "You own a plane?" Charlie nodded and took a swig of iced tea, unfazed by the verbal jabs Tully and Mara were trading back and forth, discussing his future. "I saw it on the water outside the shop the other day. You gave tours from your plane?" Charlie nodded proudly.

"What on earth are you going to do with an amphibian plane out here?" Mara said, shaking her head. "At least in North Carolina you could fly it year-round, but nobody is going to want to go for a ride when it's ten degrees in the winter."

"I haven't gotten that far," Charlie said. "But I'm not selling it, Mara."

"Just keep paying the insurance on it then. Drain your savings…"

"Gosh, sis, you're in a fun mood tonight." He moseyed up behind her, wrapped an arm around her neck and planted a kiss on the crown of her head. Mara let out a raspy sigh and held up her hands in defeat.

"I know, I know. I'm sorry. It's just… stress." She snuck a quick glance at Lucy and then turned for the kitchen. "Can I get anyone anything? Drinks?"

Paige shook her head. "Can I help do something, Mara?"

"No. I need a minute. Excuse me."

Charlie winked at Paige and followed Mara into the kitchen as Lucy tagged behind him. Paige swirled the ice in her glass and mused how concerned Charlie was about his little sister. She wished she had had someone like that in her life when she was growing up. But just as quickly as she had begun to feel blue, she reminded herself that she'd found Aunt Joan and Uncle Craig and been quite happy for the last ten years.

"He's a good guy," Tully said as if reading her mind. She nodded.

"It sounds like he has some things to figure out with his plane."

"Ah, he's only been back a short time, and the weather is beautiful. What's the rush?"

"I like your attitude, Tully. What do you do when you're not hanging out with Charlie?"

"Did he tell you we hang out a lot?"

"I guessed."

"I'm happy to have him back." Tully lounged on his chair and smiled at her for several moments. "I'm a detective."

Paige's lips thinned. "As in the police?"

Tully chuckled. "You didn't expect that, did you?"

She forced a laugh as the hair began to stand on the back of her neck. "No. I can't say I did, Tully."

"Most people don't. I've been told it's my demeanor. I've been called a teddy bear more times in my life than I can count, but I guess that's why I'm so effective."

Paige's throat clenched as if merely speaking more words would draw his attention to what she had done in her past. Nothing could be worse than talking to a cop.

"Huh…good…good for you. What sort of cases do you cover?"

"Whatever crops up."

"Do you get much crime in Roseley?"

"We have a low crime rate, certainly, but a high-profile case pops up now and again. People are people, no matter where they live. Theft… vandalism…assault…missing persons…"

"Missing persons?"

"Had a case just last year. It turned out well, thank goodness."

"Good," Paige croaked, realizing she had a death grip on her tea glass. "And you enjoy it?"

"I was made for it. See… I like sizing folks up without them knowing I'm doing it. Interesting creatures…people. When it comes to crime, sometimes the culprit is the last person you'd ever suspect." He stood and turned the shish kebabs on the grill, a brief distraction as Paige scrambled for what to do next. "These shouldn't take too long, Paige. I hope you're hungry."

"I… I'm actually not feeling all that well."

Tully's face scrunched in concern. "I hope it wasn't something I said."

Paige forced another laugh, but her voice sounded foreign, grating against her nerves. Her head was speeding a thousand miles a minute. It was time to go. *Now.*

"It could be the heat, Tully. That happens to me from time to time. I get too much sun and don't balance my electrolytes and my stomach lets me know it. I thought the iced tea would help, but I think I should get going—"

"Paige!" Lucy called desperately from inside the house. "Paige, come quick!" Paige sprang to her feet and made her way into the house as Tully followed. She and Tully made it to the living room just as Charlie and Mara emerged from the kitchen. Mara sniffled and smeared tears from under her eyes, but her body stiffened when she spotted the others.

"Paige, I don't get it," Lucy said, holding up a small card. The contents of Paige's purse lay scattered at her feet. "What does this mean?"

"Lucy," Mara said. "Did you go through Paige's handbag?"

"I didn't! Leapsters knocked it off the couch

and her wallet fell out. I was just putting it back when it flipped open by itself and—"

"By itself?" Mara said as Charlie took the card from Lucy. Paige broke out in a cold sweat as she instantly recognized it as her old driver's license. He studied it for a moment before handing it to Paige. She slid it quickly into her back shorts pocket and hurried to grab her purse.

Mara stood next to Lucy like a hen rearing to peck. "You shouldn't have looked in her wallet, Lucy. You know better than that."

"But why does it have a different name with Paige's picture?"

"Say you're sorry to Paige," Mara said.

"But, *Mom*—"

"I mean it."

"But—"

Mara insisted. *"Lucy."*

Paige wanted to assure Lucy it was okay and that she wasn't angry and that she was a good little girl. She wanted to tell her the entire truth, but in that moment, from the shock, all she could do was stand frozen as her old driver's license burned a hole in her back pocket.

"I'm sorry, Paige," Lucy said through a quivering lip. "It was mostly Leapsters's fault.

I want to go to my room now." She sprinted to her bedroom and slammed the door behind her.

"I'm sorry," Mara said. "I think she's been picking up on my stress. I can't imagine what made her rifle through your purse like that. It's not like her at all."

"Ah, she had a momentary lapse in judgment," Charlie said. "She's a good kid."

Paige slung her purse over her shoulder, eyeing the three of them.

"It's fine," she said. "It didn't bother me at all. Please tell her I'm not upset and I…" But before the words were fully out of her mouth, she caught Tully's stare. His jolly demeanor had changed. For the first time since she'd met him, she felt as if he was now sizing *her* up.

"Let's get dinner started," Mara said. "We'll let Lucy cool off for a few minutes, and then I'll go talk to her."

"I'm not feeling well," Paige said. She glanced between Charlie and Tully. "I'm so sorry to leave before dinner, Mara. It smells delicious."

Mara studied her. "Let Charlie drive you."

"It's okay. I'll ride my bike."

"Don't be silly, honey. If you don't feel well—"

"Thanks, Mara, but I'll see myself out." Paige waved sharply and beelined for the door, uncertain if she would ever return. If Tully suspected anything fishy about her now, he was a person with the means to dig deeper and discover what she'd done. He'd ask Charlie about the name on her driver's license as soon as she had pedaled down the driveway. If she was smart, heading back to Ohio within the hour was exactly what she should do.

But leaving Lucy on such a sour note made her wince. She didn't want to end it like that when she didn't know what the future held for either of them.

She could sense Charlie following her down the front walk and to the back of his pickup truck where her bike was stored. When she turned to face him, she spotted Tully watching from the doorway.

"I'll get it," Charlie said. His tone was serious, a quick departure from the Charlie she'd been getting to know, and it filled her with deep regret. Why on earth did she still have that old license in her wallet? It had been hidden in the secret sleeve behind her other cards, but apparently was still easy enough for a child to find.

She shifted her weight as he pulled her bike from the bed of his truck.

"Thanks, Charlie." He nodded and slammed the tailgate. "I'm sorry I can't stay for dinner but I—"

"It's fine."

Though the evening sun was still shining brightly, and a warm breeze teased her senses, Charlie's cold shoulder gave her a sudden chill.

"Charlie, thanks for inviting me to Mara's—"

"I hope you feel better," he said dryly as she hesitated with her hands at the handlebars.

She gazed up at him, finding his eyes wanting. She knew she didn't owe him an explanation about the driver's license, but his crestfallen expression made a place deep in her soul ache. As much as she wanted to come clean and tell him every little detail of who she was and who she had been in the past, she'd been conditioned the last ten years to do the opposite. Her safety and Lucy's safety had depended on her complete diligence to the idea that she should reveal nothing—to anyone—ever.

Words would fail her now, as much as she wanted to say something to get the old Charlie back. Desperate for anything to bridge the divide rapidly expanding between them, she patted her bicycle.

"You know, I really shouldn't ride home without my helmet, Charlie. A deal is a deal."

He stopped short. "Don't tell me you're going to wear it now."

"If I had it with me, I would."

He snorted to imply he didn't believe her. "Don't take your safety seriously just because I want you to."

"It's kind of you to care so much. I haven't had many people in my life who really care like you. If you drive me back to my motel, I'll be sure to wear it from now on."

He drew a contemplative breath and nodded. Something in his demeanor softened slightly and Paige could catch a spark of the Charlie she had come to adore over the last couple of days. Without speaking a word, he hoisted her bike back into the truck bed. Paige slipped into the front seat and gave the most innocent, friendly wave she could to Tully, now stationed at the window. He lifted his hand as Charlie backed the truck down the driveway, but he didn't retreat into the house for as long as she could see him.

CHARLIE GRIPPED THE top of the steering wheel and tried to concentrate on anything rather than Paige. He was having more trouble reading her from one moment to the next. First, she seemed happy to come for dinner, then she wanted to bolt from the house, and now she was cozying up to him—well, verbally anyway. Whatever was going on with her had to stop. He couldn't afford to get hurt again.

Then there was the driver's license. It was long expired. The name was different. He hated to ask and seal his participation in some sort of charade with her he couldn't understand, but as he caught her glancing over at him, he knew he was already in too deep.

"Are you some sort of secret agent or something?" he said. It was meant as a joke, a way to break the ice and find out what the heck was going on, but she laughed a little too hard. It made him cringe.

"Is that what you think?"

"No."

She looked out her window for a few moments before whispering. "Maybe I am a spy."

He pulled off the main drag and cut toward the sports shop. It was in the opposite direction from her motel and when he did it, he noticed her tense.

"Nah. You're too kind to be a spy."

"What do you think then? I can tell you're curious."

Charlie drove for a while in silence, considering what it was he did assume about her alternate name. After a minute he pulled the truck around behind the shop close to the beach and cut the engine. He eased back in his seat and noticed her fingers flex on the tops of her thighs as well as how she had sucked in a breath. He didn't want to let her off the hook. He wasn't the serious type, but he wanted someone to think twice before lying to him. He had to guard himself a little more intensely so he wouldn't fall into a similar situation like he had been in with Crystal. Perhaps Paige wasn't the one, like he had thought, and fate had sent her to remind him of that hard-learned lesson.

"I'm going to ask you this one time, and I want you to be honest with me. If you can't be honest, then we'll end this right here and now. You can go about your life, and I can go about mine. We'll part as friends."

She nodded. "Fair enough. But first, can I ask why you brought me here?"

He looked out over the horizon as the sun inched closer to the water. Maybe he was a hopeless romantic at heart and was betting that she was the kind of woman who you could depend on. And if she wasn't, this place would soften the blow.

"I have my reasons."

She stared at her hands for a moment before looking back up into his eyes. "Okay, Charlie."

"Is Willow Beckett your real name?"

Paige cringed at his question, or was it at the sound of the name? He couldn't be sure, but he could tell he was verbally ripping off an emotional Band-Aid.

"Yes," she said in a barely audible whisper.

He frowned and readjusted in his seat. "I don't understand. Is Paige Cartman a pseudonym? A pen name of some sort?"

"Paige Cartman is my legal name now. I changed it a long time ago."

"You didn't like Willow?"

"I still have a lot of baggage from my mother raising me, but changing my name was at least one thing I could control when I became an adult. I wouldn't have to deal with her or that name anymore."

He searched for deceit in her voice, any inkling that it wasn't the truth. He mentally kicked himself for dredging up her past. After what happened with Crystal, he didn't want to be paranoid, but he knew he couldn't trust himself the way he once had. He needed to know the truth.

"Listen, Charlie, I want to be honest with you, but with every question you ask it makes me want to bolt out of this truck and hitchhike back to my motel. The driver's license Lucy found is almost a decade old. I don't know why I still carry it with me. Even though I hated that name and wanted to be rid of it and my old life as soon as possible, I couldn't..."

He understood. It was the same reason he hadn't been able to pawn Crystal's engagement ring. He had no intention of keeping it or giving it to another woman, but parting with it was just as painful as looking at it.

"You don't have to explain. The past is difficult to shake off sometimes."

She tipped her head back and gave him a slow nod to convey he really did understand.

"That was probably something for more of a fifth date, huh?" he said.

"I've never had a fifth date before, Charlie. I'm not sure when I would reveal that to someone, but there it is."

"Do I know everything important that I

should?" He wanted her assurance, but she shook her head.

"No, but I have to leave it at that for tonight."

"Why?"

"I guess I have *my* reasons." He accepted her answer though a thousand more questions swarmed. Who was this woman who had walked into his life and flipped his world upside down in a few short days?

"Let's move on for now, because I don't want to lose the light."

"The light?" She sat straighter and followed his line of sight to the amphibian plane at the end of the dock. "Are you kidding?"

"Nope," he said opening his truck door. "And don't worry. You don't have to wear a helmet for this."

PAIGE HESITANTLY FOLLOWED Charlie to the end of the dock protruding into the lake. The small prop plane she had seen when first arriving to Roseley bobbed gently in the water.

Charlie opened the door and offered her a hand.

"I promise it's not as scary as it seems. I'm an excellent pilot."

"I'm sure you are," she said, glancing back

at the truck. "But I prefer to keep my feet on the ground."

"If you like the speed of bicycling—"

"This is *not* the same thing, Charlie. I've never flown before. And isn't it going to get dark?"

"We'll only be up twenty minutes. The gas tank is almost on empty."

"What?"

He held up his outstretched hands in surrender and chuckled.

"Just joking. This is my tour plane. I've flown this baby a thousand times. You'll be safe with me, Freckles." Paige's breath hitched at the sincerity in his voice. Whether or not this plane was safe, he at least believed she'd be safe with him. He waved her over. "Come take a look inside, at least."

Paige inched closer and peered into the cockpit.

"How many people can you fit in here?"

"Six, including me."

"It must have set you back a pretty penny."

He agreed. "More than you know."

"What would happen, exactly, if I wanted to go for a ride?"

Charlie braced his hand over the door and leaned in. She couldn't help but delight in the way his eyes had turned youthful and spirited like a sixteen-year-old kid about to sneak his dad's Firebird out of the garage.

"Well," he said, his voice a husky whisper, "you would sit in there and be the prettiest copilot I've ever had. I'd untether us and sit beside you. I'd do all the checks before take-off and as soon as that boat way out there on the water clears out, we'd take off. I'd fly you all around the lake and show you a beautiful sunset before landing you right back here. Easy peasy."

"Don't start with that easy peasy nonsense again. I'm scared of the landing, not the take-off."

"The landing is the easiest part on an amphibian. Instead of having to land on three narrow wheels, I land on these—" He pointed to the two big floats under the plane. "You'll be surprised how smooth it is."

Paige bit her lip. She was more surprised at how easy it was falling in love with Charlie Stillwater.

"I don't know…" she said, though she'd made up her mind the minute he'd called her Freckles again. She wanted him to sell her on the idea a little bit more. Mostly, she wanted him to keep leaning in so she could feel the warmth of his breath on her face. "I suppose I could give it a try as long as you promise to land before it gets dark."

She wanted him to promise, to say that bit again about how she would be safe with him, but instead, he ran his hand down the length of her arm and slipped his hand around hers. His touch sent an electric current throughout her body, shivering its way across her shoulders and down her spine. Swooning on her feet, she had to catch herself as she thought he might kiss her. Tipping his head toward the cab of the plane, he helped her climb inside and gave a quick wink that she knew she would always associate with him.

CHAPTER ELEVEN

CHARLIE HANDED PAIGE a headset and motioned for her to place it over her ears.

"Can you hear me?" he asked through the microphone on his own headset.

"Loud and clear."

"Your seat belt buckles like ones on a regular airplane," he said. "Well, if you ever fly on a commercial flight, this will look familiar. Just unlatch the metal clasp to loosen it."

She followed his instructions, cinching the belt. He could tell she was nervous, and it made her even more endearing to him. The fact she was willing to go up for her first airplane flight with him made him smile with satisfaction.

"What are you doing now?" she asked, her eyes darting to follow each movement of his hand like a cat stalking a dangling string. "You'll tell me before we take off, won't you?"

"Just the preflight checks," he said, working to keep his voice as calm and soothing as he could. "I'm going to crack the throttle. We're priming the engine by flowing fuel into the cylinders right now."

Paige grabbed his hand, throwing him off guard. He wanted to tell her he couldn't hold her hand during the takeoff process, but then she pressed it to her chest. His face perked in surprise.

"My heart's beating out of my chest, Charlie Stillwater."

Her voice crackled through the headset speaker as her eyes wildly flashed up at him. She kept his hand firmly over the spot, an area of her body he'd never touched before. He wanted to slip off his headset and kiss her there, slowly and delicately just as he'd imagined. He'd draw a cursive line with his lips until she invited more. The sun flickered off the water, making a golden backdrop behind her, lightening the hair around the crown of her head like a halo. She was nearly hypnotizing.

"You're going to be all right, you know," he said, reclaiming his hand to keep his wits about him. "Will you do me a favor before we take off?" She nodded eagerly. "Look out your window as far back as you can see. Tell me if any boats are heading our way."

Paige jostled in her seat, craning her neck to look.

"I don't see any."

"Good. We have a clear runway."

Every time he fired up the engine, the loud puttering was sweet music to his ears. How could he give up his plane? Even if he couldn't support himself giving tours around Roseley the way he had been able to along the ocean shore, he couldn't part with this sound, this experience. He had wanted to fly his whole life, and he was too young to give up on his dream just because someone else had ruined his first attempt to make it a reality.

"You look like you're doing something," Paige said.

"Water rudders…right tank has a good supply of fuel…check." Charlie noted each of his flight checks in the exact same order he always practiced. Now was not the time to get distracted by his pretty copilot or he could miss something crucial. "Elevator track… lower flaps…clear on both sides…we're going to idle out on the water."

"Is this it? Are we taking off?"

Charlie cracked a wide grin. "Don't you love this feeling?" he said. He pulled back on the wheel a bit to smooth it out.

"I'll let you know once I return home alive."

"You're doing great. We're about ready. Avionics…beacon…landing…strobe lights… headsets on…ready for flight."

"This is it!" Paige said, clasping her hands. "I can't believe I let you talk me into this."

"You'll be thanking me in about thirty seconds."

Charlie scanned the lake again for boats on either side of them before skimming his eyes over the horizon. He needed to get the prop away from the water and spray, to get the best pickup.

"Is this what a regular plane sounds like?" Paige asked over the noise and momentum of the aircraft speeding across the water.

"This is much louder. Your seat is only a couple feet off the water. It's more like the intensity of a speedboat, but not for long."

Through the windshield, a view segmented into three triangles because of an inverted brace bar in front of them, the coast on the opposite side of the lake was very distant but getting closer by the second as they sped toward it. He loved the speed, the element of excitement that was always present. He couldn't control what Crystal had done or what Paige might do down the road, but he knew how to fly a plane.

Paige threw a hand around the brace bar and looked to Charlie for affirmation that that was okay. He nodded as the pitch of the engine changed. In a matter of a few seconds the friction of the plane against the water ceased and they officially pulled up into the air, taking flight.

"Oh!" Paige called. "Here we go!"

Boats disappeared into water bugs skimming the lake below them. The brilliance of the neat green lawns cozied up against a sapphire-blue lake briefly gave Charlie something to admire more than Paige.

"Isn't it beautiful?" he said.

"I've never had a view like this before. Everything below is so small it looks fake."

Charlie chuckled. "It always does. I think that every time I fly." He slowly banked to the right before straightening them out to follow the shoreline.

"I can see why you love this now."

A small satisfaction came over him as he watched her enjoy the view. "I think I hooked you. You'll be going for your own pilot's license in no time, Freckles."

She let out a whooping laugh. "I wouldn't rule anything out, Charlie."

THE SKY HAD begun to turn to orange and pink, oil paint streaks covering as far as they could see, when Charlie aimed the plane toward the sunset. Every time he banked one way or the other, Paige's stomach floated up into her chest, suspending her breath for a few delightful moments. She felt as effervescent as champagne bubbles lifting off from the bottom of a fine-stemmed crystal flute, and with Charlie secured by her side, she wasn't sure she ever wanted to come back down again.

"I wish I could live up here," she said, without giving a second thought to how silly it sounded. The joy of cruising high above everything had momentarily suppressed her usual filter.

"You can," he said, the static of the headset doing nothing to mask the warmth in his voice. "I'll take you up anytime you want."

She believed him. He smiled with the happiness of a person whose passion had been understood and appreciated, and it made her wish for something like it too. She'd never had something of her own to love as much as he loved flying.

"I envy you this, Charlie. This passion of yours."

"Don't you have one?"

She shook her head as her eyes found his.

"I don't have much, Charlie. That's why I'm so scared of losing the few things I do have."

She thought of Lucy. Since she had found the girl and met her, how could she walk away now? It was hard to imagine a time when she could safely reveal her relationship to Lucy, but perhaps she could still be in her life somehow. Couldn't she be the kind of friend who becomes so close to the family, over time, everyone begins to call her auntie? She could be Aunt Paige. She could feel satisfied her entire life as Aunt Paige, couldn't she?

And then there was Charlie. It had been so vital in the past to push people away and not let them get close for fear they would ask the wrong questions or lead the wrong people to her. But Charlie had charmed his way into a date and then another, and if she was honest, it was because she had fallen for him the first time they'd met; it didn't have anything to do with Lucy. So maybe her life was finally falling into place. Maybe it was time for her to finally get the things she had desired her entire life.

"Do you want to see where the Water Dancers perform?" he said, snapping her out of her daydream.

"Remind me who they are again."

Charlie banked the plane toward the shore.

"The Water Dancers Ski Club has been around for eighty years. They're kind of *the* club to join on Little Lake Roseley. They perform every Wednesday night in the summer right over there." He pointed to a long beach where a floating dock displayed their large banner.

"I'd love to see that show."

"Their first show is tomorrow night. I'll take you, if you're still around."

She could tell his friendly invitation had more intention behind it. He wanted to know her timeline, whether she planned to stay. She wanted to know that too.

"So, if this is *Little* Lake Roseley, where is Lake Roseley?"

Charlie pointed. "Nine miles that way. It's almost four times as big as this one."

"Why not run a tour guide company and include both lakes? Could you get enough business from both?"

Charlie sat in silence, staring out over the water as he prepared for landing. She thought perhaps he hadn't understood what she'd said until he turned to her.

"It's not the same as touring oceanside, but it's something worth considering."

"There has to be something else you can do with this plane. You *cannot* get rid of it."

He laughed. "I'd love to hear you say that in front of Mara. I half expect her to slip a for-sale sign on the windshield when I'm not looking."

"You listen to me, Charlie," she said, her voice firm. "Don't you dare sell this plane. Roseley needs it even if you don't know why yet."

He chuckled. "You have no idea how much I want to believe you."

A booming voice bursting through the dashboard radio made Paige jump, and by the confusion on Charlie's face, she figured it didn't happen often, at least not when he wasn't giving tours.

"Cessna 206 Chuckie, this is Squad Car 27. Do you copy?"

Charlie side-glanced at Paige before responding.

"I copy, 27. Tully, is that you?"

"Yes. I'm here with Officers Randall and White."

Paige's face instantly tightened at the sound of Tully's voice. If Tully had run her name in the police database, he'd be waiting at the dock in his squad car by the time they landed. She couldn't believe she'd let herself get cornered like this. It was so unlike her. So rash, too reckless.

"How'd you know I was up?"

"A squad car spotted you. Do you have a passenger?" By his tone and directive, she knew this wasn't a social call.

Charlie smirked at Paige. "I do, and she's a lot prettier than you. Jealous?"

There was silence over the radio. Every second that ticked by without Tully's response made Paige's stomach roll in nauseous waves. What on earth did he have to say, and why wasn't he saying it? Was he afraid he'd tip her off? Did he already know what she'd done?

Finally, Tully's husky voice barreled through the line.

"We need your eye in the sky. What is your location?"

Charlie instantly straightened.

"Pier thirty at twelve hundred feet."

"Head toward pier one-twenty. Look for a speedboat."

"Make and model?"

"Jet boat. Fifteen-foot Scarab with red hull. She'll be racing."

"Copy that."

Charlie tipped the nose of the plane slightly toward the open water, descending for a closer look.

"What's going on?" Paige asked through bated breath. She wasn't completely certain Tully wasn't pursuing her. Maybe it was meant to distract her until they landed.

"Not sure. Might be a theft or the police might be looking for a person of interest. I've gotten calls like this before in North Carolina. Never had one here."

Paige scanned the shoreline. "It might be docked somewhere."

"Possible. But by the sound of it, someone is on the run."

"With so many boats, I'm not sure how we're going to know which one is our winner."

"Just look for anything suspicious."

Paige leaned closer to her window. She wanted to spot the boat and do something helpful for Charlie before she slipped out of his life forever. The sick gut-wrenching turn that had happened because of Tully's voice had revealed to her a sad truth. She couldn't stay in Roseley after tonight.

"I love this," Charlie said as she turned to admire the ruggedly handsome lines of his profile. "I could do stuff like this all day."

"Are you an adrenaline junkie?"

"I never considered myself that before, but there is something fun about the rush of it all, don't you think?"

Paige turned back for her window. Maybe it would be more exciting if she wasn't worried Tully was waiting for her when they landed.

Just then, Paige spotted a small dot on the horizon. Even at a distance she could tell the blur was racing. She could barely make out that it was a boat, let alone what color or model it was, but she knew.

"That's it, Charlie!" she said pointing straight ahead. "I know it!"

Charlie nodded and lined up the nose of the airplane. Without hesitating, he went for the radio.

"Squad Car 27, we're tracking a boat that might be your suspect. It's southwest of Caribou Island, heading east."

"Copy, Chuckie. Please pursue."

"Copy that."

"Do you think it's a criminal?"

"Hard to say," Charlie said. "This lake is so safe, it's hard to imagine anything truly sinister happening here."

"That's exactly what people say on the news after there's a gruesome murder."

"Hmm, I suppose…"

"People are people, Charlie," she said, sadly recalling Tully's prior observation, which had rung so true with her. "There are villains everywhere even if you don't recognize them at first."

"Whoa," he said. "I didn't know you were so cynical. Have you known a lot of villains in your day?"

Paige shrugged. She'd known one.

"I only meant it might be exciting to think you and I are chasing a serial killer or something. It could happen."

"If we catch a serial killer tonight, Paige Cartman, I'm getting you on the eleven o'clock news."

"No need for that," she said sharply, but Charlie just jerked his head toward the lake. They approached the speeding boat, and much to Paige's delight, she spotted the bright red paint reflecting in the setting sunlight. "I think we've got our man!"

"Squad Car 27, suspect heading north between Caribou Island and shoreline."

"Copy, Chuckie."

"Chuckie?" she asked.

Charlie turned his head at the amusement in her voice.

"It's the name of my plane," he said, circling north.

"Is your legal name Charles?"

"Nope. My dad's name was Charles, but he never liked it. After he died, my mom wanted to name me after him, but chose Charlie for my legal name."

"That was sweet of her."

"She's a sweet person, much like you."

"I don't know how sweet I am."

Charlie flashed his signature grin at her as he directed the plane lower toward the boat.

"You're sweet, Freckles. Trust me."

"Where is your mom now?"

"She and Glenn moved to Florida a couple of years ago. The humidity helps Glenn's asthma, but they'll be up for a visit in a few weeks."

Charlie's statement hung in the air. She knew she wouldn't be around to meet them and was grateful when Tully interrupted.

"Chuckie, can you get a view?" Tully asked.

"Copy, 27. We have three suspects on board."

"They look kind of young," Paige said. "Their bodies are scrawny like children or teenagers."

"You're right. This is bad."

"Why?"

"Because they've probably stolen that boat and don't know how easily they can hit the wake off another boat and flip themselves." Charlie got on the radio. "27, suspects look to be teenagers. What is your location?"

"We have two boats northbound, over."

"Copy that, 27."

Paige perched at the edge of her seat and grasped the brace bar with both hands for lack of anywhere else to channel her concern. These young men had no idea how dangerous a situation they had put themselves in. They might not understand until they were adults or in a worst-case scenario, until they flipped the boat and had to deal with whatever the outcome. What did teenagers know about the long-term ramifications on the future and how their choices at this tender age could impact the rest of their lives and the lives of others? She hadn't known squat when she had been their age, but she'd lived with the consequences of her actions, and Trudy's actions, every day.

"These kids are going to kill themselves, Paige. We have to get them to slow down, but I'm afraid lowering the plane will spur them on."

Paige studied Charlie, whose face had contorted into a road map of lines, some from worry, some from frustration. They had to do something, but what?

A surge of resolution flooded Paige's veins as she furiously unfastened her seat belt. Her hands flailed over the piles of gear on the back seat and floorboard, searching for something, anything that could help them.

"Put your belt back on, Paige!" Charlie called through her headset speakers. "I don't have time to worry about you too."

She didn't pay him any attention. She was after something, and she'd only know it when she spotted it—

"You have a bullhorn!" she shouted, hauling it to her lap. "Lower the plane, Charlie, and I'll call down to them! How do you open the window?"

"Are you crazy?"

"Do you have a better idea? You said they could kill themselves!"

Charlie's eyes darted between Paige and the speedboat as he descended closer. "The window rotates up, parallel to the wing. Hang on, though. It's worse than rolling down your window on the freeway. We won't be able to hear each other. I'll get you as close as I can. And put your seat belt back on!"

"I can't. I won't be able to lean out far enough. Get closer!"

With the bullhorn clamped between her knees, Paige opened her window, the wind smacking her hard in the face, nearly sucking her breath right out of her and onto the open air. Charlie lowered the plane nearly twenty feet above the speeding vessel. Paige angled the bullhorn out the window and clamped down on the speaker button.

"Stop! Police!" she hollered. She knew the boys might not hear her even if she screamed her throat raw. She also knew it was illegal to impersonate a police officer, but she'd done worse before.

The two passengers on board the boat turned their faces up toward the plane as they desperately clung to their seats for dear life. One scratch of the nose could send them toppling to the back of the boat, if it didn't knock them right into the crashing wake. She screamed her orders at them again as Charlie dipped even closer. If she had been a stunt-woman in an action movie, she imagined this was the scene where she'd be expected to jump into their boat. She'd had a high-speed chase once before in her life, but nothing like this. Not as the pursuer.

One of the boys slapped the driver on the back, no doubt shouting at his friend. Paige hoped he wanted the boat to stop. The driver tried to shake his friend off his shoulder while accelerating.

"Stop!" Paige shouted again. Charlie's fear they would try to evade them was coming true, and as Paige looked ahead into the distance, she spotted several boats speeding right toward them. She pointed, though she knew Charlie already saw them too. "You're in danger!"

Finally, one of the passengers made for the steering wheel while the other friend threw a headlock around the driver, yanking him back and onto the floor. They tumbled, a mesh of limbs sprawling and flailing as the boat wobbled but continued to accelerate forward. Paige cranked the window and sealed the cabin shut again.

"He doesn't know how to drive it!" she blurted.

"He needs to pull back on the throttle. The boat is out of control." Charlie grappled for the radio. "27, two passengers overtook the driver. Inexperienced driver at the helm."

"Copy that, Chuckie. On the scene in sixty seconds."

Paige looked on in fear as the two young men rolled on the back floor, slugging each other. Finally, the new driver, his hands frantically moving over the gear, located the throttle and pulled it back, quickly jarring the boat down to a manageable speed.

"He did it," Paige breathed, collapsing back in her seat.

"27, driver backed down the throttle. You should be able to board the watercraft. Over."

"Copy that, Chuckie."

Charlie peeled the plane off to the east, circling back around for another pass over the scene. Paige cheered as she saw the police officers climbing into the boat with the boys.

"I hope their parents ground them for at least a year," she said.

Charlie shook his head. "They really don't know how close they came to flipping."

Paige watched for as long as she could from

her window before she lost her vantage point. She turned when Charlie patted her hand.

"You did good," he said.

"Yeah?"

"Would I lie to you?"

She shook her head, but she knew she couldn't ask him the same question. Keeping her secrets from Charlie, who was becoming even more integral in her life story, was the same thing as lying, wasn't it? He was Lucy's uncle and as much as she wanted to make him her confidant, she just couldn't.

She'd remember this evening with him, but as soon as they landed, she would need to leave while Tully was distracted with the teenagers. She needed to return to Ohio. She needed to kiss Charlie goodbye.

"ARE YOU READY, PAIGE?"

"For what?"

Charlie jerked his head toward the windshield.

"What goes up, must come down."

She winced. "I wish you hadn't said it like that."

But Charlie looked completely at ease as the water loomed closer and bass fishing boats and pontoon boats passed more quickly underneath them. Paige sucked in a breath as Charlie began their descent. Everything she had ever seen on television portrayed the landing as the most harrowing part of the flight, and she assumed this would be no different, despite what Charlie assured her.

But as the plane skimmed the water's surface, the engine quieted so quickly that Paige frantically glanced around, believing the engine had cut out before the floats had touched down.

"What happened?" she said as the plane slowed to a drift. "Did the engine die?"

"That was it."

"That was it?" she said, releasing an exasperated breath.

"I told you landing was the easiest part."

Paige removed her headset and unfastened her seat belt as Charlie worked against the wind to pull the plane up along the end of the dock. Throwing open his door, he reached for a rope dangling from the dock's edge and hopped out.

Paige waited patiently until Charlie had secured the plane and reached for her hand. As he helped her onto the dock, she could sense his reluctance to let it go.

"How was it?" he asked as she wavered on her feet in front of him.

"I had a good time. I enjoyed it more than I thought I would. You gave me quite a show."

"Well, when you leaned out your window, you nearly gave me a heart attack."

"How about now?" she asked, smiling up at him. This time he placed her hand on his chest, just over his heart. His eyes had darkened in the setting sunlight, early twilight casting shadows over them. "Mmm, still racing," she murmured.

"Are you cold?" he said, noticing her shiver.

"A little. Warm me up?"

With a practiced ease, he embraced her. She pressed her body up against his chest as his body heat warmed the lines of her face into a dreamy smile. *He gives good hugs*, she thought as she allowed him to adjust his arms more snugly around her. They were the kind of hugs a woman could find herself looking forward to at the end of a long day. The kind of hugs that offered unwavering protection and safety and warmth. And, she decided as she tipped her face up toward his and ran her hands up his chest, the kind of hugs that led a woman to maneuver for more.

"Charlie," she whispered as he gazed down

at her. It was all she muttered before she pulled his face toward hers and kissed him tenderly for a long time.

PAIGE KNEW IT was time to secretly wish Charlie goodbye, but as he smiled at her from the driver's seat, the headlights from oncoming traffic highlighting his perfectly curled lips, she wanted to draw out their last moments together.

"Tired?" he asked as he pulled up to her motel. She shook her head. "Would you like to meet down at the beach tomorrow evening? The Water Dancers are performing, and I promised it would be a good show."

She imagined how nice it would be to cozy up to Charlie on the beach as the sun set again. They could spread out a blanket and watch the ski club and bring Lucy and Mara and...

Tully.

It wouldn't be the dream she imagined. She was only fooling herself. Tully might be distracted tonight, arresting and processing the teenagers, but tomorrow he'd run Willow Beckett in his police database. If she waited any longer, she might miss her window to leave. It had to be tonight.

"Sounds nice," she said.

"I'll pick you up."

She shook her head, forming the lie on her lips. "I'll meet you there."

"On your bicycle."

"Probably."

"Are you going to wear your helmet?" he teased.

She bit back tears and nodded her head enthusiastically. "Absolutely."

Paige slipped out of the truck as Charlie cut the engine and worked to pull her bike from the truck bed.

"How's this for curbside service," he said, wheeling it up to the bike rack. "I'll even lock it up for you."

"Thank you, Charlie," she said, as her heart sank in her chest. He really was kind. She needed more kind in her life.

He stood and faced her, his eyes falling over her with a tenderness that could make a woman forget herself. If this was their last goodbye, she didn't want it to end.

"Walk me to my door?"

"Whatever you want." She reached for his hand and led him into the motel. Their fingers intertwined the way she had always imagined holding hands with a boyfriend. She'd never had a boyfriend before, and now that she had found Charlie, she was working herself up to leave him. "I probably shouldn't come in," he said when she dug for her room key. She turned and found him serious. He leaned in toward her and rasped his lips along the contour of her ear. "This evening was perfect just as it was, and I have my gentlemanly reputation to uphold."

She curled her fingers in the fabric of his shirt. "With that wicked grin, you never struck me as a good boy, Charlie Stillwater."

"I'm the poster boy for discretion." He smirked, the mischievousness in his eyes both surprising and delighting her. She nuzzled her face to his, welcoming his mouth once again. His kisses were skilled, lips sliding over hers, tongue beckoning for more. She felt the broadness of his shoulders, gripped his muscles and tugged him closer. She wanted to lose herself with him for a spell, wanted to show him how much he meant to her.

"What about dinner?" she said, trying to regain her thoughts. "You showed me a good time tonight, but you *did* promise me dinner. I promised I'd wear my helmet, so if you don't hold up your end of the bargain, I think that reputation will be tainted."

He brushed his lips down the nape of her

neck, tickling each nerve along the way. "Hmm. I wouldn't want that to happen. Are you hungry?"

"Starving. I'll meet you in the lobby. I need to change and check my messages." She welcomed the minute breather.

"Take your time, Freckles." He winked. "I will prepare the most romantic, second-rate motel, pizza dinner you've ever tasted." She watched him stride down the hallway for a moment before ducking into her room. The light on her room phone blinked. The voice on the other end of the line was nearly unrecognizable as she pressed it hard to her ear. Aunt Joan's voice croaked, forcing her message— *call me*. Paige's fingers shook wildly as she dialed the numbers.

"What's wrong?" she spat once Aunt Joan answered.

"Your uncle was heavily sedated. He didn't know what he was doing. He's so sorry, Paige. He's *so* sorry."

"Slow down, *please*," Paige said. "What did he do?"

Aunt Joan heaved several frantic breaths as if struggling to calm herself.

"Craig was sedated, but awake. I didn't find out until I got here tonight—"

"Find out what?"

"Thorne was here."

"At the hospital?"

"He came to see your uncle. I don't know how he knew Craig was a patient. He must have been watching the house."

"What did Uncle Craig tell him?" Paige strangled the phone receiver. She knew it was going to be bad. She just wasn't sure how bad.

"He doesn't remember for sure, but he remembers calling Lucy by name."

"He can't find her with just a first name."

"And he knows your name."

"Does he?" Paige sank to the floor. If Thorne knew her address, he certainly must know her new name. "Could he find me? Could he trace me to Roseley?"

"Yes."

"How?" Paige waited for Joan's answer and when it didn't come, she shut her eyes tightly. "Tell me he didn't mention Roseley, Aunt Joan. Please tell me he didn't—"

"I don't know." Joan's voice was pained and soft. "He doesn't know for sure."

She imagined her aunt holed up along the vending machines or in the bathroom, having a meltdown all alone in some corner of the hospital, and Paige wasn't there to comfort her, because she was in Roseley.

"It's going to be okay, Joan. It'll be fine."

"It won't. We thought getting you out of town would be best. We thought if you weren't here with us…if he couldn't find you…if he couldn't see you…but now…you're there all alone…"

"I'm not alone."

"Is Charlie with you?"

Paige thought of Charlie waiting for her in the lobby. She should tell him. She should tell him about Thorne and about her past and about where Lucy came from…

"I'll be fine," Paige said, her voice more of a command. "Go get some sleep. I don't have my cell phone anymore, but I'll buy a new one in the morning and call you. See if you can sleep. Uncle Craig needs you to stay rested, stay strong."

"It's going to catch up with us, you know. I just hoped it wouldn't happen until—"

"Go to sleep, Joan."

"I will. But you need to too. Good night, love."

Paige fumbled to return the handset to the phone and stared off across the room.

Thorne would find his way to Roseley

now. If he was coming, it didn't matter now whether she was here or not, because he didn't want her. He had never wanted her. All along, all this time, all he had ever wanted was Lucy.

CHAPTER TWELVE

CHARLIE KNOCKED LIGHTLY on Paige's door. He had ordered the pizza and bought a couple of sodas out of the lobby vending machine. He had waited patiently for her to arrive, but after forty-five minutes of watching the lobby television, he went in search of her.

He waited at her door, listening for shuffling on the other side, but it was quiet.

"Paige," he called, knocking again. "Are you okay?"

He didn't think she'd have cold feet about eating a piece of pizza in the lobby. He had made it clear this was a dinner with no strings attached. He didn't want to rush things with her or scare her off. He wanted to lay the groundwork for a courtship that could lead to...what? Marriage? Family? Building a life together? They were all the things he thought he had been working toward with Crystal no more than a couple months ago, before everything came crashing down.

But now, after the evening they'd had, he wanted to pinch himself. Between pursuing the stolen boat and holding Paige in his arms, he knew he wanted more of both those things. He wasn't sure exactly what the future held, but for the first time in months he felt as if he was pointed in the right direction.

"Paige, love," he called tenderly. "Is something wrong?"

Finally, he heard the dead bolt unlock. Paige creaked open the door and stared up at him. Her green eyes were laced with red veins, while tears smeared across her blush-pink cheeks. She pulled the door open farther and shuffled back into the room, her unspoken invitation making him uneasy. What on earth had happened since he'd left her?

Just as he latched the door behind him and moved closer, she burst into tears, burying her hands in her face.

"I don't know what to do," she whispered. Charlie ran his hand over her back until she turned and buried her face in his chest. He wrapped his arms around her and felt her shudder against his skin.

"Talk to me, Paige. I can help." But she stayed silent, gently shaking from the tears that soaked through his shirt. Who was this woman he held in his arms? He had to admit that as much as he liked and admired her, he didn't really know her. "Is it your uncle? Did something happen?"

She nodded, making him hold her tighter. Together they swayed in the small motel room as he waited for a sign she wished to disclose more. When she finally looked up at him, her eyes were pleading.

"I won't be able to sleep tonight if I'm alone," she said in a shaky voice. "Would you stay here with me tonight?"

He brushed the hair off her face. He needed to figure out what he was dealing with to get offered such an invitation. "Did your uncle pass? Is he gone?" She shook her head. "Did he take a turn? I'll go to Ohio with you, Paige, if you need me to."

"No," she said, taking his hand and pulling him toward the bed. "I need to sleep. I need my mind clear tomorrow and to do that, I need to close my eyes. Will you stay?" Her voice melted him, the desperation in it triggering every protective instinct he possessed. He wanted to shelter her from whatever had hurt her.

He stretched out on the bed as she nestled her body into his. Her head instantly found the nook under his shoulder. He stroked her face as he would lull a child to dreamland and her eyelashes fluttered before resting on the tops of her cheeks. As neither of them had thought to turn out the light, he found himself admiring the uniqueness of her face in the warm lamp glow. He counted the freckles punctuating the slope of her nose. He watched her lips part as her body relaxed, and she drifted fully into a deep sleep. She was a true beauty.

"I'm in trouble," he whispered, though to no one who could hear him. "So much trouble."

CHARLIE STARTED AWAKE to his cell phone vibrating in his pocket. He glanced at the motel clock.

6:00 a.m.

He gingerly slipped his arms from around Paige and ducked into the bathroom. Over the course of the night he had switched off the light and pulled a blanket over the two of them. He'd spooned her body, heavy with a sleep he could only imagine she hadn't gotten in years.

"Tully?" he said. "Just because you're an early bird doesn't mean I have to be. What on earth?"

"Sorry, buddy. Did I wake you?"

"What is it?"

"I came by your place last night but didn't see your truck."

"The evening went longer than I expected."

"I see." Tully's voice was serious. He was most likely at the station, working a case. He was a workaholic when on a case, barely sleeping until he'd solved it. He was a guard dog of sorts, his teddy bear temperament shifting into grizzly when innocent lives were in jeopardy. It was a quality that also made him the most fiercely loyal friend Charlie had ever known, and after Crystal, Charlie wasn't about to take a friend like that for granted.

"Are you at the station?"

"I'm sorry, Charlie. I had a late night and arrived here a couple of hours ago. I forgot what time it was."

"I'm awake now. What's wrong?"

"I had a talk with Chief Marley, and we wanted to speak to you—"

Charlie turned at the rap on the bathroom door. "Hang on, Tully," he said, pulling it open. "Mornin', sunshine."

Paige's sheepish smile greeted him, her messy blond locks tossed over her shoulder.

"Everything okay?" she muttered, glancing at his phone.

"I should be asking you the same thing. What happened last night?"

She shrugged. "Are you going to see Lucy today?"

His eyebrows lifted. "Uh… I guess, yes. Why?"

"I need to fit her for her costume. I'm going to finish it today."

"I'm sure that would be fine. Are you hungry for breakfast?"

She nodded and motioned she needed to go in the bathroom. "I'll get dressed."

Charlie slipped out before she latched the bathroom door. "Okay, Tully. Why did you call again?"

"Did you spend the night with Paige?"

"Yeah, but just to sleep. Her uncle…he's dying."

"I'm sorry to hear that." Charlie waited for Tully to continue. He didn't know how many more times he needed to ask why his friend called before he spit it out. "Can you come into the station this morning?"

"We can swing by after breakfast."

Tully was silent for several more moments before he cleared his throat. "Don't mention it to Paige."

"Why? What's going on? Is this because of

last night?" Charlie asked. Tully cleared his throat again, but his tone was still serious.

"Yes."

"Are you giving us a medal of honor or something?" Charlie chuckled. He couldn't understand why his friend was being so evasive. This must be how other people, those who encountered him when he was on the job, felt around Tully.

"You'd like that, wouldn't you?" Tully said, his voice finally breaking into a chuckle. "I'll see you when you get here."

Charlie slipped back into the room as Paige emerged, a toothbrush in hand.

"Would you believe I actually have an extra one of these?" She smiled, holding it out to him. "Aunt Joan is a bit obsessed with buying toiletries in bulk."

"Thanks."

"Charlie," she said, resting her head against the bathroom door frame. "I'm sorry about last night."

"I'm not. It's not every night I get to sleep beside a beautiful woman." She rolled her eyes as he continued. "Do you mind me asking what upset you?"

Her face fell somber. "My world might be falling apart."

"Am I supposed to know what that means?"

"*I* don't even know what that means."

He contemplated her answer for a moment. She wasn't the dramatic type, trying hard for attention or sympathy. Something had happened last night when he went for pizza, so perhaps over breakfast, she'd warm up enough to tell him what it was.

"Who was on the phone?" she asked.

"Never mind. I have an errand to run after we eat." And with that, he shoved the toothbrush in his mouth, and gave her a wide, warm grin.

PAIGE TIPPED BACK the last of her coffee and studied Charlie. She had been so upset to hear about Thorne, she had collapsed with exhaustion into Charlie's arms. She hadn't slept well since the night Joan and Craig had suggested she look in on Lucy, but once she'd cozied against Charlie, she didn't even remember falling asleep. It was as if nothing bad could happen if Charlie was there beside her.

But in the morning light, over breakfast, she remembered she had to decide what to do about Thorne. She loved Lucy and as much as it would hurt, she needed to warn Mara and Peter about Thorne. Warning them would mean exposing who she was and what she had done. Given she'd been getting to know them and Lucy over the last few days, masquerading as a visitor passing through Roseley, they'd never trust her again. She was jeopardizing any chance of seeing Lucy again or perhaps, being a part of her life in the future. But she had an obligation to come clean now, didn't she? If she truly loved Lucy, she had to tell them.

Paige admired Charlie. He was oblivious to what danger lay ahead for her and Lucy as he smiled up at her from over his cup of coffee in the folksy diner. The Copper Kettle had a fair amount of charm and Charlie seemed to love it. He'd explained how the prices were low, the food was decent and the waitstaff didn't try too hard. He'd made her laugh at a moment when all she wanted to do was cry.

Paige considered laying it all out for him: who she was, why she was in Roseley, who was coming for Lucy. He could be an ally and help her confess to Mara and Peter. He could be another person to help protect Lucy. But every time she opened her mouth, her throat clamped in a vise. How exactly did she begin a confession like hers and what on earth would he think? She wasn't just jeopardizing her future with Lucy, but with Charlie. Severing their connection would be so painful...

As they drove off from the diner, Paige was so lost in thought, considering what she would say to Charlie once she worked up the nerve, she didn't notice where they were until they swung into the parking lot.

"Is this the errand you have to run?" she asked, sitting straighter in her seat. The Roseley Police Station was the last place she wanted to be and yet here they were, pulling up into the closest parking spot.

"Yep," he said, throwing the truck into Park and cutting the engine.

"I'll wait out here for you. You won't be long, will you?"

"Come on in. It's chilly this morning."

"Leave me the keys," she said, flattening out her palm with an urgency that made Charlie chuckle.

"You're not going to bail on me, are you, Freckles?" As she frowned at him and motioned for him to fork over the keys, she had to admit she wasn't quite sure. He began to hold out the keys before jerking them back with a jingle. "Come in. What else do you have to do?" And before she could protest further, he hopped out of the truck and strode up to the doors.

Paige wiped her palms down her thighs and swallowed hard. What else could this man make her do with that lopsided grin of his? Reluctantly, she slid from the truck and shuffled toward the door.

Inside, the fluorescent hallway lights flickered like in a horror movie. She squinted against them and followed Charlie through a double set of security doors.

"What exactly do you have to do here?"

"Tully needs to see us."

"Us?" Before he could answer, they spotted Tully coming from a nearby office. He stopped short and waved them over. A hefty man, about sixty years old, rose from behind his desk.

"Hey, man," Charlie said, grasping Tully's hand.

"Good morning, Paige," Tully said, nodding to her. Paige managed a thin smile as her eyes shifted to the older gentleman. "I want to introduce you to our chief of police, Chief Marley."

"Mornin'," Chief Marley said, shaking both their hands. "I understand you two are to thank for helping apprehend those boys last night."

"I don't know how much help we were," Charlie said, "but we were happy to do it."

Paige nodded as her eyes darted toward the door, looking for any more uniformed officers.

"Glad to hear it," Chief Marley said. "Look here, Charlie. Tully and I were talking about the situation last night and he mentioned you just arrived back in town."

"Yes. I lived out of state for several years."

"What are your plans for the future?"

Charlie glanced at Paige before shrugging. "I haven't decided."

"What are your plans for that plane of yours?"

"I'm trying to come up with a way to keep it, if that's what you mean."

Tully cleared his throat. "We have an idea for it *and you*."

"Which is?"

Tully looked to Chief Marley, who settled back on his heels and readjusted his belt. "Last night wasn't the first time we could have used a plane on the force, but it was the first time we not only had one, but were able to move so quickly to catch a perp."

"Those boys were too young to know what they were doing," Paige said. "They're not perps."

Chief Marley's bushy eyebrows met together. "They were doing something that could have gotten themselves and innocent folks killed. The fact that you were able to give us their location so quickly probably helped avoid a tragedy last night."

"The force needs you on staff, Charlie," Tully said, cutting to the chase.

Charlie shifted from one foot to the other. "I don't know what to say. I'd be happy to help whenever I can. You know that, Tully."

"No, Charlie. That's not what we're suggesting." Chief Marley came around from behind his desk. "To be on staff in this department, you'd have to go through the police academy."

"Become a police officer?" Charlie looked at Paige, who stood speechless. Charlie didn't strike her as the police officer type, but the more she mulled the idea over in her mind, the more she could see the possibilities. He was helpful. He was good at diffusing situations with his words and demeanor. He was cool under pressure. He liked and knew the area. It wasn't a ridiculous idea.

"Do you want to do more things like you did last night?" Tully asked, a sly smile curling the corner of his mouth.

"You know I do," Charlie said.

"Then you have something to think about," Chief Marley said, handing him a brochure. "They just rolled out an accelerated program. You can be in the first class if you sign up immediately. It's not a lot of time to consider it, but on the other hand, perhaps it's great timing too."

"Thanks, Chief," Charlie said, grasping his hand in a firm shake. "I appreciate the suggestion, and I'll give it some serious thought."

"Glad to hear it, son. And it was a pleasure to meet you, miss," he said, turning his attention to Paige. "Tully has one more surprise for you."

Tully held out a copy of the local morning newspaper. "You two even made it above the fold," he said. Paige's stomach lurched as she stared at the front photograph.

"Is that the photo from Holy Smokes?" Charlie said, taking the newspaper.

"A little bit of good publicity never hurt anyone. They wanted a few comments last night about the police chase, and I still had the picture on my phone…"

"It's great, buddy, although I don't know

what we did that was worthy of all the attention."

Paige knew the mistakes she'd made the past few days to garner so much attention. But it was the attention of only one individual she was worried about. If Thorne had already turned his focus to Roseley, this picture would confirm he was in the right spot. There was no hiding now.

"You look good, Freckles," Charlie said, hip-checking her as he passed her the newspaper. Paige quickly scanned it. They had cropped Lucy out of the photograph. She could breathe a sigh of relief for that, at least. And they had only mentioned Charlie by name. She was, thankfully, listed as just a passenger.

Tully led them out of the office and toward the front door. She tried to plaster on an expression that showed anything but the sickness she felt, but she knew Tully had homed in on her.

"What are you two celebrities up to today?" Tully asked. Paige turned to Charlie, who seemed lost in thought. He had no idea how much this newspaper article jeopardized her and Lucy. She needed to tell him before it was too late.

"You two go ahead," Charlie said, motioning them forward. "I have another question for Chief Marley." As he disappeared back into the office, she turned to find Tully studying her. His eyes narrowed.

"When did you stop going by Willow?" he asked. She stiffened, the mere sound of that horrible name bringing back memories she had worked so hard to repress.

"You don't know what you've done," she said, matching his dark expression with one of her own. Tully had forced her hand more than he knew. The more she thought about it, the more anger surged within her.

"Tell me, then."

She shook her head. "I can't."

"Can't or won't?"

Paige kept her lips together to keep from spilling out every scary thought she had harboring inside her. Tully stepped closer, so intent, so honorable.

"I'd like to let you pace this, Paige. I know you need to find the right time to tell Charlie whatever truths you're keeping to yourself. Heck, you've only known each other for a few days. Who am I to dig the skeletons out of your closet? But I'm Charlie's friend first and foremost so I'm loyal to him above all."

"You're a good friend, Tully. I see that."

"A good friend watches the other's blind spots, and he definitely has a blind spot where you're concerned. My job is to make sure he doesn't get hurt again."

"Again," Paige whispered, recalling Charlie's experience with Crystal. She was going to break his heart again. The realization made her want to slink out of the room.

"Have you run my name in the police database?" she asked, her question shooting out of her mouth like a bullet. Tully's surprise was clearly obvious.

"What do you think, *Willow*?"

She thought he hadn't. Otherwise this would be an entirely different conversation.

"I'll tell Charlie everything he needs to know today. Stay out of his ear until then, Tully. Please."

"Why should I?"

Paige glanced back at Charlie as he smiled and shook Chief Marley's hand again.

"Because I love him dearly. I don't want to see him hurt any more than you do. Please, Tully."

She held his stare for several beats as Charlie joined the two of them. It was only when

Tully's face flinched in agreement that Paige broke her stare and clasped Charlie's hand.

"Everything okay?" she asked as he squeezed her hand affectionately.

"I accepted Chief Marley's offer for the accelerated program. It starts next week."

Paige slipped her arm around his waist and gave him a hug.

"Congratulations."

"Thanks. Now I need to find a way to tell Mara."

Tully's stare softened in a fake smile. "Good luck with that one."

Paige pulled Charlie to the door before Tully could change his mind. She needed to tell Charlie the truth about who she was even if she wasn't sure how to do that.

CHAPTER THIRTEEN

PAIGE HAD SPENT the morning quickly cutting out the fabric for Lucy's costume using the desk in her room as a makeshift worktable. It had been an easy pattern, holding true to its claim that it could be completed in just a few hours. Even Charlie could have figured it out, if he'd had the mind to. And though it was anything from a work of art, Paige could hardly wait to see the dress on Lucy.

Before she had hopped out of the truck later that morning to begin the dress, Charlie had kissed her softly.

"Are you sure I can't talk you into a couple more hours together before I start my shift at the sports shop?"

"No," Paige had said, stroking the side of his face. "As much as I'd like to, I want to get this costume constructed so I can fit it on Lucy after school."

"You're so responsible. She'll really appreciate it."

Paige had shrugged off the compliment. Responsibility had nothing to do with it. If she didn't complete it now, she'd never get it done in time. More importantly, she wanted a legitimate excuse to see Lucy one last time. She needed to touch her, even if it was within the confines of fitting her in a simple dress. Once she told everyone the truth about herself, she wasn't sure she'd be allowed near Lucy again.

Paige finished the dress in record time and smoothed it out, lightly steaming it with the motel iron. It wasn't great, but it was pretty good.

Her motel phone rang just as she hung up the dress to cool.

"Hello?" she said, waiting for her aunt's voice to answer over the line. But it was silent. No, it was worse than silence. She could hear breathing on the other end. Someone was there. "Hello?" Paige pressed. Just as she was about to ask again, the line clicked dead.

Paige slowly replaced the receiver and began calculating. If Thorne had learned about Roseley the night before, he would no doubt already be in town, even if he had hit rush hour. But how on earth would he have found her so quickly? Perhaps if he'd called all the local motels until he had found hers…

Paige began tossing items into her suitcase in a frenzy. She couldn't take any chances. She couldn't risk opening her room door and finding Thorne's dead stare meeting her. If he made it to her motel before she left, he could follow her to Lucy. Her best option was to hope he wasn't at her motel yet.

Determined to carry her suitcase, the sewing machine and Lucy's dress in one trip, she peeked into the hallway before hurrying to the exit doors and to her car. Safe inside, she fired up the engine before stopping and resting for a moment. This would be it. It was time to tell Charlie and Mara and Peter the truth.

As tears slowly streamed down her face, she pulled out of the parking lot and headed straight for the sports shop. Charlie would be at work, but perhaps Lucy would be finishing up with school soon. As she made the short drive, she thought of Aunt Joan and Uncle Craig. She had intended to call them once she'd finished the dress. She didn't want them to worry, but without her cell phone, she couldn't stop to check in with them now.

She thought of Uncle Craig and how sick he was. He would now have to deal with her mess from the past. He was one of the most important people in her life, and as she faced

Thorne again, he wouldn't be around long to help her or protect her this time. She'd lose him and Charlie and Lucy soon enough. The realization hurt, but she didn't have time to think about that. It was time to tell the truth—the whole truth—and fast.

CHARLIE GRUMBLED UNDER his breath as Mara popped a hand to her hip.

"What do you mean you're going to the police academy?" she said, nearly spitting her words at him from across the counter.

"What's so difficult to understand?" he said. "It's a good opportunity."

"Opportunity to do what exactly? What do you want to be a cop for?"

"I think I might like it."

"You think? Don't you know for sure?"

Charlie's eyes narrowed. "Why are you trashing this? You haven't even stopped to listen to me."

"Fine," Mara said, throwing up her hands. "Why do you want to do this?"

"I helped apprehend those kids last night—"

"With your *plane.*"

"So? With my plane or not, it was great. I want to do more of that."

"What if you join the force and they don't

want you to fly your plane anymore? And what about murderers and thieves and…criminals?"

"I'll deal with those too, but I'll also get to help people."

"You help people here."

"In the shop?" Charlie said, wincing. "Selling life jackets and water skis?"

"Well…you do. And it's safe."

"Come on, Mara."

Mara reached for his hand and cleared her throat to try again. "I'm worried you're jumping in too quickly again."

"Again? Why do I think you're not just talking about the police force?"

Mara squeezed his hand. "Because I'm not. There's Paige too. After Crystal…"

Crystal. How that name still stung whenever he heard it on anyone else's lips. She had done him wrong more than any sad country song could ever express, and his bruised heart was all that was left in her wake. Well, his bruised heart and a plane he couldn't afford. If he could salvage them both, he'd consider himself a lucky man.

"I could spend the next few years just bumming around this place, before finally working up the guts to pursue a new passion, Mara. I don't want to be scared to try again."

"Try what?"

"Try for a new career I love…"

"You love it already? You don't know the first thing about it."

"I do, Mara. I'm *excited* about this."

She shook her head in defeat. "Then it's been a busy week for you. Excited about the police academy…excited about Paige…"

"You're not losing me, you know." He pulled her into a hug and forced her face into his armpit. She squealed the way a baby sister would.

"Seriously, Charlie. I'm too old for this."

"Aw, sis," he laughed as Peter joined them from the back room. "I love you too."

"What's going on out here?" Peter asked.

Mara escaped from Charlie's hold and smoothed her hair. "He wants to go to the police academy, Peter. The *police academy*."

"It doesn't sound odd to me," Peter said, flipping through a store inventory binder.

"Of course not," Mara said, clearly exasperated. "You're all big dreams and great ideas but no details or planning."

"That's why I have you, baby cakes," he said.

"Don't butter me up. You still have a long way to go to make things up to me, you know."

"And you won't let me forget it," he said, puckering a loud air kiss.

"Am I the only rational thinker around here?" Charlie joked.

"What's irrational about your brother becoming a cop? I think it's great, man," Peter said, turning to Charlie. "I wouldn't mind having a cop in the family. Could you get me out of a couple parking tickets?"

"You're impossible," Mara said. Charlie looked around the shop. It was empty aside from the three of them, but a quick glance at the front window showed Paige pulling up in front of the store.

"Paige is here." He smiled. "I wondered when she'd arrive."

"What does Ms. Wonderful think of your new career endeavor?"

"I'm not sure. I hope she's supportive."

"Any idea if she's staying or not?"

Charlie shrugged. There was a lot about Paige he didn't know yet. Her itinerary was the least of his concerns as of late.

"If I have to dig deep and really be honest, Charlie—"

"Please do."

Mara sighed. When his eyes met hers, hers softened, conveying a genuine happiness for him. "I don't want you jumping into things too quickly after awful Crystal but…" Mara tipped her head thoughtfully and watched Paige fumble her way out of her car. "Paige is lovely. It's nice to see you happy again."

"Even if that means becoming a cop?"

Mara groaned. "Are you really going to leave me after you've just gotten here?"

"Sis, I was only helping out until…"

"I know," she said, following Peter into the back room. "I know."

Paige pushed her way into the shop and beelined for Charlie, sewing machine under one arm. She slid it onto the counter before hurrying to him.

"Aren't you a sight for sore eyes," he said. "Business has been painfully slow."

Paige scanned the shop before moving into his personal space. Her mouth opened as if to say something before snapping shut. Sensing she was upset again, he eased his arms around her. She melted, allowing him to enfold her into his embrace.

"Hi, Paige," Peter called, strolling out to the counter. At the sound of Peter's voice, Paige stiffened and pulled away.

"Peter," she said. "I didn't know anyone else was here."

"Guilty as charged. You'll be seeing a lot more of me from now on."

Paige looked up at Charlie as if searching for more clarification.

"Peter decided to sell his stake in the sports marketing business."

Peter leaned against the counter, pausing before elaborating. "Believe it or not, Mara and I don't usually bicker as much as you've witnessed. I'm sorry you've seen us fight at all. Ugly, isn't it?"

"All couples argue."

"Nah, not like this," Peter said, crouching to retrieve a few files from beneath the counter. Charlie quickly nodded to Paige to punctuate Peter's assertion. He'd never seen the two of them fight as much as he had in just the short time since he'd returned to Roseley. Their household was nothing but stressed to the max anytime he visited. But once Peter had announced he was quitting sports marketing, it was like a release valve had been loosened. Most of Mara's hot steam had been escaping all day, thank goodness.

"I made a bad decision leaving the shop to start a new business," Peter continued, standing. "Mara is so capable and hardworking I thought she could handle this place on her own. She was so supportive in the beginning, I didn't take the time to consider if I *should* get into sports marketing. I was so happy working here with her, building this place from the ground up with her. I've been missing that this past year. Being away from her and Lucy, being on the road a lot made me miss…my life. It's a pretty darn good one."

"What was that?" Mara said, beelining out of the back room and to the counter.

"Peter was telling Paige how much he missed you and can't wait to work with you all day, every day," Charlie said.

"Oh, you did not!" Mara howled. "You'll be sick of me within a week."

"Baby," Peter said, "I've been in love with you since you were fifteen and sneaking out of the house to meet me by the boat docks. I could never get enough of you."

Paige sighed, resting her head against Charlie. Maybe she was a romantic too, he thought. He lowered his gaze, sensing a sadness emanating off her. He would ask about her uncle when they were alone. He didn't want to stir up painful feelings in front of anyone else. He kissed her on the top of her head, making her tip her face up to him and smile. As the afternoon light streamed in from the front window, it caught the flecks of gold in her green eyes. They were tear-filled, mesmerizing and…

Charlie pulled back slightly, readjusting his focus. Something about the shape of her eyes had him doing a double take. Her eyes widened under the weight of his stare as Mara babbled in the background about recent orders. It was Mara who finally made Paige pull her gaze.

"Did you want to tag along, Paige? Charlie promised he'd close up the shop for me, didn't you, Charlie?"

"Tag along?" Paige asked.

"To pick up Lucy."

Lucy.

Charlie released Paige, now examining her face with a cop's intense suspicion. He checked the slope of her nose, the fullness of her mouth, the edge of her hairline. Did he see similarities because he now thought he should? Had he really seen something so familiar in those green eyes or was he only being paranoid? Had Mara's talk about Crystal made him start looking for red flags where there weren't any?

"We'll grab her from school and hit the Water Dancers' show," Mara continued. "You really shouldn't miss it, Paige. I look forward to it all week."

Paige's cheeks had begun to flush again, like they had the day she'd pitched copy to him and Mara. The deep, blotchy red marks were creeping up her neck to her chin and face. She brought her hand to her face as if to hide it, but now he saw it all. The missing pieces were rapidly falling into place: those eyes, her interest in Lucy, Dr. Bob's phone call the other day.

"Get out of here, you two," Peter called. "We'll meet you for dinner on the beach. I have a hankering for a cheeseburger."

Before Charlie could speak, Mara had whisked Paige out the door. He stood rooted in the middle of the shop watching them drive away, knowing Paige Cartman's green eyes had once again thrown his world off-kilter. But this time it was in one of the worst ways possible.

CHAPTER FOURTEEN

PAIGE RODE ALONG as Mara clamored on and on about everything on her mind. She talked about town, pointing out shops that had been on Main Street for generations. She rambled on about the sports shop and Charlie and... Lucy.

Paige knew the best life for Lucy was anywhere but with Thorne, even if that meant living with parents who fought all the time. But what Peter had said in the sports shop sounded promising.

"Peter said I'd be seeing a lot more of him now."

Mara smiled. "You will, thank goodness. That man finally came to his senses."

"About?"

"His sports marketing business."

Paige nodded, wondering if that translated to a better life for Lucy as Mara heaved a breath to explain.

"Things between the two of us became

strained last year. Strained is putting it mildly. I'm sure Charlie must have mentioned something about it to you. He returned to Roseley for personal reasons, but I can't say I was disappointed to see him. Things were so bad with Peter and me, I appreciated his moral support."

"You and Peter don't usually bicker?" Paige tried for the last word as delicately as possible.

Mara belted a laugh. "Now *that's* putting it mildly. We used to be so happy. That's why the past year has been so awful. When you know how great it *can* be but then it isn't… ugh…"

"It must have been hard on Lucy."

"Has it ever." Mara's eyes misted with tears. "My sweet little girl…"

Paige was grateful to see a tenderness in Mara she had been looking for over the last few days. Mara had been so anxious, constantly moving and working and doing. Seeing her now calmer and tender, especially at the mention of Lucy, felt reassuring.

"What changed?"

"When Peter came to me with the proposal to buy in to his friend's sports marketing start-up, I thought it sounded like a good idea, and financially it was. The business looked like it would boom. I thought I could handle things at the shop on my own, and Peter promised to help me when he could. We had been a well-oiled machine until that point, partners in business, partners in marriage, and I convinced him he needed to give the start-up a try. We married so young, I always worried he didn't get a chance to do anything adventurous. I didn't want him to regret not trying it and resent me as a reason for playing things safe. But as his commitments with the start-up grew, so did *my* resentment."

"What made him decide to quit?"

"Lucy had a meltdown last night, even after that episode about your driver's license. I forgot another thing for her school. *Again.* And she accused me of not being there for her anymore. Then, of course, it made me have a meltdown. I called Peter and laid everything out on the table—I'm tired of this arrangement, it's not working."

"What did he say?"

"He said he's been ready to quit for months. He misses us so much when he leaves that when he's gone, all he does is daydream about being home. When I told him to get home as soon as he could, he said his bag was already packed." Mara smiled. "Love that man."

"Does Lucy know?"

"We'll tell her tonight."

"I think that's wonderful, Mara." Paige nearly whispered the words, the relief that things would improve for Lucy washing over her in waves of gratitude.

"Yeah?"

"Yes. I can tell Lucy is very important to the both of you."

"Yes, well, we're both so grateful to have her."

"Tell me about adopting her."

Mara's face eased into a nostalgic smile. "We just celebrated her tenth birthday, but it's hard to believe she's that old. It seems like just yesterday we got the phone call."

"Did you go through an adoption agency?"

"Initially. Peter and I always knew we wanted to adopt. We were high school sweethearts and discussed adoption earlier than most couples. I had a terrible illness as a child and afterward doctors discovered…well, they learned it would never be possible for me to conceive."

"I'm sorry."

"I'm not. Knowing from an early age sort of helped. Well, I guess it helped as much as it could, considering. Peter knew from the start, and we both decided we'd apply for adoption as soon as we were married. The process takes a lot longer than most people realize."

"How did you get matched with Lucy?"

"We had been working with an agency for a couple of years and every time we thought we were getting a baby, something would fall through. The birth mother changes her mind sometimes. I can't imagine how difficult a decision that would be for any mother."

Paige closed her eyes and nodded her head, her empathy on display right alongside Mara. Mara really couldn't imagine what it felt like to ease a sleeping infant into someone else's arms forever. As she clasped and unclasped her hands tightly, she hoped Mara never knew what it felt like to hug a ten-year-old Lucy goodbye for what would be the last time.

"A doctor we had worked with over the years contacted us one morning. We were still in bed when he called to say he'd be at our house in an hour. We thought we had everything prepared for a situation like that, but nothing really prepares you for the moment when someone hands you your child."

"How did you come up with the name Lucy?"

"We didn't. It's standard to change a baby's

name when they're so young, and we had had a few girl names selected. But when Dr. Hathaway placed her in my arms and told us she had been named Lucy by her mother…well, she looked like a little Lucy. Plus, it was the least we could do to honor her mother, considering what she'd done for her. And us."

Mara stared at Paige, whose eyebrows lifted in curiosity. She wanted to hear Mara's impression of what had happened. She wanted to know what Dr. Hathaway had told her all those years ago. What was the story they would eventually tell Lucy when she was older?

"What—what do you mean…for her?"

"Lucy was a rescue baby."

"Rescued from what?"

"Dr. Hathaway didn't have many details for us. He also felt the less we knew, the better. Her birth mother had gotten caught up in a very unhealthy relationship with the birth father and she was scared for her safety. She wanted to give Lucy a better life than she had had. To have that kind of courage…" Mara placed her hand over her heart as her eyes welled with tears again. "Well, how could I change her name after hearing that?"

"That was kind of you," Paige said, wiping her own eyes.

"Do you think so?"

"I do," Paige whispered, trying to muster the courage to segue into her confession. She needed to tell Mara that Thorne was coming for their girl.

"It's the shop," Mara said, pointing at the cell phone vibrating in the center console. "Would you want to go in and get Lucy for me? She should be waiting just inside the doors."

Paige slipped from the car, composing herself, and beelined through the front doors of the school. She cringed at how easy it was—too easy—to get into the school. Shouldn't they have a double set of locked doors or security or something? She supposed the time of day was a large factor and the children weren't still primary school aged. Still, if she could just walk in, so could Thorne. The fear of him slipping into the school to get Lucy sent a cold chill along her spine. She shook away a shiver as she promised herself she would tell Mara as soon as they were at the ski show. She had no choice but to just blurt it all out. Once Mara got over the shock that she might have unintentionally led Thorne to Lucy, she'd probably be angry, furious even, when she realized Paige had been masquerading as a stranger all this time. But she had to do it.

"Paige!" a joyful voice called. Paige scanned the swarm of children hustling past her to line up for their buses. And there, not twenty feet away, was that perfect little face, beaming.

"I'm sorry I looked in your wallet," Lucy said, stopping just short of her. Paige shook her head in surprise. So much had happened in the last twenty-four hours, she had forgotten all about it.

"You're forgiven," she said, reaching for her. Lucy hesitantly slipped her arms around Paige's waist. "I'll always forgive you. Okay?" Lucy nodded. "Do you want to see your costume?"

"Did you finish it?"

"Yep. I have to fit it on you, but it should be all set."

"Where's Charlie?"

"Working at the shop. Your mom is outside."

"I don't want to see her."

"Why?"

"I yelled at her last night. I made her cry and…"

"Things are going to be better now, kiddo. I promise you that." Lucy searched her face for understanding, but all Paige could do to clarify was sling an arm around her shoulders and give her a squeeze. "Come on. Your mom is excited to see you."

They followed the stream of students outside as a school bell rang and more students poured out of classrooms. Mara honked the horn. She'd parked at the end of a row. Paige and Lucy hurried around vehicles and people to the car when Paige noticed something odd out of the corner of her eye. That hair. That wild flurry of messy brown hair. She turned, doing a double take. The children rushing past her made her frantically work to readjust her eyes against the afternoon sun. Was he here?

"Are you coming?" Lucy asked before sliding into the back seat. Paige fumbled for the car door handle, glancing back behind her again. Her heart thudded in her ears. He was there, somewhere in the crowd, watching them with those ink-black eyes. She knew it.

By the time she flopped into the front seat, pulling the door shut with a frantic slam, Mara was revving the engine.

"Everything okay? You look like you're escaping from prison and on the lam."

"What? Of course not."

"You might have to soon enough," Mara continued as she pulled out of the parking lot. "My brother wants to see you immediately. Goodness was he ever short with me. He wants us back at the shop right away. Did you forget to kiss him goodbye or something?" Mara smirked as Lucy burst into giggles, but Paige slunk down into her seat. She had a feeling she already knew the reason and worried the lid on her past would be blown off for everyone to see before she had explained herself.

CHARLIE HAD PACED the same aisle of the sports shop, grateful for no customers and no one around to distract him. He'd had something on his mind he needed to work out and any distraction, no matter how little, would be a rude intrusion.

He kept replaying the instant he looked upon Paige's face and saw something familiar there. He had been so shocked he hadn't been able to form the words or questions that now grated on his mind: Who are you *really*? Are you here for Lucy? Are you her birth mother?

After at least ten minutes on his own, Charlie dug for his cell phone and dialed the only person he truly trusted.

"What's up, buddy?" Tully's deep, familiar voice somehow managed to calm his nerves with only those three words.

"I think she's lying to me, man."

There was a long pause on the other end of the line. He waited for Tully to follow up with questions, wanting to clarify what he meant. Instead, his silence sent Charlie rambling.

"This morning there was something so oddly familiar about her face. She blinked up at me with those pepper-green eyes and it struck me for the first time. She's not here to write. She's not here for work. She's here for her *daughter*. She's here for Lucy." Again, all that met him on the other end of the line was more silence. Charlie ran a hand through his hair and slammed his hand on the counter. "Damn it, Tully. Are you still there?"

"I'm running her name now. I wanted to do it this morning. I regret not trusting my gut."

"Which name?"

"Both."

"No." Charlie didn't want to resort to that. He didn't want to build a case against Paige and have her defend herself against it. He knew she'd had a troubled past and still had issues in her life to sort out. He wanted to know the truth, but he wanted it to come from her.

"Charlie," Tully began. "I know you're smitten but—"

"*No,*" he said again. "I want to talk to her first and give her a chance to sort this all out."

"When?"

"Now."

Tully sighed heavily into the phone. "There's nothing wrong with checking, Charlie."

"If that was true, you would have already done it." Charlie finally managed a smile. "Though I suspect you have a finger hovering over the submit button right now."

"If she's Lucy's birth mother, come to take her away, isn't it better to know sooner than later?"

Charlie leaned back against the counter. Tully was right, so what had him hesitating?

"I'm in love with her, man."

Tully paused on the other end of the phone. "I know. But how much can you really love a person without *knowing* them?"

Charlie considered this. Did he really know Paige? When they talked, when he looked in her eyes, he thought he did. He thought he knew her heart, but now...

By the time Mara's car had pulled up in front of the sports shop, Charlie knew he needed a direct answer from Paige, as much as the fear of the truth made him cringe. He had met them on the sidewalk, not wanting to wait another second longer.

"Hi, Uncle Charlie," Lucy sang, slipping past him into the shop. "Are you coming to the ski show with us?"

"Not until later, kiddo. I have to keep this place open for your mom."

"What's so pressing?" Mara said, patting Charlie lovingly on the cheek.

"Nothing, sis."

"It didn't sound like nothing on the phone."

"Don't worry about it."

Mara opened her mouth to protest, but then caught the seriousness of Charlie's stare. She nodded and pushed into the shop, calling out a hello to Peter.

Paige hung back near the car, teetering on the curb edge as he stared at her. With her hands slung in her shorts pockets and her head tipped to the side, she looked guilty as all get out. He just hoped it wasn't for the reason he suspected.

"Hi, Charlie."

"Paige," he said. "If that's your real name."

"I told you it wasn't." He scoffed. Paige eased closer to him as he stayed within the shadow of the door awning. Her hair glistened like gold in the sunshine, but her squinting made it difficult for him to discern any sincerity in her eyes. "I need to talk to you."

"Go ahead," he said. His body stiffened as he braced for a confession. He was waiting for the truth and for it to all be over between them. The thought made him ache deeply from heart to gut.

She slowly slipped her hands into his and stepped into the shadows with him. Only then could he see her eyes were glistening with tears.

"I want to be completely honest with you, Charlie. I want to tell you everything, but I can't right now. I must do one thing first. Please believe me when I say it's the right thing to do."

He shook his head. After the year he had had, it was difficult to trust anyone again. And now, as he suspected Paige had been lying to him and his family, he was supposed to trust this?

"That's a lot to ask, don't you think?"

"I wouldn't ask it unless I had to." She slipped her hands from his and tenderly grazed them up the front of his chest, caressing the nape of his neck. Her body was drawn close to his, pressing against him like she had when she'd kissed him on the dock. His wits demanded he pull away and get some answers. He needed to know the truth. But his senses, drowning in her scent and the softness of her hands running through his hair, failed him. "I love you, Charlie," she said, breathing the words onto his lips before she drew him into a kiss he couldn't surface from. He embraced her fully and let himself dissolve into the complete rapture that was purely her. He loved this woman too. He had let himself get carried away with the kindness of her words and the joyfulness of her laugh. He'd fallen in love, and now, he didn't know if she was kissing him because she loved him or because she was saying goodbye.

Paige held him tightly as she grazed her lips to his ear and whispered gently. "I never thought I would love anyone until I met you, Charlie. You've changed my entire world, and I promise to tell you everything. I promise. But not yet."

"Why?" he said, his whisper more of a demand.

"Because I can't."

"You're going to break my heart—" he began, but before he could finish, she kissed him again and harder this time. He could feel her hot tears on his face. He wasn't sure she was going to let him up for air as she seemed to need to convey something in her kiss that she couldn't manage with words. So he let her.

"Whoa. Sorry to interrupt," Mara chortled, pushing out of the front doors and heading around the back of the building. "Lucy and I are heading over now, Paige, if you want to join."

Paige pressed her forehead to Charlie's before peppering a last kiss on his lips.

"I'll join you," she called, her voice a forced, cheerful reply. She wiped the tears from under her eyes and slipped on sunglasses before turning toward Mara and Lucy.

He knew he was in trouble. He knew he couldn't think clearly when Paige was near him. And as he watched the three women he loved most in the world head off toward the beach, he knew something earth-shattering was coming that he wouldn't be able to escape.

CHAPTER FIFTEEN

THE WATER DANCERS' SKI SHOW drew a crowd bigger than what Paige first imagined Roseley could hold. As hundreds of people congregated on the beach and the water skiers in their sparkling sequined costumes darted to take their positions, the announcer on a loudspeaker welcomed the crowd.

"I'm starving," Lucy said, pointing to the concession stand. Paige was too anxious to eat, even as the warm aroma of roasting hot dogs wafted through the late afternoon air. She needed to say goodbye to Lucy. She needed to tell Mara the truth about who she was. And most importantly, she needed to warn her about Thorne. Her stomach clenched, making her bring a self-conscious hand to her side to try to soothe the pain away.

"Tonight is more of a dress rehearsal before the season begins," Mara explained, waving to passing friends. "You should see this place in a half hour."

"Paige is here!" a voice called, making them all turn. CeCe and Dolores hurried up alongside Paige, CeCe squeezing Paige's bicep. "Come to the sandwich shop tomorrow. My book club is getting together, and I want you to meet everyone. Dolores will be there, won't you?"

"She's still supposed to stop by the tea shop, CeCe."

"Thanks for the invitation," Paige said. "I'll try." She wanted so much to shake these lovely women off so she could focus on talking to Mara, she didn't even care that she lied.

"I saw Paige and her beau at the fabric store yesterday," Dolores said, ripping apart a piece of hot pretzel and offering it.

"It was for my storybook costume," Lucy said, accepting the pretzel and popping it into her mouth. "I drew a picture of a dress I need for Storybook Characters Day, and Paige sewed one overnight."

"Ha!" CeCe scoffed. "Youth can get away with whipping up a dress at a moment's notice and getting it to fit. When you reach my age—"

"Oh, CeCe, leave it alone. I've listened to you complain about your age for the last twenty-seven years," Dolores said.

"If you want me to stop, buy me a lemonade," CeCe said. "I'm melting in this heat."

Dolores grinned. "Come on, old woman. I'll even spring for nachos."

CeCe laughed as they labored to walk away in the sand. "Enjoy the show, Paige. Best entertainment in town!"

"Does everyone come out for this show?" Paige said, eyeing the swelling crowd.

Lucy nodded. "All my friends come."

"Every Wednesday?"

"Yep! All summer!"

Paige could see the appeal. Along the long stretch of gently sloping beach, families had spread blankets and umbrellas, coolers and lawn chairs.

"Do you see any of your friends?" Paige asked, searching the faces of the growing crowd. Was Thorne here? Would he have followed them from the school, looking for a chance to confront her or snatch Lucy?

"There's Mary Alice!" Lucy said, pointing. "Can I go, Mom?"

"Don't you want to eat first?" Paige quickly suggested. She wanted a few more minutes of Lucy before she told Mara the truth. She feared those minutes together would be their last.

"Later. Please, Mom?"

"Here's a few dollars," Mara said, handing her a wad of cash. "Grab a few hot dogs for you and your friends and meet us over by the flagpole."

Lucy barely squeaked out a thank-you before scampering down the beach to a gaggle of girls her age.

"Don't you want to keep an eye on her?" Paige suggested, her pulse racing at the thought of Lucy disappearing into the crowd.

"I have to work so hard not to hover around her," Mara said. "But heaven knows my mother never knew what I was up to at that age. Charlie and I had free rein of this place our entire childhood. She'd kiss us in the morning, and we wouldn't come home until dark, smelling like lake water, sweat and dirt. My father used to say we smelled like good old-fashioned sunshine." Mara laughed. "I love those memories. Anyway, I know most people on this lake. She'll be fine."

"But you don't know *everyone*," Paige warned, following Mara to an open patch of sand by the flagpole. "A stranger could snatch her and disappear before you had time to blink."

"Hey! Don't get me thinking about that," Mara said. "I'm already prone to worry."

Paige continued to scan the crowd, darting her eyes to locate Lucy every few seconds. She was happily chattering with a gang of preteen girls.

"It feels good to relax for a moment," Mara said, flopping down on the sand. She closed her eyes and tipped her face up to the sun. "And I wouldn't mind getting a little color on my cheeks."

Paige slowly sank to the sand, the pit in her stomach dropping deeper by the second. Maybe she should have told Charlie first. Maybe he would have helped her tell Mara about Thorne. What had she been thinking doing this by herself? She'd always had her aunt and uncle to help her through the hard times. Was she already steeling herself against any help, knowing they wouldn't be around forever?

Mara peeked open an eye to discover Paige still watching Lucy.

"You're making me feel grossly negligent, Paige," she laughed. "She's fine over there. No one's going to hurt her with everyone watching."

The announcer's voice crackled over the loudspeaker. He was happy to say that the show would be starting shortly, just as soon as the skiers took their places. He mumbled on about buying tickets to the 50/50 raffle and pointed out how the concession stand was now proud to serve Perk's Pizza. Paige wrung her hands. As soon as the announcer powered off his microphone again, she blurted her best attempt to explain.

"What if someone *did* want to hurt her, Mara? What if her father was here for her? You said she was put up for adoption to escape him, right? Isn't it better to be safe than sorry?"

Mara released a sigh, her closed eyes still turned to the sun.

"Don't make me think about that. It would be more likely her birth mother was here, especially after what's happened this week with Dr. Hathaway."

"Mara—" Paige began, her voice a cold mix of urgency and panic.

"Yeah?"

A little child sprinted past, kicking sand on them. Paige didn't flinch.

"Mara, there's something you need to know about Lucy's birth mother…"

"Huh?" Mara shielded her eyes and turned to Paige. Paige clasped her hands desperately to her chest, her lip quivering beyond her control.

"Lucy…*our* Lucy… I need to tell you, Mara… Oh, I'm so sorry it's taken me this long…"

Darkness shrouded Mara's eyes, her face contorting from confusion to sickening realization.

"Ladies and gentlemen," the announcer began. "You know it isn't summer until the first Water Dancers' show kicks off the season. With four new Water Dancers joining the crew this year, you're in for a real treat tonight. Keep your eyes on the youngest and newest members of our team—seven-year-old Brayden, and his nine-year-old big brother Bentley. They are going to take their very first loop for you. Please put your hands together for the Hanover brothers!"

The crowd erupted in a supportive cheer as two little boys gripped the rope handles and braced to slide off the floating dock and onto the water. Paige didn't look to see if they managed to stay on their skis. She couldn't tell by the cheering crowd if they had succeeded or not. All she was focused on was Mara's face, etched in horror as she straightened and hustled to her feet.

"Who? *You?*" Mara spat as Paige scrambled after her. "All this time? It was *you*?"

"Please, listen," Paige begged as Mara's eyes flashed brilliant. "I love Lucy. I don't want anything to happen to her—"

"You heard me cry to Charlie and all this time it was *you*? Dr. Hathaway's phone call just as Charlie met you... I never suspected a thing...and all this time..."

"Mara, I don't want to hurt Lucy, but her birth father...a man named Jared Thorne... I think he's here... I'm so sorry." Paige reached to touch Mara's arm, but Mara jerked back.

"Get away from me!" she shrieked, eliciting dozens of nearby people to turn in alarm. "Where is she? Lucy!" Mara stumbled in the general direction of Lucy, frantically searching for her daughter.

"Mara, I'll help you," Paige called, struggling to keep her footing in the sand as she followed. Mara's slim frame somehow managed to part the crowd, as if her maternal instinct to get to her daughter had empowered her with a supernatural force. Happy-go-lucky faces blurred in front of Paige, the smell of sunscreen and hot dogs and lake water swirling around her in a dizzying array. She was only a few steps behind when Mara reached the startled little girl. Without an explanation, she tugged Lucy in the direction of the sports shop.

"Mom? What is it? I haven't bought my hot dog yet."

"Mara," Paige called, running alongside them. "I need to tell you about Thorne—"

"Shut up," Mara snapped. "Get away from us. Get away from Lucy." Lucy looked back, her frightened emerald eyes bobbing before Mara tugged her to face forward. Paige fell away, letting the gap between them grow with each passing second. It had all gone so wrong so quickly. Things were going to fall apart now, and it was all her fault.

CHARLIE RANG UP one of many customers standing in line. The Water Dancers' show was always good for business, drumming up steady foot traffic until closing time, but with each slam of the cash register drawer, he hated all of it. He needed to be somewhere else.

"Want some help?" Peter asked, shuffling in from the back. Charlie nodded as the bell over the front door rang, signaling yet another customer. This time, however, when he looked up, Tully was in the doorway. His face was solemn, darkened even, and Charlie knew he needed to leave.

"Take over, Peter," he said, as Tully led him outside. "What is it, Tully? Don't tell me you ran her name."

"I didn't have to. A person of interest report came in for her."

"Person of interest? For what?"

Tully shook his head. "Brace yourself, Charlie."

"For what?" His gut twisted as he prepared for the answer.

"Kidnapping."

Charlie teetered back on his heels, the word socking him in the jaw like a sucker punch. Tully readjusted his hand on his belt buckle, waiting for the sudden shock to pass.

"You mean…kidnapping Lucy?" Charlie finally managed.

"Looks that way. Her supposed birth father came into the station. He's an odd-looking son of a gun but his story adds up. The timeline, Lucy's age…it doesn't look good."

"At worst I thought—" What *did* he think? That Paige was Lucy's birth mother coming to see her after all these years? That possibility had been palatable because he thought Paige to be so loving and kind. Even as he had suspected it this afternoon, he believed she wouldn't do anything to pull Lucy from her family, from him and Peter and Mara. He didn't think she'd endanger Lucy in any way. But now...with a birth father in the picture and kidnapping charges surfacing...

"Do you know where she is? I have to pick her up for questioning."

Charlie shook his head, though he knew the first place he'd check—*alone*. "I have to find her," Charlie mumbled, running a hand through his hair.

"Don't warn her, Charlie. She's not worth it. If she's done what this guy claims she's done..."

Charlie managed a nod. All he knew was that he needed the entire truth from Paige this time, because his niece's future and well-being hung in the balance.

PAIGE STUMBLED ALONG the beach, letting the cheers of the crowd fade into the distance with each passing step. Her car was packed. She knew what she should do—leave town and never look back. But as she watched the skiers skim across the lake, like shiny, gold water bugs, all she could think of was Charlie. How could she leave without giving him an explanation? He had trusted her to tell him the truth. After Crystal had broken his heart, he had chosen to trust her now. She knew a man like that didn't come along every day, nor did she fall in love every day.

Paige had just turned toward the public access road to head back toward the shop when she spotted him.

Thorne.

His coal-black eyes were unmistakable, even from thirty yards away, and they were marked for her at an alarming pace. Paige tried to swallow but her throat had gone bone-dry. The crowd, so happily cheering on the ski show, wouldn't come to her aid if she needed it.

She had only known Thorne for a few months, but it had been enough time for her to predict what he'd do next. He'd want to know where Lucy was, and by the look in his eye, she knew she'd no sooner waft off a bloodhound than get rid of him now. He felt he had a claim over Lucy, and no one would convince him otherwise. She was stronger than the teenager who'd faced him ten years ago and better capable of confronting him, but she still wished she didn't have to, especially alone.

A truck rumbling from behind Thorne made him break his focus on Paige. It sped alongside him, up the public access road to the beach, sputtering gravel as it passed by him.

Charlie.

"Get in," he called, but Paige had already broken for the passenger door. Charlie cut a U-turn and aimed them for town. "I take it that's him," he said once Thorne was a dot in Paige's side mirror.

Paige confirmed it with only a blink. She wondered how much Charlie knew. As Charlie drove in silence, Paige scrambled to piece together the timeline since Mara had run off with Lucy. She couldn't have gotten back to the shop and explained it this quickly. For Charlie to know anything about Thorne, Tully would have had to tell him.

"Did you talk to Tully?" she asked as Charlie made a turn through a woodsy area just outside of town.

"He wants to see you at the police station," he muttered. "You're listed as a person of interest for kidnapping, but you must already know that by now." He pulled into a small picnic area, a remote nook tucked within mature aspen trees. Aside from an aged picnic table and a staked sign for a trail leading farther into the woods, it looked untouched. Charlie cut the engine and eased out of the truck. He made his way to the picnic table, and she knew he was waiting for her. He wanted an explanation, and she'd have to confess all of it now. It was time.

Paige slipped from the truck and drew a deep breath. Straightening her shoulders, she perched on the picnic table beside Charlie.

"I'm not sure where to start," she said matter-of-factly. Charlie snorted and faced her.

"Start at the beginning. I think I deserve it, don't you?" He did. She wanted to.

Charlie leaned into her line of vision, his eyes cutting straight to her heart. He looked like he was biting back fury toward her. Maybe he was furious at her or maybe he was furious to be put into a situation where Lucy's future was jeopardized. She didn't blame him for the fire behind his eyes. She hated it, but she didn't blame him.

"I'll tell you everything, Charlie."

"Are you Lucy's birth mother?"

Paige swallowed hard. She needed him to understand why she'd done it. She needed him to understand what she had dreamed of for Lucy, so she took a breath and spoke the first of many truths.

"No. I'm not her birth mother."

CHAPTER SIXTEEN

CHARLIE NEARLY FELL off the picnic table as the fierceness of her eyes locked on his.

"I don't understand," he said, grabbing the back of his neck. "If you're not her birth mother then who are you? And how did you know her father was coming for her?"

Paige nodded as if they were all good questions.

"As you know, my mother, Trudy, had a host of problems. For one, she was an addict. For another, she had undiagnosed mental health problems that were never treated. They were probably the reason she began using in the first place. And as you already know, I was raised by my grandmother, who was the last stronghold of discipline and foundation in my mother's life. When she died, my Aunt Joan, Trudy's twin sister, and Uncle Craig tried to take me. They knew Trudy was toxic, but before they could make their way to Tennessee—that's where we lived at the time—Trudy had whisked me off."

"She and your aunt were twins?"

"Joan and Gertrude. My grandmother always said they were as different as salt and sugar. Looking back, I now understand how things went off the rails for her, but as a teenager, what could I do about it? She wouldn't accept help or guidance from my grandmother when she was alive, and she refused to listen to my Aunt Joan when Grandma died. When I think of how things might have been different…"

"Go on," Charlie said, detecting the guilt and desperation in Paige's voice. "What happened when Trudy took you?" Out of instinct, he touched her hand to encourage her along. The anger that had been brewing on the drive to find her was suppressed for now. For the moment, he wanted to help her tell her story. He wanted answers and he could tell when Paige blinked at his touch, she wanted to set down the secrets she'd been carrying for years.

"Trudy couldn't keep a job to support us. She…oh, Charlie… I'm not exactly sure what she did for money." She looked away as if the shame of it all had been hers. "Every now and then we'd end up crashing with so-called friends who had a working phone. I'd try calling my aunt to tell her where I was, but sometimes I wasn't exactly sure. We moved so much, sometimes in the middle of the night. We'd catch rides with people we didn't know. It was awful."

"Were you ever...hurt?"

Paige met his eyes. Hers widened as she violently shook her head. "No. Despite all the unsavory characters Trudy introduced into my life and our transient lifestyle, I was never physically hurt."

He managed a grateful expression. He could only imagine what a life like that would have been like for her. As he thought back on the woman he'd come to know over the last few days, he wondered how she had grown into a person of such love and kindness, someone so concerned for her aunt and uncle and tender and sincere with him.

"Just after I turned seventeen, Trudy got into a terrible fight with one of her friends. She swiped his car keys so we would have a place to sleep that night. I figured the police would come looking for the stolen car and then call my aunt, but the next day we met

Thorne. And let me tell you, I hated him from the moment I laid eyes on him."

"He was the man on the beach?"

"He hasn't changed much. Eyes as dark and deep as black holes, an untamed mass of hair and an unwavering belief that he is special."

Charlie frowned. "What's that supposed to mean?" Paige rubbed her temples as if there was so much to explain, and she couldn't get the words out fast enough. "Just keep going," Charlie said softly.

"Thorne offered us a ride to his Oklahoma homestead. It was a hike from where we were living in northern Tennessee, but my mother excitedly accepted. He promised a beautiful place where he said, we would be treated like the queens we were. He had a thing about people who were special."

"Did he think you were special?"

"He thought my mother was. She was a twin, remember?"

"And that was good?"

"It was to him. He had a lot of ideas about where to find special people, and whenever he told my mother she was one of them, she'd fawn all over him. I tried to stop her from going with him, but she wouldn't listen. I was scared for her, Charlie. I knew if she left with him, I'd never see her again, so I went along too. Thorne had been in Tennessee recruiting new followers to live at his homestead. Unfortunately, he had found us.

"He didn't believe in any conventional methods of doing anything, so there was no sort of official marriage ceremony between him and my mother. But it didn't take long for the people of the homestead to understand he and Trudy were a couple."

Charlie grimaced. "This sounds like a cult, Paige." She closed her eyes and he immediately realized he'd touched a nerve. "Did you live in a cult?"

"For several months. Just long enough, in fact, for my mother to start showing."

"Pregnant?"

Paige nodded sadly. "Thorne was ecstatic, but I knew we had to get out of there as soon as possible. I tried to convince my mother to leave with me, but she refused. They only had one phone at the homestead, and I wasn't permitted to use it so I couldn't call my aunt. Any thoughts I entertained about leaving on my own felt selfish. How could I leave my mother pregnant and with Thorne? What choice did I have? I had to either leave without my mother or stay and try to protect her."

"So, you stayed," Charlie said gently.

"She might have made a lot of bad decisions over the years, but she was still my mother. I still loved her."

Charlie nodded. Of course, she wouldn't leave her mother. The conviction of her words reminded him of the woman he'd been getting to know the last few days. She had acted out of love. That much was still consistent.

"Thorne didn't believe in conventional medication or hospitals or help of any kind. When a woman went into labor…well…she'd better trust she could pull it off on her own. My mother, unfortunately, couldn't. I don't know what went wrong or what killed her, but she died the day after giving birth." Paige stared intently at Charlie. "Her baby girl survived."

Charlie's face contorted. "Is Lucy your half sister?"

Paige nodded. "Haven't you noticed we share the same green eyes?"

Charlie recalled the moment he'd seen the familiarity in her face. There was plenty that wasn't the same but those eyes… Once he had seen the similarity, he couldn't understand how it had taken him so long.

"They're unlike any I've ever seen."

Paige smiled at this. "My grandmother told me her mother and grandmother had had them too. In fact, the color has been passed down to the women in my family for generations, including Trudy and Joan. I'm sure Trudy's eyes helped convince Thorne we were some of the 'special' people he was searching for."

"They're rare and so green," he said.

"The rarest," Paige sighed as if recalling some link to a past she missed. "With my mother gone I knew I was in deep trouble. The homestead was locked and loosely guarded. It was also in the middle of nowhere. If I took off running, I wasn't sure where the heck I would go. And with a baby.

"I told Thorne I wanted Joan present for my mother's funeral. He hated the idea of inviting anyone to the homestead he hadn't yet vetted. So I lied and said that not only was my aunt a perfect resemblance of my mother, but she was also single."

"He let you call her?"

"That same day. She said she would be there, *alone*, in two days. I was able to talk in code, saying over and over how Thorne was letting her come because she was single, and he wanted to meet her. She figured out quickly that something was very wrong. Uncle Craig came too and dropped her off at a nearby bus station where Thorne picked her up. When I think of how much faith Uncle Craig must have had to drop off his wife, not knowing exactly what she was walking into…"

"He did it for you."

"They both did. He's a good man, and he loves me. Joan is the strongest woman I think I've ever met. She was Trudy's complete opposite, in nearly every imaginable way."

"Why didn't they call the police?"

"They could have, and the police would have helped me leave, but what about Lucy? She was Thorne's baby, not mine. We only had one shot to get the both of us out of there.

"When Joan arrived, Thorne wouldn't leave us alone, and if he had to duck out for even a minute, he made sure we had other people there as our chaperones. He hadn't wanted to tell Joan about Lucy, but I made sure to mention on the phone that Trudy had died in childbirth. She needed to understand ahead of time why I hadn't left the homestead. I needed her to understand that she wasn't coming for just me.

"Joan convinced Thorne she wanted to live at the compound too to help take care of me and the baby. Then she lied and said she had children of her own, who she'd left with friends. She said she wanted to return home and bring them to the compound."

"Thorne let her go?"

"Joan was very convincing. You can sell anything to anyone if the people you love are in danger."

Charlie bit his tongue at this, wondering what exactly Paige had been able to sell to him over the past few days. He admired her levelheaded thinking and determination to escape the homestead, but any trace of deceit in her brought back too many old feelings from when Crystal had fooled him. He knew the situations were entirely different—Crystal's fueled by selfishness and Paige's fueled by selflessness, but still…

"Are you okay?" she whispered, noticing he'd turned away.

"I'm having a hard time with this. To know this was Lucy's beginning and that you were involved in such a creepy world…"

"I'm sorry I didn't tell you all of this earlier, but can't you understand how I couldn't? It's not something I could tell in pieces—to begin talking would mean I'd have to tell it all. There's no option for in between. Aunt Joan and Uncle Craig and I promised never to mention anything about Lucy ever again because the mere mention of her name could risk her safety. I would do anything to keep her from going back to Thorne."

"How did you manage to get away?"

Paige closed her eyes. "The night after Thorne dropped Joan at the bus stop, she and Uncle Craig returned and parked in a wooded area about a hundred and fifty yards from the compound. They waited nearly all night. I don't know what they would have been thinking, not knowing if I was coming or not. I was awake all night, waiting for a chance to run. Finally, by four o'clock in the morning, I was able to wrap up Lucy and break for the wooded area. It wasn't long before I heard voices behind me and four-wheelers powering up. When Uncle Craig saw lights flash on at the compound, he gunned it. They picked me up with seconds to spare.

"Uncle Craig just kept driving. We didn't stop for a break for six hours straight. No car seat for Lucy, no nothing. We made it across four states in record time."

"How did Lucy end up with Mara and Peter?"

"We knew the safest place for her was, unfortunately, away from me. Thorne would be looking for me as a way to find Lucy. Aunt Joan contacted an old friend of hers, a doctor who had always had a soft spot for her, and he agreed to help expedite a private adoption."

"I don't think Dr. Bob told Mara or Peter any of this."

"He doesn't know any of it. Joan said I had been in an abusive relationship and wanted to give the baby up for adoption. We pretended Lucy was my child."

"It's as easy as that?"

Paige's eyes moistened with tears. "There was nothing easy about any of it."

He sucked in a breath. "Of course not. I'm sorry. Is that the real reason you changed your name?"

She shrugged. "The name Willow is a part of my past I never want to revisit, Charlie. After I changed it, we moved to Ohio. Thorne had only ever known Joan by her first name. He didn't have much to go on to find me. But now, after all these years, he's managed to track me and Lucy here, and for that I am truly sorry."

He ran a hand down his face. He believed her, but what good did *sorry* do now?

"Why did you come here in the first place, Paige?"

"It's been ten long years thinking about Lucy and praying for her. I wanted to know if she was okay, safe, happy. I wanted to meet her and feel a connection to...my family."

"Okay," he muttered. "But doing that has jeopardized her future with her own family."

At this, Paige's face twisted in misery. "I know that," she cried, bringing a hand to her mouth. "I never meant for him to find her. All I ever wanted to do was make sure she was all right."

"And what was I, then?" Charlie said, moving to his feet. If her trip to Roseley had been to find Lucy, then what had he been? Collateral damage? She obviously had had no intention of staying in Roseley, therefore no intention of pursuing things with him. As he lumbered toward the woods, his body aching in places he didn't know could feel rejection, he realized everything he had felt for Paige was built on a foundation of straw and lies. "I'm no more than a chump to you, huh?"

"Anything but," Paige said, following. "Charlie, I never meant... I mean, I never thought..."

"What? You'd find such an easy mark?" His gut wrenched as he put it all together. This was what he got for taking a chance on love again and man, had he deserved it. She had just convinced him she had had feelings for him. She'd used him and he'd let her. He knew he should have been more cautious and taken things more slowly, but his heart was always skipping off ahead of his brain. He had made the same mistake in love all over again.

Paige scowled, shaking her head violently. "Of course not. How could you think—"

"That you used me? Do you think I don't see what's happened here? I see now that you must have facilitated our meeting so you could get access to Lucy."

"I didn't! Charlie, I wouldn't."

"That day at the sports shop. That day I invited you along to meet Lucy, did you already know I was her uncle?"

"Right then I did, yes, but…"

"You made me feel something for you when all this time I was just a way to get to Lucy."

"Charlie, no," Paige pleaded, reaching for him. She tried to pull him to look at her, but the flick of hurt and betrayal was too much.

"I *am* a chump. *Again*." He couldn't believe he'd been so blind. Paige's face burned hot and red as tears welled.

"You came along at a time when I didn't think I could love anyone, Charlie. I've never met anyone like you before. You made me fall so deeply in love with you I began to question everything, especially how I could live a future without you. That's why I didn't leave after I met Lucy. That's why I can't bear to leave now. I never meant to hurt you, Charlie."

"But that's exactly what you did. How could I ever be certain you didn't flirt with me just to get what you wanted?"

"Because all along I've wanted you!" Paige clasped her hands to her heart. Her words echoed against the aspen trees, ringing in his ears and trying to navigate a path to his heart. He had never wanted another woman as much as he had wanted her. Even with the little voice in the back of his mind warning him not to move too quickly, not to be too impulsive, he hadn't been able to stop. He'd fallen in love with her completely, and that's what made the hurt cut so deeply.

"And Lucy," he said. Paige stopped, bringing her hands to her cheeks. "You wanted me *and Lucy*."

"She's my family. I wanted to be a part of her family." Hesitantly Paige came closer and peered up into his eyes. "I wanted to be a part of your family, Charlie. I wanted to be yours, and I still do. Please believe that."

He wanted to curse her for making him listen. Even if she had met him out of coincidence and they had fallen in love that night at the bar, talking and dancing, where did that leave them now? How could he accept a woman into his life who was partly responsible for a brewing custody case over Lucy? If it came to that, his family would never forgive her or ever accept her. And how could he?

"That night at the bar," he said. "When you had to leave so suddenly. Tell me the reason why."

Paige's face fell as she recalled the memory. "I knew I had to give you up, because I had no intention of staying in Roseley. You were turning out to be everything I had ever dreamed of in a man, Charlie. Every minute we spent together would just make the inevitable harder, and I didn't know if I'd recover."

"Did you know the night in the bar that I was Lucy's uncle?"

Paige grazed fingertips over his hand. "I didn't know until the pitch meeting with Mara and Peter."

He hated her answer because it made it harder to write her out of his life. If she'd felt the same way he had felt that night, it made saying goodbye more difficult. Fate had a wicked sense of humor, pairing the two of them up only to land a shocking blow like this. He needed to clear his mind.

"Take the truck," he said, handing her the keys. "I'll find my way back."

"Charlie, please," she said, tugging on his arm. "Please don't leave me like this."

"I don't know if this is real!" he snapped. "Can't you see that?"

"It's real," she said, pleading. "I promise you, it's more real than anything I've ever known."

"But I don't know you anymore."

"You know me. You know how I feel about you," she whispered, pulling his face closer to hers. "It's real, Charlie. I promise, it's real."

When she kissed him, he wanted desperately to believe her. To believe everything he'd thought was true. His fingers entwined in her golden locks as he cradled her head with one hand and ran another down her back. He kissed her with the longing of a soldier heading off to war, though he didn't know if he'd find his way back into her tender embrace ever again now that the truth had come to light.

"What have you done to me?" he said, pressing his forehead to hers.

"Charlie," was all she could manage as she clasped his face between her palms and cried. He could believe anything and everything she told him in this cozy, secluded spot where nothing could hurt them.

She'd captivated his heart from the moment he'd first seen her in front of the sandwich shop. It was crazy to admit it now or ever, but in that moment, he had been certain he would fall in love with her. She'd drawn him in like a daydream he'd happily revisit over and over. By dinner that night, he had already been visualizing a forever with her.

But what did he visualize now? Where would they be after they'd reemerged to a reality where Lucy could be ripped away from her family? The grim possibility jolted him back to his senses.

He pulled away as she reached to keep him. Putting several paces between them and avoiding eye contact as self-defense, he called back to her.

"Take the truck to the shop, Paige. Like I said, I'll find my own way home."

"Charlie, please!" she shouted after him, but he slipped into the woods and out of sight before she could convince him to stay.

CHAPTER SEVENTEEN

PAIGE DROVE WEARILY back toward the shop, her body numb and weak. Applying pressure to the gas pedal took all her effort, as did keeping the truck on the road. Finally, as her tears clouded her vision too much to see, she pulled onto the gravel shoulder and parked. Charlie had left his cell phone in the center console. Fumbling her fingers along the numbers, she dialed home.

"Hello?" Uncle Craig said hesitantly.

"It's me."

"Honey, are you okay? I've been dialing the motel. We're going out of our minds sick with worry. Thorne—"

"Is here in Roseley. He went to the police and they want to see me as a person of interest in Lucy's kidnapping."

"Come home," Craig said. "Don't talk to the police. We'll get you a lawyer and build a case. Heaven knows Joanie and I need representation for what our part was in all this.

Once a court hears who Thorne really is, they'll understand what you did. What *we* did. We'll face this together if you just come home."

"They hate me, you know," Paige said as she dried her tears. Somehow, talking to Uncle Craig managed to toughen her up. He never frowned upon a person crying or breaking down, but something in his steady voice helped Paige think.

"Who does?"

"All of them, but Charlie most of all. He thinks I used him."

Craig started softly. "Didn't you?"

"Of course not." Paige's tears had dried completely at the suggestion. She was ready to verbally come out swinging and say everything to Uncle Craig that she had meant to tell Charlie. "I didn't ask to meet him. *He* approached *me*. He invited himself to lunch, and he invited me out to dinner, and he was the one who was completely kind and charming and impossible to stop thinking about. Even if I hadn't learned he was Lucy's uncle, I would have—"

She caught herself, imagining their conversation on the sidewalk when he'd said he was Lucy's uncle. At that point she had been intent on never seeing him again. She had wanted to, of course, but the truth was, if he hadn't been Lucy's uncle, that conversation would have been their last.

"What am I going to do now?"

"Come home."

The cell phone began to vibrate in her hand. Paige pulled away to check the caller ID. It was Tully.

"I have to go," she said. "I have to clear things up first. Tell Joan..."

She knew she'd only return to Ohio if the police let her, but she sensed Uncle Craig already understood.

"I'll tell her, honey." Paige clicked over to the other line.

"Where are you?" Tully's voice boomed. Even using his urgent, commanding tone, there was still something she liked about him. He was protective and honest and just. If circumstances were somehow different, she imagined they could have become friends.

Paige drew a breath. "It's Paige. Charlie is wandering around somewhere in the woods. I have his truck and phone."

"Then where are *you*?" he asked. "It's really you I need to see immediately."

"Are you going to arrest me?"

"Do I need to?"

Paige tipped her head back against the headrest. "I did what I thought was best for Lucy. I'll take the consequences, whatever they are, Tully."

"Good." His emphatic one-word answer said it all.

"I'll meet you at the station." Paige dropped the phone into the center console and pointed the truck toward the police station. She loved Lucy dearly, and if given the chance to do anything differently, she wouldn't change a thing. Lucy didn't belong with Thorne any more than she belonged with the devil himself, and she was ready to say that to anyone who asked, including face-to-face with Jared Thorne.

AT THE POLICE STATION, Paige recognized Mara's car and Tully's truck. She assumed Thorne was already there, waiting for her to arrive, and the thought made her wish Charlie was by her side.

Cutting the engine and drawing a determined breath, she made her way into the station. An officer buzzed her through the security doors. On blue scoop seats, Lucy and Mara huddled together. Mara looked distraught, but Lucy's head popped up excitedly once she spotted Paige. She slipped from her mother's arms and sprinted straight toward her.

"Lucy!" Mara commanded, but the little girl didn't look back. She sprang toward Paige and this time, instead of stopping short, leaped into her arms.

"Hey, sweetheart," Paige whispered, squeezing the life out of her. "I'm sorry you have to come here."

Lucy stared up at her. "Mom's mad at you."

"Yes. Do you know why?"

Lucy shook her head as Paige faced Mara, stalking toward them. Mara wrapped a protective arm around her daughter.

"Thorne is talking to Tully. He says he's her—" She jerked her head down at Lucy.

"He is. But I'm not her..." With Lucy listening, Paige hoped Mara understood. The situation would be solved if only she *was* Lucy's birth mother, but justice had its limits. Mara's narrowed brows lifted in surprise.

"I don't understand. Aren't you the one who contacted Dr. Hathaway the other day?"

"Not quite. Can we talk?"

Mara glanced back at Peter, who had

emerged from Tully's office. His sunken face led Mara to dig through her purse.

"Lucy, I want you to sit right here near Officer Kirk and play on my phone. I have to speak to Daddy and Paige." Officer Kirk glanced up from his paperwork and nodded.

"Can I do one of the game apps?" Lucy asked.

"Whatever you want, sweetie." Mara smooched a kiss to her temple and ushered Paige toward Peter.

"We should have been suspicious of you all along, huh?" Peter said, his voice grim.

"Peter, she's not her birth mother. You'd better spill it, Paige, and quick. That Thorne fellow is talking to Tully."

Paige nodded. For the second time that day, she relived the worst period of her life and tried hard not to leave out important details. The story came easier this time, but so did the tears. Neither Mara nor Peter had interrupted her, letting her tell the entire story from start to finish, and when she was through, they stood slack-jawed before her.

"Thank heavens you got her out of there," Mara said, glancing back at Lucy.

"What else could I do? My only regret is that he's found her now. That's on me, because

I came here, led him here. And I'm sorry I lied to the both of you. It was never my intention to jeopardize your family."

"There's nothing that can be done about that now," Peter said. "What you need to do is tell Tully everything you told us."

"No," Mara said. "She shouldn't have to see Thorne. Just one look at him makes my skin crawl. You don't have to go back there, Paige. We'll wait until he's left before we talk to Tully. We'll wait until—"

"No." Paige shook her head. She'd have to face Thorne in court eventually so she might as well march in and face him right now. She wasn't a seventeen-year-old girl anymore. She was a woman with a strong mind and a strong will, and she couldn't live in fear anymore. "He's expecting a fight for Lucy and that's exactly what I'll give him," Paige said, turning toward Tully's office.

"Hold on, honey," Peter said, taking her elbow. "You're not going in there alone. You never have to go in there alone ever again."

Paige saw the determination and sincerity in Peter's eyes and when she turned, Mara's face reflected it too. Mara reached for her hand and squeezed it tightly.

"We're in this together. Got it?"

Paige nodded, and she did.

CHARLIE ARRIVED AT the police station and stopped short when he saw Lucy. He nodded to Officer Kirk before plopping down on the chair beside her.

"Hey, munchkin," he said. "Where are your mom and dad?"

"They're in Tully's office with Paige."

Charlie had spotted his truck but had figured Paige had dropped it off and headed for Ohio. He knew she was packed and ready to leave. Heck, she'd made it clear enough times over the last day that she needed to return home. He just hadn't understood why at the time.

"Have you been out here a while?"

"I've played eighteen rounds of Alien Explorer."

"Do you have any idea what they're talking about in there?"

"Not really. Mom made us leave the ski show before it even started. Then she started sobbing to Dad. Then Tully called and we had to come here." She peered up at him with round eyes. "Is this because I found Paige's driver's license? I already told her I was sorry."

"Nah, it's not about that." He wrapped an arm around her and gave her a little squeeze.

"Don't worry. Your mom and dad are just working through some questions with Uncle Tully."

He'd no sooner uttered the words when Tully appeared. He raised his eyebrows at Charlie when he spotted him, before turning to hold open the door for the others. Officer Kirk straightened and took a few steps to stand in front of Lucy when Thorne emerged. As he passed, he made a little finger waggle at Lucy but didn't utter a word before exiting the station.

When Paige exited the office, she looked lost in thought. She didn't notice Charlie until she was nearly right on top of him.

"Charlie," she gasped, readjusting her stance.

"What happened in there?"

Paige glanced at Lucy. "Walk me out?"

He nodded. "Lucy, stay here with Officer Kirk. Your mom and dad are coming now." He followed Paige out into the evening sunset. "It's amazing the difference a day makes," he said, staring at the horizon. Her eyes followed his gaze toward the pink and purple clouds in the distance before returning to look at him. He knew she was thinking of their plane ride as well. How could she not? He'd had trouble thinking of much else for most of the day until…until he wasn't thinking about it anymore.

"Thorne filed a police report. He demanded I be arrested for kidnapping, but Tully is hesitant to do that after hearing my side of the story."

"I doubt he has much of a choice if Thorne is her father."

"Tully's been in contact with the police department back in Ohio. There are criminal charges to sort out and then custody things to sort out. The fact that Lucy has been living with Mara and Peter for over ten years makes things very complicated."

"Can they really make Lucy go to live in that cult?"

Paige wrapped her arms around herself. "Oh, Charlie, I don't know. I saw so many strange things when I was living at Thorne's compound but no smoking gun to prevent him from getting custody." Her tears made his gut twist, the gravity of the situation hitting them both again and again, like waves crashing against the rocks. "Just when I get a grip, I begin to think about it all over again."

"Me too," he said.

"What should I do?"

"What *can* you do?" He didn't want to say it but the only thing she could do now was testify that Thorne wasn't fit to be a father, and she'd stolen Lucy to protect her from him. Maybe if a court believed Lucy had been in real danger...

"Do you hate me?"

His eyes met hers, and he knew he should tell the absolute truth. There had been enough secrecy over the last several days.

"Never."

"Never?"

He nodded. "I admire your courage. I'm worried you'll get prosecuted for it now."

"I don't care. I'd do it again." He believed her.

"I would have done the same thing..."

She shifted on her feet when he didn't continue. He understood why she kidnapped Lucy and was thankful for her action. Lucy was one of the biggest joys of his life and she'd certainly enriched the lives of everyone around her. She had deserved better than the distorted life Thorne would have given her.

To think of Paige holing herself away in Ohio, keeping a low profile, keeping the secret for all these years just to protect Lucy, it made him realize she was a stronger person than he was. He would always hold Paige in his deepest respect and be eternally grateful to her for not leaving Thorne's compound without his little niece.

But the day's revelations had made something shift within his soul, and the last holdout he'd had to trust again had crumbled. For days he'd believed he and Paige were falling in love with each other. To now discover she'd had an ulterior motive, a desire to use him to get to Lucy, made his heart begin to harden again. He was all too familiar with this betrayal, this tune of playing the fool. He believed Paige when she said she'd fallen for him before she knew he was Lucy's uncle, but still, places deep in his soul had already begun to ache and throb. The aftershocks, he was certain, would last long after Paige was gone.

"I can't do this now. Do you need a ride back to the shop?" he managed to say. She accepted his invitation by shuffling to the passenger side of his truck.

"How did you get here?" she asked.

"Walked."

"From the woods?"

"And hitchhiked."

"Isn't that dangerous, trusting a stranger?"

It could be. He'd figured he'd already been

burned by trusting a stranger once this week with his heart. All that was left to risk now was a shell of his former self.

CHAPTER EIGHTEEN

CHARLIE STEERED TOWARD the sports shop. Now that things had come to light with Thorne, Paige had no other reason to stick around town. He assumed she'd want to get back to her car and make her way to Ohio…

But he didn't feel like asking her. He was so exhausted as the events of the day had worn on his soul; he didn't feel like uttering a single word more. As Paige sat in silence, staring out the truck window, he relaxed into his seat and embraced the quiet. It was the vibration of his cell phone that broke the silence.

"Hey, sis."

"Is Paige with you?"

"Yes, she's here." He flicked a glance and found Paige hanging on his every word.

"We're heading back to the house. Bring her with you."

"I don't think she'll want to come—"

"She must. We need to work this all out,

and Paige is essential to that conversation. Meet you at home."

Mara hung up the line before Charlie could protest. He dropped the phone back in the cup holder and continued to grip the steering wheel. He could feel Paige's eyes boring holes into the side of his face. A full minute ticked by without her asking for clarification on his phone conversation before he finally explained.

"Mara wants you back at the house to straighten things out." Paige still stared at him. "What?" he said, his eyes darting at her from the road.

"Do *you* want me there?"

"It doesn't matter."

"It matters to me."

"I can't make an emotional turn of one hundred and eighty degrees in less than an afternoon, Paige." There were a lot of things he had wanted over the last few days that had dissipated faster than a kiss evaporating on his skin. He'd gone from wanting Paige to be his wife to not knowing if he could trust her again. He had to focus on helping Mara and Peter protect Lucy now. He didn't have time to sort out his complicated feelings for Freckles.

They were first to arrive at the house, so

Charlie let them in. He flipped on the kitchen light and stared around the stark white countertops. The entire place now looked so barren and cold. A threat to his niece's future was all it took to crush his optimistic nature.

"Want a drink?" he managed, shuffling to the fridge. Paige nodded, sliding up onto a counter stool across from him. All Mara had was some sort of fruity red punch. He poured two glasses and stood across from Paige, eyeing her.

"You're never going to forgive me, are you?" she whispered. He clenched the glass in his hands. He didn't know what he would forgive her for, exactly. She hadn't intended to hurt him. She hadn't lied to him about being related to Lucy for any reason meant to hurt him. She had wanted to protect Lucy as they all did, but still, he somehow felt used.

"What else do you have in common with Lucy?" he asked, trying for a polite distraction. Paige smiled and ran a finger around the rim of her glass.

"I don't see much of myself in her, if that's what you mean. I was a shy kid and Lucy is a ball of light."

Charlie bit back a smile. He knew exactly what she meant. "She's going to set the world on fire, that's for sure. Although maybe you would have been different, given a different childhood?"

"I don't know. There's no way to tell, really. How much is nature versus nurture?"

"Does she remind you of anyone in your family?"

Paige looked thoughtful for a moment. "Aunt Joan is a force of nature, but I wonder how much of that was developed because she had to be strong. First she had to navigate years of drama with her twin sister and then she had to take care of Uncle Craig when he got sick…"

Charlie nodded, remembering her uncle. "Have you talked to them recently?"

"Not more than a few words. I should call."

"There's a lot to update them on, huh?"

Paige took a sip of punch. "They'd be here by my side if they could."

"Are you worried this new development will affect your uncle? I mean, this kind of stress…"

He immediately regretted his words when Paige wavered on her seat. Moving around the island, he was to her side in a blink, but what he wanted to do there, he couldn't be sure. He couldn't hold her, but he still needed to be near. Paige forced a smile, as if appreciative of what little he could offer.

"I'm okay," she said. "This kind of stress isn't good for him, but the three of us knew Thorne might find Lucy eventually. I only hoped he wouldn't until after Lucy had turned eighteen and aged out of his legal hold."

"Were you the one to name her Lucy?" Charlie asked, the question coming to him in a moment of curiosity. "Or was it your mother?"

"Me. It might be unbelievable, but I can't remember the name my mother chose before she died. I was very moved when I learned Mara and Peter kept it."

"I can't imagine her as anything but a Lucy."

"Me neither. Now that I've met her..." Paige took his hand, her soft fingers delicately weaving against his. "You've changed my life, Charlie. You'll never understand the gift you've given me these last few days."

"Introducing you to Lucy."

"I've loved her from afar for ten years, so to finally get to hug her and know her has filled a deficit in my heart. Yes, you did that." Paige rose, taking his other hand in hers too. "But I meant how I feel about you, Charlie."

He squeezed her hands tightly before releasing them. It was too much—this desire to both embrace her and pull away at the same time.

"I have to take a shower," he said, making for the hallway as Paige stared after him. "They should be here soon. Make yourself at home." He could use some time alone before everyone arrived and they rehashed the worst of the day. He left her sitting under the warm glow of the kitchen lamp as he shot for the shower. He wanted hot water on his skin and a hard smack in the face for rushing too quickly into another heartache.

By the time he emerged from the bathroom, he heard voices chattering downstairs. He hoped they weren't pressing Lucy too hard. That kid was innocent and sweet and didn't need to hear all the scenarios of what might happen to her. The first scenario was that he'd beat Thorne to a pulp if he even tried to come near his niece.

As he towel-dried his hair and tugged fresh clothes on, he heard an unfamiliar voice in the kitchen. It was an older woman's voice, that much he was certain, but he couldn't place her. CeCe? Dolores? His brain flipped like a rolodex, trying to pinpoint who it was. When he at last made his way to the kitchen, he saw a woman, sixty years old, but with Paige's likeness. Her tired face lifted as Paige rose to her feet for introductions.

"Hey, Charlie," Paige said, waving him forward. Mara, Peter and Tully looked up from around the kitchen table. The new woman's blond hair, though graying and askew, might have clued him in, but it was her hazel-green eyes that made him certain. Even with the lines and puffy circles earned after many sleepless nights, no doubt, nothing could disguise the relation.

"You must be Aunt Joan," he said. Joan reached out a hand, but Charlie pulled her into a hug instead. Joan let out a little laugh, accepting his embrace. As he glanced around the kitchen for Uncle Craig, he gathered she'd had to make a difficult decision: fly to support her niece or stay with her sick husband. It would be an excruciating decision and one he could honor with a hug.

Paige's face softened at the sight of them, and her eyes seemed to convey a thank-you with only a blink.

"Charlie, we were filling Joan in on what happened today. She flew in and surprised me."

"I knew you'd tell me not to come, but Craig insisted. He told me to 'go get our girl.'"

"How did you find us?" Charlie asked.

"When my plane touched down, I called the police station to give my account of what happened before Thorne muddied everyone's opinion."

"You talked to Tully, didn't you?"

"I picked her up from the airport myself," Tully said.

"You really do know everybody in this town, Tully," Mara said. He chuckled.

"I'm still working on it."

Charlie looked around the room. "Where's Lucy?"

"We dropped her off with a friend for an overnight," Mara said. "I don't want to scare her. Watching movies and eating junk food should be the most of her concerns."

"Aren't you worried Thorne could take her while she's gone?" he asked.

Tully smiled. "She's with Stephen Kirk's daughter." Charlie got the point. Officer Kirk was one of the toughest cops in Roseley. He'd no sooner let a person come near Lucy than he'd let someone harm his own kid.

"I'm glad she's having fun," Joan said. "But I sure did want to meet her."

"You're her aunt," Charlie muttered, the realization dawning over him. She had more

WHERE THE HEART MAY LEAD

connection to Lucy than even he did. Joan smiled and patted him lightly on the arm.

"There will be time enough for that. I want to hear what the plan is to keep that lousy con man away from our girl." Joan took a swig of coffee and slapped the table with a resounding force, making even Tully sit a little straighter. He muffled an amused smile, before spreading out paperwork from the station.

"There are a lot of factors involved here from a legal standpoint and a custody-standpoint," Tully began. "Paige, when you and Joan took Lucy, you crossed state lines. That makes things more challenging and unfortunately a lot worse for the both of you."

"How challenging, though, can this really be?" Paige asked. "I can't imagine any person in the world could learn about Thorne and want to send Lucy to live with him."

"The law is not as simple as that."

"It should be. If I had to do things over again, I'd take Lucy in a heartbeat. I could never have lived with myself if I had escaped and left Lucy there." Paige turned to Tully. "What do we do next?"

"Hire a lawyer—"

"Done," Peter said. "We meet with our legal team in the morning."

Joan reached for Mara's hand. "Are they any good?"

"Best in the tristate area. Do you have one?"

Joan nodded. "I will by tomorrow."

"How much did Dr. Hathaway know?" Tully asked. Aunt Joan shook her head.

"We told him Lucy was Paige's child, and the father was a danger to her. That's it," Aunt Joan replied.

"Can you get in trouble for talking to us, Tully?" Paige asked. Tully shook his head.

"Charlie's family is my family. I'm here as a friend first and foremost, Paige. I did recuse myself from the investigation this evening."

"Does Paige need to stay here in Roseley?" Joan asked, bringing everyone's eyes to her niece. "I only ask because I have to return to Craig in the morning. As much as I didn't want to leave him, I had to fly out tonight to make sure she was okay." She turned to Paige. "You know I couldn't stay away thinking of you facing Thorne all alone—"

"I wasn't alone," Paige said, taking her aunt's hand. "You should fly home first thing tomorrow. I'll be right behind you, as long as I'm allowed to leave."

"You need to check in with the police within one hour of arriving back home," Tully explained. "They'll monitor you and be the first to make contact in the event you are brought up on criminal charges, which you will be. Don't leave town, and don't evade them. It makes you look guilty and hurts the case."

"Why hasn't she been brought up on charges already?" Mara asked.

"The police need to first prove Lucy was kidnapped. They need to prove Thorne is her father, as he says he is, and that things happened the way he described them. They're most likely interviewing Dr. Hathaway and will come knocking on your door shortly. Paige, don't be surprised if they show up possibly as soon as you get home."

Charlie lowered his eyes to his lap. Paige would return home to help Uncle Craig fight for his life, and he'd stay in Roseley to help Mara and Peter fight for Lucy. It seemed backward somehow that they couldn't be together to fight for their families side by side. He didn't envision a future with her anymore, but as much as he now felt distanced from her, it was hard to bid her goodbye.

PAIGE BROUGHT MARA a cup of hot tea as the others continued to talk around the kitchen table. The house was dark and quiet except for the warm yellow light fixture hanging over the kitchen table and the others' voices, which had dropped to murmurs. Mara had shuffled to the adjoining living room, wrapped herself in a shawl and cuddled at the end of the couch, her legs tucked up to her chin.

"I should be fixing *you* tea," Mara said, accepting the hot mug with a weak smile. Paige shook her head and covered Mara with another blanket before resting on the floor beside her.

"I'm so sorry, Mara. I can't imagine what you're going through right now."

Mara stared at the hot tea before shifting her gaze to Paige.

"Somehow I think you do. The way you told the story of escaping with Lucy—"

"I was scared out of mind the entire time."

"But you kept going," Mara whispered. "You're brave, kid."

"Right now, all I see is the mess I created. If I had never come to Roseley, Thorne might never have found Lucy."

"He would have found her eventually. If you hadn't come, he might have just taken her. At least now we can see the devil we need to fight."

"She can't go back to Thorne, Mara. I'd take her again to keep that from happening."

"No one will let that happen," Charlie said from behind her. Paige turned at the sound of his voice, growing hoarse as the evening had passed.

"Will you stay, Paige?" Mara asked.

Paige's mouth fell agape. "I wouldn't think you'd want me to."

"Of course we do. Stay here tonight. Stay until this gets fixed."

Paige's heart leaped, but then she saw Charlie's face fall cold. She couldn't spend any more time in Roseley after seeing the hurt he harbored because of her.

Then there was Aunt Joan and Uncle Craig. Paige's intentions when she'd first arrived in Roseley was to check on Lucy and return home to her family. Things hadn't panned out as she had hoped, but now the right people were aware of Thorne and could step in to protect Lucy. Just one look at Charlie reminded her that there wasn't anything holding her to Roseley anymore. And just one thought of Uncle Craig made her certain of her answer.

"Thank you, Mara, but my uncle needs me."

Mara plucked a wisp of hair back off Paige's face as Charlie returned to the kitchen. She bit back another apology, knowing Charlie would never trust her again. He'd never love her again like he once had and she knew that loss would haunt her. Paige took a deep breath and let it out slowly. Mara tipped Paige's face up, her dark eyes falling sad.

"You and Lucy really do share an uncanny resemblance. It's in those eyes of yours, windows into an old soul. It's funny I never noticed it before."

Paige dropped her head to Mara's lap and Mara stroked her hair for a long, long time.

PAIGE WOKE THE NEXT morning to Joan packing her bag. They had stayed at Mara and Peter's house until late into the night before making their way to the motel for a few hours of sleep. Something about huddling around the kitchen table with a group of people who loved Lucy as much as she did seemed to help soften the fears for the future. Only a few days earlier, she had imagined being welcomed into that family as a cherished auntie, a person they embraced wholeheartedly as family. And now, all she wanted was for them to not resent her forever.

Paige rolled out of bed and noticed the light on the motel phone blinking. As she hadn't remembered it blinking when they'd arrived that night and couldn't recall it ringing, it confused her. When she retrieved the message, she gasped at Thorne's controlled voice on the other end of the line.

"Good morning, Willow," he said. Instantly, she remembered the first time he'd ever spoken her name. She and Trudy had been sitting outside the stolen car they'd parked and slept in at the edge of a grocery store parking lot. From a distance, she'd watched Thorne walk toward them with an eerie calm and confidence that had made her want to run. When he'd approached, she had been frightened by his black eyes, irises so dark there was no distinguishing them from the pupil. When she learned he believed he was something special, something not of this world, his unnatural eyes conveyed he might not be wrong.

Paige had slunk away, retreating to the back seat of the car as her mother happily chatted. Trudy had invited and teased Paige to come meet her new friend, but Paige refused. Finally, after he had watched her through the back seat window, listening to Trudy continually call for her to join them, Thorne had seemed to lose his patience. With a forced smile pinning back his lips, he had tapped on the glass and whispered, "Good morning, Willow."

Paige shuddered at the memory as she waited for more of Thorne's message. But when the line cut off, signaling he had spoken no more, she replaced the receiver and sat back on the bed.

"What's wrong?" Joan said. "Who was it?"

"Those eyes. Those black eyes." Paige remembered how he thought he was special and how he thought he was going to live forever. He was so different from the other men her mother had been romantically involved with and yet something else about him made him stand out from the pack.

Then, the realization hit her so hard and so fast she sucked in an audible breath. Her arms flailed for Joan before finally clasping Joan's shoulders and shaking her.

"I have to get to Charlie. I have to tell him Lucy can't be Thorne's daughter and we can prove it."

PAIGE PACED THE HALLWAY of Mara and Peter's house later that morning, waiting for Tully to turn up. As Charlie sat on the bottom stairs watching, he yearned to calm her. He considered how good it would feel to squeeze her to him, but then where would that leave them?

When the front door opened, it was Lucy

who came galloping into the room ahead of Tully.

"Paige!" she said, hugging her. "I didn't know you were going to be here."

Paige dropped to her knees to better hold the little girl. "I have to go home to Ohio today, but I wanted to come say goodbye."

"Why are you leaving?"

"My uncle is really sick, and I want to take care of him. I am so glad I got to meet you, though. You're my favorite little girl."

"That's what Uncle Charlie always tells me."

"Be good and listen to your parents and Uncle Charlie, okay?" Paige fumbled behind her back before holding out the dress. "What do you think?"

"I love it!" Lucy squealed, clasping the dress in her hands. "The shade of purple is perfect."

"Well," Paige said, holding it up, "I wanted something nearly as beautiful as you." Lucy giggled and showed it off to Charlie.

"It looks great, kid."

"I have to show Mom."

"She's on the deck." What he didn't say was that she was talking to their defense team.

"This is goodbye," Paige called, making

Lucy turn. She embraced Lucy one last time before the little girl skipped away. "And that's it," she whispered, standing. Charlie moved near. He wanted to offer comfort but instead motioned toward Tully.

"Tell Tully what you told us," Charlie said, shoving his roaming hands into the front pockets of his jeans.

"My mother dated a lot before she met Thorne. She attracted the wrong kind of guy every time. Anyway, I pieced together the timeline from when we arrived to Thorne's homestead to when she announced her pregnancy. It's possible Lucy is Thorne's child, but I have good reason to think she's not."

Tully settled back on his feet, resting a hand at his belt loop. "Which is?"

"Her eyes. Green eyes, especially eyes as green as mine and Lucy's, are a recessive trait. They're the rarest eye color there is. My mother said my father had blue eyes, allowing me to inherit hers. But Thorne's eyes are so dark and certainly a dominant trait, I think it would be incredibly rare for Lucy to have green eyes if he's her father—"

"Improbable, Paige, but certainly not impossible."

"It's enough to go on, though, isn't it?"

Charlie said. "A DNA test could settle this before it goes much further?"

Tully agreed. "A DNA test is necessary regardless of your observation, Paige, but knowing this might help conclude things more quickly."

Paige nodded. "Before Lucy hears about it and worry disrupts her life." That was what she was most concerned with.

Tully said, "Have you told Mara and Peter?"

"We just did, Charlie and I together."

Charlie inwardly sighed at her words. It would be the last thing they would do together. Next week he'd start in the police academy and pursue new beginnings for himself. He'd have to work hard, but he'd eventually put memories of Paige behind him.

Tully touched Paige on the shoulder. "I think Lucy is going to be okay."

"Will you let me know, Tully?" she said. Charlie knew she didn't dare ask him. She knew, as well as he did, that things between them were over as soon as she walked out that door.

"I'd be glad to."

Charlie held open the front door. "I'll walk you out," he said after Paige hugged Tully.

Alone with her on the front stoop, he said, "Did your aunt fly home?"

"Early this morning. She's already with Craig by now. Thank heavens for direct flights, huh?"

"How's he doing?"

"Fine for now. I should make it home by tonight."

"They're lucky to have you."

"Lucy is lucky to have *you*."

He shuffled his feet along the concrete walk, glancing back at Tully, who moved away from the front window, where he'd been watching.

"I guess this is it," he said with a weak smile. "Drive safely, Freckles. Wear your helmet, huh?"

"Charlie…" Her voice quavered, making him shake his head.

"You have a life in Ohio, and I have a life here in Roseley. Whatever we had the past few days…" He trailed off, not sure how to define it. "I'm grateful for the time we shared together."

"I'll never look at the sun setting over the water without thinking of you, Charlie." He hoped this wouldn't be the case for him.

The next fifty or so years of sunset flights would be torturous otherwise.

"I hope your uncle…" He didn't know what to say. He wouldn't be there to hold her when Craig died, and it seemed inevitable he would soon. "I'm sorry about your uncle," he finally managed.

"Thank you."

"You should go before the traffic picks up."

Paige hesitated. "After the pain Crystal caused you, I didn't want you to get hurt again, Charlie."

"I know." And he did, but it didn't soothe the heartache any better.

"Goodbye, Charlie." He watched her drive away, following her until she turned and disappeared into the morning sunshine.

"Well, Freckles," he sighed. "I won't be able to look at another sunrise now without thinking about you."

CHAPTER NINETEEN

CHARLIE FOLLOWED HIS field training officer, his friend, Officer Stephen Kirk, into The Sandwich Board. Field training was turning out to be a breeze compared to the police academy, and learning under Stephen was a best-case scenario. Stephen had asked for Charlie to be assigned to him, and he'd greatly appreciated it. It helped having someone he trusted level with him about the job.

"Good afternoon, Officers," Angelo called, making his way to the end of the counter. "Coffee?"

"Decaf, if you would, Angelo," Charlie said. "And a pastrami on rye."

Stephen grabbed a water bottle out of the refrigerator as CeCe hurried at the sound of their voices.

"Charlie—" She stopped short and fanned herself with her hand. "*Excuse me.* I mean, *Officer* Stillwater."

Stephen smirked. "He hasn't done much yet to earn that title."

"Well, you're still a police officer," CeCe said with a proud grin. The past year had seen many changes for him, most of them positive. *Most* of them. "Are you seeing anyone, *Officer* Stillwater? My niece is moving to town, and she's quite the looker."

"We talked about this, CeCe," Angelo said, handing over the sandwich. "You're supposed to be discreet."

"I *am* being discreet. I'm *discreetly* letting him know that a beautiful single woman who is searching for a good man will be arriving to town shortly, and he should be on the lookout. Neither of them is getting any younger."

"Casual, honey," Angelo said with an eye roll. "What can I get you, Officer Kirk?"

"Nothing for me, thanks. Just waiting for the greenhorn."

"Have you caught any villains recently?" CeCe asked.

"I'm going to take off, Charlie. I'll see you tomorrow." Stephen pushed out into the sunshine as Charlie took a sip of his coffee. His field training officer was a serious man, short on words and patience.

Angelo kissed CeCe's cheek. "I love her,

Charlie, but my wife isn't really one for discretion or decorum."

"What was that?" CeCe said, taking a playful swat at Angelo. "You're making fun of me in front of Charlie."

"He should be so lucky to have a woman like you." He planted another smack on her cheek.

"All I'm saying," CeCe said in a hushed voice, "is that you and my niece would make a fine couple. She's very sporty. She takes good care of herself, if you know what I mean. I wouldn't set you up with anyone else, Charlie."

Charlie hadn't dated since Paige had left, almost a year ago. Completing the police academy and starting a new career had helped take his mind off of her, for the most part, but on lonely nights when he took his plane out for an evening flight, he couldn't keep from helplessly drifting to thoughts of her. Sometimes it was all he could do to keep from wishing she was sitting beside him when he looked at his passenger seat. It was hard to understand how something that felt so right one day was lost to him the next. Perhaps all he needed to snap out of his funk was someone new.

"When does your niece arrive?"

CeCe's face brightened. "I'll give you a call when she gets here."

Charlie shuffled back toward the door with CeCe smiling after him. He hadn't committed to a date, but maybe it was a step in the right direction.

CHARLIE ARRIVED AT Mara's house at the same time Tully did. Even though he had moved into a house of his own, he appreciated Mara's frequent invitations to come for dinner. He knew Tully appreciated them even more.

"Tough day?" he asked, cutting a line across the yard toward Mara's front stoop.

Tully nodded. "I've been looking forward to Mara's cooking all day."

"You should take some cooking lessons. Might make you even more appealing to the fairer sex."

"Nah. I'll never settle down. I'm not the marrying kind." It was Tully's standard tagline and one Charlie had heard him utter since the time they were kids, building tree forts and jumping off the docks to get Tully's mind off his family.

"Never say never, man," Charlie said. "The right woman will take you off the market in a heartbeat."

Tully huffed as they made their way to the back deck. "Don't put your money on it."

"I'd take that wager," Peter said, overhearing them approach. He smiled and led them inside. "What's the bet?"

"Good! You're here!" Mara called.

"She's been up to her shenanigans again, be forewarned," Peter said.

"What great idea has she come up with this time?" Charlie asked, but Peter shushed him as Lucy raced over and crashed into Tully's arms.

"Mom said I can have a birthday party this weekend. Wanna come?"

"It's her first boy-girl party," Peter groaned.

"Are you old enough for that?" Tully raised an eyebrow.

Lucy giggled. *"Tu-lly."*

"I'll come by and keep them all in line for you."

"I only invited one boy—Axel."

"Axel?" Charlie said with a discerning eye. "I'm wearing my uniform."

"Uncle Charlie," Lucy said giggling. "He's really nice."

"No one named *Axel* is really nice."

"He is!" Lucy howled, as Charlie tickled

her. "Mom said we can get a splash pad and a Slip 'N Slide."

"I said I'd think about it," Mara said as her cell phone chimed with a message. "Paige was supposed to text tonight about—" Mara stopped short as Charlie's eyes narrowed. He shifted on his feet.

"Do you stay in contact with Paige?" he asked as Tully motioned for Lucy to follow him into the kitchen. "I know you sent flowers from all of us for the funeral…" He recalled learning that Paige's uncle had passed only two weeks after she'd returned home. He had just started at the police academy and wasn't able to make it to the funeral. It was probably just as well he hadn't gone, he repeatedly told himself.

Still, Paige would have had to mourn her uncle, and the thought he hadn't been there nagged at him. He'd even called Aunt Joan's house to offer his condolences. Twice, in fact. But he'd only ever left voice mails, and Paige had never returned his calls.

"After I contacted her about the DNA test results—"

"We dodged a bullet on that one." Peter sighed. "If Thorne had been her father… I don't know what we would have done." It had been a relief to them all. Without knowing Lucy's birth father and Paige being next of kin, she and Joan had been within their right to give Lucy up for adoption.

"We continued to stay in touch," Mara said.

"I offered my condolences. Did she tell you?"

"We only talk about Lucy."

Charlie didn't know what angered him exactly. Mara had been of good heart to contact Paige about Thorne not having any relation to Lucy. And there was nothing wrong with keeping her updated about Lucy, as she was her half sister. Perhaps, he thought, he was just angry at himself for not being there for Paige when the time came to let her uncle go.

"Are you all right?" Tully said quietly as Mara sorted the food on the counter.

Charlie clenched his jaw. "Fine."

"Help yourself," Mara called, handing out plates. "Buffet style tonight with paper plates for the win."

"Why is Paige texting you now?" Charlie asked, his mind unable to shift gears to polite table conversation. Lucy's head popped up from squirting ketchup.

"Did Paige text you, Mom? You said I could talk to her."

"You did?" At Charlie's words, Mara looked to Peter again.

"Of course. She's family," Peter stated.

"Family," he said, pushing his chair away from the table.

Mara tipped her head in confusion. "What's wrong?"

"Nothing," he said, huffing his way out of the house. As much as he hated speaking to his family like that, he couldn't find a way to settle his frustration. He strode to the edge of the lawn, not sure if he wanted to drive home or to his plane or somewhere far away. He stood in the middle of the road, contemplating his options, when he realized he'd been followed. "I needed a minute," he said in a grumble.

"You've been taking quite a few minutes the last year." Tully crossed his arms over his chest.

"Counting, huh?"

Tully shrugged. "Only because it's out of character for you."

"I didn't know Mara was in contact with Paige or why it's been a big secret."

"Judging by how you just reacted…"

"You think she was right to keep it from me?" Charlie spun around to stare his friend in the eye. Tully studied him, his face giving away nothing.

"I think you're mad at someone, and it isn't Mara."

Charlie snorted. "I forgot you're the expert, Detective."

"Nah," Tully said. "But I am your best friend. I can see you miss her."

"I'm trying not to."

"How's that going?"

Charlie ran a hand down the length of his face. "I'm going to need another minute."

"Do you think she intentionally did anything to hurt Lucy?"

"Of course not."

"Do you think she was trying to be deceitful? Trying to scam you or use you? I've got to tell you, Charlie, I've met plenty of liars and cheaters in my line of work, and at worst, I think she had just gotten in over her head when she met you."

"At first, when she confessed who she was, I thought she was using me to get to Lucy. But whenever I let myself replay our time together, replay the times where I felt a real connection—"

"What?"

"I find myself thinking I made a terrible

mistake not fighting for her to stay. Sure, she had to go back to Ohio to nurse her uncle until he died, but now…"

"But now what?"

"How can I get over what we had? How can she?"

Mara stuck her head out the front door. "Can you two wrap it up? The burgers are getting cold!"

"What am I going to do?" Charlie said, heading back toward the house.

"I don't know," Tully said, punching him on the shoulder. "But I'll have fun watching you figure it out."

PAIGE SUCKED IN A breath of early summer air, letting it fill her lungs and populate every cell of her body. It was a good day to be young, to be alive, to be free. She coasted her bicycle along the concrete before pulling to a stop in front of the coffee shop.

"Hey, darlin'," Polly called, waving a pretzel rod at her. Paige locked her bike and went over to her friend.

"Isn't the benefit of pretzel rods that you don't have to come outside to smoke them?"

Polly grinned and pretended to take a puff. "When the weather is like this, I still like to come out for a quick smoke break. My hands and body have a muscle memory I can't seem to shake."

"Mind if I join you?" Paige accepted a pretzel rod from Polly's bag. She looked out over the shops of her hometown, but all she could see was Roseley. It had been a year since she'd left Charlie and Lucy, but every day, she still longed to be back with them. Things here in Ohio had lost their appeal. And she couldn't help remembering how quickly folks in Roseley had befriended her. They'd had a way of embracing her, welcoming her into the community. And then there was Charlie. How could anyone here ever replace him?

Paige bit off a piece of pretzel. She wondered if she had her own muscle memory from her brief stint in Roseley, yearning to hold Charlie once again. But because her time spent there had been so brief, she reminded herself that muscle memory wasn't the same as deep longing.

"Coming in for coffee?"

"Not today. I'm meeting Joan."

Polly paused, following Paige's line of sight to the Mama's Cakes shop. "Hmm. It's about that time of year. Should I wish you a happy birthday today or tomorrow?"

"Actually, my birthday is in October."

"October?" Polly said with a scowl. "I always thought June. Madge was just telling me about the masterpiece she's been working on for the last two days."

"October," Paige said with a satisfied sigh. She could tell people things like that now. She could stand on the curb and carry on a conversation with a woman she had always wanted to befriend. She could now be more than an acquaintance to whomever she chose because there wasn't anything to hide from now, except, perhaps, a broken heart still trying to heal.

"I'm glad to see you out and about, kiddo," Polly said. "I'm glad to hear your aunt is too. If you change your mind about coffee, pop on in. Your usual table in the window is open."

Paige thought about Roseley. She wanted a usual table in Angelo's sandwich shop. Wouldn't it be lovely to sit and write in the window there, the place where she'd first shared lunch with Charlie? Although she'd probably never get any work done with CeCe stopping by every few minutes to dig into her social life.

She chuckled at the thought as Aunt Joan came hustling up the sidewalk.

"I made record time," she said, wiping sweat from her brow. "But, boy, am I out of shape. You'd think hustling around the hospital would have kept me more fit. Retirement might be the death of me."

"Are you ready?"

Joan nodded. "Should we call from here or inside?"

"I said I'd call right at four o'clock. Let's stand out here and do it. Having to get a table and explain to Madge will take too much time and—"

"Do it."

Paige dialed Mara and put the call on speakerphone. She hoped Lucy would answer, but it was Mara's chipper voice that greeted them.

"Hello, Paige and Joan! Is that you?"

"It's us," Paige said, as she and her aunt huddled at the phone.

"Where on earth are you? It sounds windy."

"Is it?" Paige squinted at her aunt, who pantomimed a look of confusion. Though they were outside, there was hardly a baby's breath of a breeze. "We can go inside if that helps."

"Are you at home?"

"No. Grabbing a cake for the big day."

"Are you at a cake shop nearby?"

"It's a ceremony of sorts. This year is even

more important since we get to talk to the birthday girl while we eat her birthday cake." Joan's smile stretched wider in anticipation as she hurried Paige through the front door of Mama's Cakes. She held up a hand to stop Madge from interrupting as they slid next to each other in a small booth. Paige held the phone between them like a precious stone.

"Is she there?" Joan asked, her voice shaky as her hand clutched Paige's arm. There was a slight pause.

"I'm so sorry," Mara said. "I know we said four o'clock, but Lucy isn't here right now."

They stared at the phone as if the device itself had crushed their spirits, coldly, unapologetically.

"Is everything okay? Are you and Peter having second thoughts about us talking to her?"

"No, of course not," Mara said. "She's very excited to talk to the both of you. She just isn't here right now."

Paige wrapped an arm around her aunt. "We can call back when it's more convenient—"

"No, no. Don't call back. I'm not exactly sure when she'll, uh…"

Paige strained to hear. She thought she could hear Mara whispering to someone in the background. Was it Peter? Did he have second thoughts about them fostering a relationship with Lucy? Did Mara not know how to tell them? Was it *Lucy* having reservations?

As Mara began to piece together a long, unintelligible excuse, a sinking thought crept into Paige's mind. What if Charlie didn't want them to talk? She'd hurt him so deeply after he'd already been hurt by Crystal. She had yet to forgive herself the past year for wounding him when all she'd wanted to do was love him. If she couldn't forgive herself, how could he?

"It's okay, Mara," Paige said softly. "You don't need to explain anything to us. If Lucy wants to call, she can."

"You're still going to get cake, aren't you? Please tell me you're getting cake."

"We sure are," Joan said, piping up in her usual toughened spirit. Paige could count on her to not let them wallow.

"I'm glad. Enjoy your cake, and we'll touch base soon."

With that, the line went dead. Paige placed the phone on the table, each of them staring at it instead of each other. After several silent minutes, Madge shuffled to the table.

"Did you want to see it?" Madge asked.

"Hmm?" Paige said, finally lifting her watery eyes.

"The cake. Do you want to eat it here?"

"No," Paige muttered. "Pack it up. I don't want to eat any—"

"Nonsense!" Joan said, clasping her hand. "We'll eat it here. This is the day we eat the cake. We *buy* the cake and we *eat* the cake and we savor each bite of expensive cake because it's how we take time to appreciate what we have. Heaven knows Craig would. We're eating two or *three* fat slices of whatever you baked up for us, Madge. Bring out the cake!"

Paige began to laugh hard through her tears as Joan slapped the table and began a hearty laugh of her own. Madge brought the cake over on an opaque pearl platter.

They stared at the white-and-blush-pink-swirl cake, topped with white dollops of buttercream frosting and freshly sliced strawberries. It was impossible to not think about Uncle Craig at a moment like this.

"You know what Craig would do, don't you?"

Paige began to laugh harder. "He'd pick off the biggest strawberry and pop it into his mouth before we had a chance to stop him."

"That man!" Joan chuckled, the cake cutter shaking in her hand. "Who needs plates? Let's just dig in!"

It was the bell jingling over the front door that made Paige look up, fork poised. As if an apparition in a dream, a fresh-faced angel came bounding toward them.

"Lucy!" she cried, scrambling out of the booth just in time to catch Lucy in a full hug. "What on earth!"

"Surprise!" Lucy squealed, smiling so hard her pink cheeks rounded like the cake's strawberries.

"How did you find us?"

"Dad was searching for cake shops online while Mom talked to you. We all thought you'd be home, but you threw us for a loop!"

"This is Lucy?" Joan said, clutching her hands to her chest. She bent down to peer into her niece's eyes. "You're the spitting image of your mother, except for that mass of gorgeous dark hair."

"This is your aunt, Joan." Paige introduced her only two living relatives so they could meet for the first time. Lucy shook hands and said hello before smirking at Paige.

"You should go outside," Lucy told her, pointing at the door.

"Your parents?" Paige guessed. She looked,

already knowing in her heart, or was she merely hoping for, the person waiting on the other side. She rushed over. Standing next to her bicycle, running his hand over the handlebars—

She threw open the door and all but leaped outside. Her voice caught. "Charlie."

"I had to see you right away." He moved toward her with an urgency that made her stomach turn somersaults.

"Thorne?"

He shook his head. "Gosh, no. Ever since he came looking for Lucy last year, the FBI has been investigating him, so you never have to think of him again. I'm so sorry if my tone worried you. That's not what I—" He chuckled awkwardly in a way she'd never seen him do before. Despite her confusion, she smiled as the sound of his laugh crackled throughout every inch of her body. "I planned what to say on the trip here, but looking at you, I can't remember where to begin."

"Charlie, I'm so sorry."

"What?" he said, pulling her into the shade of the awning. As he did, the warmth of his hand spurred her on. Once she began, she could no longer hold back the tide.

"I'm sorry I hurt you. I fell in love with you the first moment we met—I'm sure of it. I had never let anyone get close to me, but from the moment you spoke and smiled at me…oh, Charlie, I was yours. I didn't want to use you or hurt you or lie to you or do any of the other things I did. All I wanted to do was love with you, and I ruined it all for us."

He moved with confidence, closing the short distance between them. "Ah, hey, you're stealing my apology right out from under me." He cupped her cheek as his face fell, serious. "I thought I was angry with you when all this time I was angry at myself for letting you slip away. I'm sorry I wasn't here when you lost your uncle."

"I had Joan."

"I'm grateful for that, but I should have been here. I should have held you in my arms the entire time." She nestled her face harder against his palm as he continued. "I'm in love with you, Paige, and I'm sorry if I let too much time—"

Before he could finish, she drew his lips to hers in a long, slow kiss that made the passersby stop and smile.

With Joan and Lucy at the doorway, he whispered, "Will you marry me?" He slipped a ring on her finger. "Lucy helped me pick it."

"Are you real?" she whispered, tracing the

crinkle lines around his eyes as he smiled at her. Several beats passed and she nodded, admiring her new ring in the sunlight. "I guess this means I'm moving to Roseley."

When she found Joan's eyes, there was nothing residing in them but happiness.

"Mind if I tag along?" Her aunt was beaming.

"Really?" Paige said, turning to her aunt. "Will you come with me?"

"There's nothing left for me here. My best friend is gone and—" she hugged Lucy to her side "—all my family will be in Roseley. It's as good a place as any to start again."

"You'll love it there," Paige said, holding Charlie like she'd never let him go. "*I* love it there."

Charlie kissed the freckles on the bridge of her nose.

"Then you'll marry me, Freckles?"

She pecked a kiss to his lips. "Easy peasy."

* * * * *

*For more great romances from
Elizabeth Mowers and
Harlequin Heartwarming,
visit www.Harlequin.com today!*